"Take one planet. Hit it with one 'nuclear-winter'-producing meteor. Let stand several centuries, then combine with one native species of furry, sea-going late Victorians crossed with more obstreperous days of the Dutch Republic; one permanently disabled, human-crewed, politically correct starship; and one particularly ruthless local empire. Stir well. What do you get? *Voyage to Eneh* . . . and a hell of a good read."

—David Weber, author of *Echoes of Honor*

"*Voyage to Eneh* combines an interesting, unusual world, fascinating aliens, believable people, complex politics, and some of the liveliest naval action this side of the Battle of Jutland. It's a first-rate piece of work that will leave readers wanting much more."

—Harry Turtledove, author of
Household Gods and *Darkness Descending*

"*Voyage to Eneh* is a good sea story . . . with that SF tang. The great age of adventure isn't fourteen or over—it lives and Roland Green writes his share of it. I thoroughly enjoyed the book."

—S. M. Stirling, author of
The Island in the Sea of Time and *The Ship Avenged*

"Green knows how to tell a stirring tale; his battle scenes in particular stand out. Fans of military SF will enjoy this tale and its naval spin, and will look forward to its sequels."

—*Publishers Weekly*

"Green's knowledge of naval warfare and nineteenth-century technology imparts a distinctive atmosphere to this trilogy opener. Complex alien and human politics as well as gripping land and sea battles make this SF adventure a good selection."

—*Library Journal*

Voyage to Eneh

Book One of *The Seas of Kilmoyn*

ROLAND J. GREEN

TOR®

A TOM DOHERTY ASSOCIATES BOOK
NEW YORK

To the memory of the late Dr. Oscar Parkes, M.B.E., whose love for long-vanished warships inspired my own—and with the passage of time, the work of which this is the first volume.

cast of characters

Human

BAER, Justin
Junior commander aboard human-crew *Lingvaas*.

BORLUND, Sean Lincoln
Originally Study Group trainee; later Farer and commander-trainee aboard mixed-crew *Lingvaas;* junior commander aboard human-crew *Lingvaas*.

CHAYKIN-SCHMIDT, Roald
Junior Farer aboard human-crew *Lingvaas;* "nephew" of senior Study Group Security commander.

HOUYLAN, Bridget
Senior bearer-partner of Sean Lincoln Borlund; one child by him; Observant.

KLIMOVA, Justine
Farer; oiler aboard human-crew *Lingvaas*.

KUND, Sharil
Second Captain (Executive Officer) of human-crew *Lingvaas*.

DROJIN, Vuikmar
Rinbao-Daran merchant of Kertovan descent; Imperial spy.

EJKMUS, Ludon
Junior commander at Fort Huomikki.

FAIND, Egose
Farer aboard mixed-crew *Lingvaas*.

FOBEEN, Acht
Captain of armored cruiser *Shuumiba* in Expeditionary Fleet.

GUUNDZOUSA, Ye'mt
Teacher watch chief; senior instructor aboard mixed-crew *Lingvaas*.

I HMILRA, Elandra
Wife of Othan I Hmilra.

I HMILRA, Jossu
Senior Captain Over Captains; of old Captain-born stock; commander of Expeditionary Fleet to Eneh.

I HMILRA, Othan
Son of Jossu I Hmilra; aspiring politician and entrepreneur.

IMPANSKAA, Ijo
Captain of armorclad *Byubr* in Eneh campaign.

JUINJIJARSA
Rinbao-Daran mounted-scout commander.

KEKASPA, Moi
Saadian; chief of Jossu I Hmilra's private intelligence service; aliases include "Jornja" and "Sikoe Yuurn."

Voyage
to
Eneh

chapter 1

IT WAS NOT the sunbrighten Reverence bells or the lamptenders' cries that awoke Watch Chief Ehoma Tuomitti. It was the noise of hammers in the shipyard just downhill from the reliefhouse.

Tasting sleep in her mouth and feeling something more pleasant in her loins, Tuomitti lay on the pallet, eyes closed, and tried to make out the different kinds of hammers. Mauls driving steel wedges into timber. Sledgehammers driving wooden wedges under light hulls or perhaps knocking them out—the yard finished a double hand of fishing craft and ships' boats every midtide.

Carpenters' hammers, finishing deck planking or cabin woodwork. The dull thud and wheezing of the big steam-driven hammers, driving in shores for a new building way or perhaps braces under some larger ship. (Wasn't there a new gunboat within a few commons of launching?)

Then, drowning out everything else like a watch chief with a speaking horn, the fierce rattle of the riveters. Not much of that being done by hand here anymore, she judged—it was all the new rammed-air riveting hammers.

Whatever they were using, if the riveters were at work already, that meant she had overslept by long enough to be shamed, if anybody learned. If she did not

woman said. "Pardon me if it makes me tremble, though not in awe."

Tuomitti gave the other a mocking parody of the gesture used by Daughters of the Rock in giving a blessing. "Your pardon is gladly granted."

"At what price?"

"Price?"

"It will be sunglow, maybe even fulldark, before a watch chief *gives* anything. Has either come while I slept?"

"You *slept*? The Great Tides are overtaking you, my friend. But of course, the snaggle-toothed are never—"

"I need no teeth at all to put greenmist leaf in your morning hoeg."

Tuomitti clasped her hands over her muzzle in mock horror. "My tongue abases itself. Hot hoeg, please, without greenmist leaf but with whatever sweetener you have."

The woman bared teeth that were stained and gapped but mostly straight, poured two cups of hoeg from the pot on the stove behind the brazier, then pulled out a plate of cakes and a pot of sweetbreath spread.

"Let me put a fresh pot up to boil, and I'll be joining you," she said.

Tuomitti was halfway through her first cup and second cake when the other joined her. They clinked cups.

"To a prosperous Great."

It was one of the few goodwishes that both relief-keepers and Farers could agree on. They were more likely to illwish one another. But Tuomitti's hostess Kappala Naytet had come ashore only after three injuries and two motherless children made it prudent, proper, and even necessary. Before that she had been at sea for more Greats than Tuomitti, enough that the smoke-darkened print of her first ship showed a high-seas paddlewheeler.

Naytet fell on the cakes as if she had eaten even less than Tuomitti. When the plate bore only crumbs, she

"That well may be," Tuomitti agreed, reluctant to continue any conversation along this line. She had been aboard *Valor* too long and learned a warrior's closed mouth too well.

A tidal bore of guests howling for food, drink, and baggage saved both women from embarrassment by silence. Tuomitti snatched her seabag, returned her friend's farewell gesture, and bolted for the door. She was outside in the fog before she could recognize any of the din-makers or they her.

The fog thickened as she strode toward the water. Certainly more foghorns were blowing, both afloat and ashore. Piping whistles and brass trumpets from light craft added to the din. Tuomitti preferred this to silence. That would mean the fog was keeping everything at the quay, with no ride out to *Valor* until the murk thinned.

SEAN LINCOLN BORLUND REMEMBERED TO DUCK AS HE stepped through the door from the passenger lounge onto the afterdeck. Humans averaged ten centimeters taller than Kilmoyans, and at a meter eighty-six Borlund was taller than most humans. He had bruises and cuts on scalp and forehead from mantelpieces, beams, and door lintels that offered plenty of clearance for ninety-nine out of a hundred of either race.

The afterdeck was nearly deserted. *Aygsionan* carried few passengers this early in the season, and most of them were either still at breakfast or farther below, preparing to debark.

Borlund had been too excited to sleep, and had come on deck to catch his first glimpse of the Hask Delta and Saadi. All he saw was fog that seemed to grow thicker the closer they drew to the land. He stared futilely into the murk until frustration and hunger drove him below to snatch a plate from the buffet.

What drove him out on deck now was more than curiosity. *Aygsionan* was closing the mole at barely steerageway, with lookouts posted everywhere from the

tains and boatsteerers in Saadi Bay were on direly urgent business. She'd heard every signal except the three-three-three of a ship at anchor, although she might have missed some of those. Also, a ship anchoring in this murk was as likely to be run down by somebody underway as they were to ram somebody else if they kept moving at dead slow.

Please, Lord of the Waves, let them at least be able to see the channel markers.

The murk ahead of her turned solid. Tuomitti stopped abruptly, her nose a finger from the side of a large van. She thumped the wood with her fist, only afterward noticing that it showed lettering in Saadia as well as Kertovasi.

"Apologies, Farer," a plaintive voice came from the driver's seat. "There's no but all the wagons in town ahead in the Fish Street, and none of them moving. Know you a better way to Likug Wharf?"

"If I can ride with you, I think I can find one," Tuomitti said. If one was going to contemplate this murk for the rest of the morning, one might as well do it sitting down.

She stepped around to the far side of the van, to avoid frightening the dreezans. She could tell from the accent as well as the lettering that she was dealing with a Saadian, who weren't always careful about crowd-training their dreezans.

"Beg your pardon, Lady," the driver said, as Tuomitti climbed up. "I can't offer much comfort for your kindness, but—"

"The most comfort you can offer for now is a moment's silence," Tuomitti said. She pulled out her handkerchief and wiped the puddled mist off her side of the skin bench, then sat down. The driver looked at her sideways, as if wondering whether he'd lost any real chance for a friendly chat. A Kertovan watch chief might be "Lady" only by gross, almost servile courtesy, but she was under no obligation to speak to a Saadian van driver unless she was desperate for conversation.

"There's something in that, Ma'am," the driver said, in a tone that was at least neutral.

THE FOG GREW NO THICKER AS *AYGSIONAN* CREPT INTO the harbor, but no thinner either. Her own whistle hadn't sounded three-three-three yet, but Sean Borlund had been hearing the anchoring signal from all around for a good twenty minutes. Whistles, sirens, horns, drums, pipes, bells, and more than a few sets of leathery lungs called out in three languages and half a dozen dialects that Borlund recognized and more he did not.

More passengers were coming on deck, even though they could hardly see the bow or the masthead, let alone their landfall. Borlund recognized the look on the few human faces, and supposed most of the Kilmoyans had the same thought: better to be on deck staring into the fog than below staring at a bulkhead. On deck human or Farer had a chance to swim for it if some iron prow suddenly loomed out of the murk and drove through *Aygsionan*'s side—

"*Kanik!*"

The obscenity shrilled in Borlund's ear, and a hurrying shape with a Kertovan headcrest slammed him back against the cabin bulkhead. The back of his head struck hard metal. Pain flared all the way to scalp and ears. With blurred vision, he saw the rapidly receding silhoutte of a deckhand with an armload of small cartons.

Borlund rubbed his head, surprised that neither his fingers nor what turned out to be a fire-hose bracket showed blood. What did that Farer have under his tail, to be in such a hurry that he couldn't keep a lookout ahead? Borlund had a brief vision of uncovering the theft of lifeboat rations or something else portable and receiving a civic award.

He wiped salty droplets from his skin and laughed quietly. It would take diplomacy, subtle negotiations, and perhaps a few not-so-subtle bribes to have a Dry-

be worth braving smoke, ancient fish-fat, and even foul-mouthed Kertovans.

EHOMA TUOMITTI AND THE DRIVER COMBINED THEIR ignorance without achieving knowledge. At times they were as completely lost as Tuomitti had been the time she was shipwrecked on an island off the Luokkan shore and had to flee inland to avoid the pirates. She thought afterward that the fog must have crept into their brains through their wide-open ears, as they listened for any guiding sound to fight its way through the din from the harbor.

At last they found themselves on a street sloping the right way, which said "waterfront" to both of them even if Tuomitti hadn't recognized a couple of the relief-houses and at least one drinkshop. They waited behind a steamhauler in its turn waiting for a railsteamer to pass. While they waited the driver dismounted and oiled the hides of his dreezans in a couple of places where the harness chafed.

Then at last the railsteamer hauled its train off into the murk, one of the trainmen walking ahead of it with a lantern and two more lanterns hung from the open guard wagon at the tail end. Steamhauler, van, and all the vehicles and walkers behind them bumped and rattled across the double tracks, and onto the Stone Road along the quays.

As they turned south, Tuomitti looked back at the little quayside station. It was hardly more than a brick hut with a long passenger shelter stretching fifty paces from either end. But when they'd crossed the tracks, Tuomitti hadn't been able to see the far end of the passenger shelter. Now she could not only see it but also make out the shape of the freightyard gate beyond it, and even the wrought-iron Hand of Wealth over the heavy timber lintel.

She didn't dare say it aloud, fearing that both the

chapter 2

THERE WAS SILENCE aboard *Aygsionan* but not around her. Off in the grayness, Sean Borlund heard bells, gongs, and trumpets, as nervous souls tried to generate a reassuring echo or even reply. This thick a fog could make even Farers wonder if they were not the last thinking beings left on the face of a world at last swallowed by the Mist Demons. . .

From close to redside came the rasping whistle of a pair of Seakin, surfacing to breathe through their double blowholes. Then they would dive again, to make their way out to sea in the narrow space between the deepest keel on the surface and the tallest wreck on the bottom.

Saadi Bay held many of both. It had been a port long before the Kertovans established their Protectorate, and human marine archeologists drooled at the thought of a license for extensive diving anywhere in the seventy-by-forty-klick stretch of water inside the hundred-meter line. None of it gave any trouble to the Seakin; their organic sonar was ahead of anything likely to be built on Kilmoyn for two more generations.

Borlund opened the hall door. The smells inside struck his nostrils like a padded club. For once he didn't mind the Kertovans who wriggled a shoulder at him, then moved out of his path.

A few of the Saadians who made up about a third of the hall's population followed the Kertovan example,

On a planet skewed by a millennium of survival pres-
sures toward conservation, it seemed less wise.

"Table or counter?" the steward repeated, in a voice
that made it clear he loathed indecisive clients regardless of race.

"Counter," Borlund said. He realized that he's used
up too much adrenaline in the past few hours, antici-
pating all the problems he might face on joining the
Study Group and conjuring up solutions to each one. If
he sat down at a table, by the time *Aygsonian* moved
again he might have his head down on the wooden
mosaic tabletop.

The steward condescendingly waved him toward the
counter at the rear of the salon. Only half the stools and
even less of the rail space was taken, mostly by Saadians.
Borlund was relieved to see no humans. Polite conversation at least was rigid etiquette when two humans met;
Borlund was feeling neither polite nor conversational.

He shifted his carrybag to his right hand and steered
a course for the counter.

BY THE TIME THE VAN REACHED THE BOAT LANDING,
Tuomitti had decided that she'd seen only an eddy in
fog that elsewhere lay as thick as ever. They finished the
last hundred paces with the driver on foot, leading the
number-one dreezan with one hand and holding his
whip out in front of him to probe the way.

Tuomitti walked alongside the wagon, expecting
every moment to fall or be pushed by a wheel into the
water. Twice she had to swing around the outside of
slippery bollards.

It was after this that she broke out the carrystrap on
her seabag and slung it across her back. No Farer liked
that pose, which made one look like a graveltoe land-
fighter under one of their spine-bending packs. At least
no street squatters were going to see her and call rude
remarks or toss overripe vegetables.

ness of all, which would be leaving. Her charity toward Saadians or anyone else stopped short of letting them see her not knowing what to do next. It was a vice, she knew, but one hard to avoid once one put up the lantern badge of a watch chief.

Eventually she heard the squeal of iron wheels on stone as the cart turned, the whining and belching of dreezans routed out of a comfortable drowse to pull their load again, and the fog-dimmed *pok!* of the driver's whip as he worked his team up to a walk. It took longer than Tuomitti expected for the team to vanish into the mist.

She decided that to keep a light conscience, she would go seeking that boat or *something* that would take her back to *Valor.* At worst, a search of the waterfront might let her rally a few more strayed *Valors*, to make up a party when the fog did let them see farther than an oar's length beyond their noses.

Tuomitti rose from the bollard, as slowly as if the fog had rusted her joints, and began her walking.

THE COUNTER ATTENDANT LOOKED TO BE ANOTHER Kertovan-Saadian cross, with maybe a trace of ancestry from somewhere up the Finnugh Valley. He wore a work smock, with his hair in a purely Saadian style, as well as an expression that seemed to accuse Sean Borlund of being personally responsible for the fog: No doubt the attendant had some plans of his own for when the ship was safely ported, something more pleasant than waiting on pallid, hairless, smelly Drylanders.

"Hoeg or gruuyan?"

Hoeg was made from various combinations of dried seaweeds, gruuyan from a root vegetable that looked like a potato with a glandular condition. Gruuyan was a high-status drink, also high-priced (two slyn a cup, by the sign), and much easier on the human palate.

Borlund told his taste buds to go back to sleep and ordered hoeg.

engines, Borlund was convinced that either the fog was lifting or *all* the captains and boatchiefs on Saadi Bay had direly urgent business elsewhere.

TUOMITTI FOUND TWO FERRIES WITH STEAM UP, NEIther of them any use to her, running as they did to Yuirpesi and Kylomaak. The ferry to the Fort Huomikki landing was nowhere in sight, since it ran at all tides and was probably caught somewhere in the fog if it had ever left the fort.

She hoped any of her shipmates caught aboard the ferry were at least having a good drinkfest.

At the boat landing beyond the ferry piers, Tuomitti thought at first she would have the same sodden luck. Half the boats were drawn up on the shingle; half of those in the water were empty. Some of the grounded boats were overturned, their crews huddled for shelter underneath. One comfort-driven soul had knocked out the drain plug from his boat, run a sprayed-iron pipe through it as a chimney, and built a fire to warm his shelter. Nothing short of his boat catching fire would get him on the water today.

In her younger days Tuomitti would have been tempted to wander over to the chimney-boat and plug the chimney, then wait until the boat's owner came storming and coughing out to settle with his visitor. Fuller of years and rank and needing to at least pretend to greater dignity, Tuomitti could only mourn the passing Greats and go on.

The Tide of Wonders was not yet passed, however. Toward the end of the shingle, shadowed by the breakwater guarding the ways of the next half-dozen building slips, lay a steam launch. She was an older model, doubtless sold out of Fleet service ten Greats ago. Her boiler was more patches than original metal, but she rode clean and high, brave with fresh paint.

She even had paying passengers aboard, judging from the pulled-down curtains of the passenger cabin

"*Valor,*" Tuomitti said.

That got her such looks that she surreptitiously examined her garments to see if anything improper was showing. *Valor* seemed to be a potent name with these folk. Or perhaps it was Captain Over Captains Jossu I Hmilra, *Valor's* senior owner?

"Where she moored?" the chief asked.

"Too far from Iojuk," the merchant began.

"Ah—I believe, Goodfarer—"

"Yes, I asked you, Watch Chief."

"South Anchorage, Fort Huomikki. About nine casts west of the arsenal pier, when I came ashore last night."

"This fellow's first," the boat chief said. She pointed at the merchant, rather as she would have pointed at a pile of dreezan dung. He seemed deaf to her tone and blind to her gestures.

"But I can take you out to *Valor* if the fog and your money be right, afterward."

Tuomitti had no chance to ask about the money. A high, slightly quavering voice hailed them from the shore.

"Boat? Did I hear that you are going to Fort Huomikki?"

"What's it to you if I am?"

"I go to my husband there."

The accent would have told Tuomitti that the woman was Saadian, even if her headscarf and the embroidery on the blanket wrapped around the bundle in her arms hadn't already made that plain. The blanket quivered, and Tuomitti saw that the woman was holding a baby.

"After you land me at Iojuk—" the merchant began.

The boat chief frowned. It made her look almost pleasant. "Long time on the water for a baby. Eh, Watch Chief?"

Farer was appealing to Farer. Tuomitti stared at the merchant. Something about those ears—

Of course. Most likely, the woman's husband was a commander in the Saadian legion at Fort Huomikki.

Tuomitti mentally counted her remaining money. She'd be lean-pursed until next pay, unless she could arrange a loan with the store chief, although he and this boat's owner were the same breed when it came to charity. Better that than having a mother and babe stranded in this murk.

"You'll lose nothing by it," she called, then reached for the babe. The boat chief jumped down from the wheel mount to take it from Tuomitti, leaving the Drilion even shorter of words than he was of ear tufts.

Relieved of her burden, the woman splashed boldly into the water and scrambled aboard with an agility that spoke of both youth and health. She was wringing out her skirts when Tuomitti boarded, but hissing steam and the clang and clatter of stoking made speech impossible.

As the propeller churned up mud from the bottom, then foam from the water, Tuomitti saw that at long last the fog had truly begun to lift. A land breeze stroked her cheek. Then the boat was underway, and the land breeze mixed with the passage wind, while the gurgle of water at the prow joined the chuffing of the engine.

AYGSIONAN'S ANCHOR WAS UP BEFORE SEAN BORLUND could finish his snack and reach the deck. As he mounted the ladder, he heard cheering. Under his boots he felt the changing rhythm of the engines as the ship got underway.

The only problem was that as he reached the deck, he heard more cheering from vessels still invisible in a fog that was clearing but far from gone. The first line or two of *Aygsionan*'s anchormates were visible even to Borlund's unaided eye from the deck; they could be avoided with ease if they were commanded with minimal skill and caution.

Five times as many ships had to be still veiled in clammy gray, as opaque as a Captain-Born matron's nightrobe and even less decorated. When *they* all got underway, this corner of Saadi Bay was going to become

teeth and strain cheek muscles, not to mention drawing blood from his upper lip.

No humans had been lost or even present when the passenger packet *Ilraamen* ripped her bow open on an unseen coal barge and took two hundred passengers to the bottom with her. That disaster was still in every manual of seamanship or child's book of cautionary tales printed in the fifteen Greats since the disaster.

Visibility was definitely improving. Before the last of the barges was out of sight, the South Anchorage off Fort Huomikki was in sight, almost to the breakwater that divided it from its cousin to the north.

Half a dozen warships shared the anchorage, barely a quarter of its full capacity. One lay alongside a coal hulk that must have started life as a particularly fine four-master. The graceful lines still showed under years of accumulated grime that no waves could now touch, and three masts survived as derrick stumps. Smoke curled up until it was lost in the haze, from the steam winches aboard the warship and the hulk, and from the tug waiting patiently at the hulk's bow.

With binoculars Borlund could have turned the ripples of movement on the two decks into the organized, brutal chaos of coaling ship. The Kertovans designed their more modern ships with dozens of labor-saving devices, driven by small steam engines fed off auxiliary boilers, hydraulics, or even electricity. It still took a full day to transfer the thousand tons of coal a big cruiser could swallow, then another day for the crew to clean their ship and themselves. (And even then, the beans, biscuit, and pasties tasted of coal dust for a week.)

A small armorclad was standing out as *Aygsionan* passed the buoys marking the mouth of the dredged channel to the anchorages. A long half-submerged ram, a hull like a potato sliced lengthwise, with a single tur-reted gun forward and a fat funnel aft—she had to be an *Illik*-class harbor-defense vessel, the ones known as "the floating turds."

The whistle changed pitch and signaled one-one-three—"Farer overboard." Doubt became impossible; duty became certain.

Borlund ran forward, already unbuttoning his coat.

THE SCENE ON THE BAY WAS EVERYTHING TUOMITTI had feared and somewhat more. Everyone was trying to get underway at once, and a hundred craft varying in speed, turning circle, and crew skill were on the move.

Tuomitti began to regret her eagerness to return to *Valor*. It was law, duty, and custom, as well as necessary to her authority as a watch chief. It had also bound her to a ride about as pleasant as steering a raft-fort into a narrow channel with cable-guided bomb-boats converging on her from both sides!

The boat chief had not offered her the courtesy of the "bridge," which was just as well. There was hardly room for one grown Farer on the wheel platform, and on deck Tuomitti could stay between the Drilion and the Saadian woman with her babe. The Farer didn't really think the merchant would push the woman overboard, but it might help keep the peace if he knew that he would follow if he tried.

After the third near-collision, the woman turned pale and went to the railing. Tuomitti gently but firmly took the babe, while the woman thrust her head over the side and gave her breakfast to the fishes and the Seakin.

"Bearing sickness, by any chance?" Tuomitti asked.

The woman rinsed her mouth with a dipper of water from the jug racked on the cabin bulkhead, and shook her head. Then she smiled for the first time.

"It may not be long, though, after I join Paevo. He is one of stout loins. Ah, pardon."

Tuomitti grimaced. Sometimes the formalities between jouti and tuunda were more than a trifle wearying. She had to accept the apology, or be more offensive than the woman would have been by not offering it at all.

"Granted. But I have fertile kin, and because one is

thought, but there was an outbound coastal packet hard in the wake of the railroad ferry—

Two whistles and one living throat screamed almost in chorus. Tuomitti wanted to chop the edge of her hand across the Drilion's throat, to silence him.

Even more, she wanted to wish away the rusty iron prow looming over the launch, so close she could almost have touched it with an oar. The ferry hadn't hidden the northbound steamer, but it had obscured just enough to make the boat chief misjudge distance.

The distance between prow and launch shrank, then vanished. An iron wall came at Tuomitti, as fast as a shot from a hostile gun or an opponent's fist in a brawl, as slowly as the incoming tide. She saw rivets so clearly that she could count them, a horrified face peering out of a port, the launch's stern driven under—

She had just realized the deck was no longer under her feet, when she was in the water.

leg into a stanchion and the shin of the other into a bollard, and yelled again. Nobody heard him this time either. He stopped to rub his bruises and remember that a boat might not be needed.

Kilmoyans' ancestors had been a semi-amphibious biped, and they themselves still looked like a cross between an ape and a seal. When they lived near water, like the folk along the Hask or the coastal Saadians, or by and on the sea like the Kertovans, they learned to swim as fast as they learned to walk, and better than any human could hope to emulate. That was one reason for the humans' cover story of being from the heart of a Skyfall-ruined continent in the southern hemisphere: they needed to account for their almost grotesque clumsiness (by Kilmoyan standards) in the water.

It was just possible that nothing would happen today to give Borlund a new round of nightmares. Anybody from whatever small craft that had died under *Aygsionan*'s prow who'd made it safely into the water might already be swimming clear of danger, waving to show the crew on deck where to throw the floatbelts to those who hadn't put on their own. . .

He wanted it to be that way. He wanted it badly enough to taste the wish. He didn't think his wanting would make it come true, so he kept walking. As the deck cleared before him, he began to run again.

EHOMA TUOMITTI HAD SURVIVED MOST OF THE PERILS of the Western and Greater Seas, as well as lesser bodies of water. In fact, she preferred natural dangers to some of the modern high-powered machinery aboard *Valor*. A Farer could fight wind, waves, or even rocks and shoals, but not high-pressure steam that could fatally sear lungs with three breaths or engines that could pulp the hand of an oiler reaching to lubricate a bearing.

Now she was fighting both water and machinery, but the water was the lesser danger. Enough of it over her

"Did Skoi make it out?" Tuomitti shouted. Or at least she began to shout. The pain in her face and eye reduced her to a croak. The boat chief still heard, and waved one hand in a circle, to signal that she didn't know.

Tuomitti didn't know either, but she wasn't hopeful. If the stoker hadn't made it out of the engine compartment and got well clear before the boiler exploded, he was not only dead but gutted like a hylerksh ready for salting down.

Something large broke water just behind Tuomitti. She whirled, making blood drops fly and stabbing her head with new pain. She half-expected to see a green-gullet; instead she saw the stoker's body. Literally—his head was gone and something had laid his chest open like an axe blow.

That was everybody—no, it wasn't, and the missing two were the worst of all. Forgetting her pain, Tuomitti screamed:

"Hoy! Where's our Saadian friend? Goodwife, where are you?"

The boat chief echoed her. The Drilion merchant merely seemed to draw himself up higher in the water. The stoker's body was mute. The whistles, horns, and voices continued, but they seemed to be a great distance away and getting farther every moment.

Blood loss. Scalp and face cuts will bleed freely, even when they're not deep enough to cost you an eye.

BY THE TIME BORLUND REACHED THE FOREDECK, everybody forward had rushed to greenside. So many were leaning over the railing that he expected the ship to list, and floatbelts, floatrings, deck furniture, and anything else that would support a swimmer were raining over the side. Right now, anybody in the water was in as much danger of being hit on the head by their would-be rescuers as of drowning.

The Kertovans' long "bond with the sea" had driven a good many lessons deep into their culture. One was

one ahead and another smaller one off to her—right? She thought she could still tell left from right and redside from greenside.

She nearly blundered into the boat chief, which drew a nasty laugh from the Drilion merchant. She'd almost rather he'd panicked, so that they could have let him drown with a reasonably clear conscience. Somehow, though, he'd managed to find a floatbelt buoyant enough to keep even him afloat. Why had the Gray Lord done such a miracle for a Drilion, and not for the woman and her baby?

No miracle, Tuomitti realized. Even her dim vision now showed her a dozen belts, rings, deck chairs, and other oddments bobbing on the water, flung down from one of the two ships. The boat chief had a ring under one arm and was pushing out a belt to Tuomitti. Then, seeing that the other Farer was hurt, she trod water while she pushed out the ring, easier to put on.

Wonderful. Now I can stay afloat long enough to bleed to death.

But Tuomitti would be cursed if she'd give that Drilion the satisfaction of dying in front of him. She dredged up the strength to pull on the ring, and found she did feel better. She even found her voice.

"Where's the woman?"

"Gone to the bottom with her brat, like as not," the merchant said.

Tuomitti found another reason for staying alive: to permanently maim the Drilion if the woman and babe came back, or kill him outright if they were gone. The boat chief's eyes said that she might help the Fleetfarer.

The second ship now lay straight ahead. It also seemed to have shrunk or backed away. No, something was coming toward them, only a half-cable away. A boat, your standard service boat that half the ships on the bay carried, high at prow and stern, low amidships for easy work with anything in the water—

And a Drylander sitting aft, steering, while four row-

"Best we don't laugh. If any are dead from this, their spirits may hear."

He had to repeat himself twice, before his north-islands-accented Kertovan reached the woman. At least he supposed it was his accent. Any Saadian woman with the price of a ferry-launch ticket was likely to know Kertovan fairly well.

Before she could reply, he heard someone hailing them, from redward. It seemed to come from the water, not from *Aygsionan*'s deck. Looking around, Borlund saw that *Aygsionan* had backed off a good cast or more and dropped anchor again. The hail came from a boat approaching them, with four Saadians rowing, one Kertovan sitting in the prow and directing the rowers, and what looked remarkably like a human woman in the stern, bending over somebody out of sight in the bottom of the boat.

"Slow—stop!" the Kertovan said. The oars trailed in the water, then were thrust out level and dripping as the boat's momentum carried it the rest of the way toward Borlund.

The woman struck out, covering the last few meters to the boat as fast as a racing swimmer. Four calloused hands reached down, gripping both her and her remaining garments. The garments did not survive the strain, and the woman tumbled into the boat almost naked.

She didn't wait to borrow as much as a cloak before she was at the gunwale again, reaching down for her child—definitely a son, Borlund saw, as he held it up. The baby was nestling against his mother's nearly bare torso and a Saadian was wrapping them both in a blanket before Borlund could struggle out of the floatjacket.

The urge to keep it as a souvenir yielded to the knowledge that he really hadn't done all that much and now desperately wanted out of the water. He'd avoided appearing before the Study Group Directors sleepless from nightmares; now his danger was pneumonia or at least a bad cold. He gripped the gunwale, heaved him-

Weil actually laughed. "Stay that way. I want to get back to that Drilion we had to leave when we saw you and the family."

"The what?"

"You didn't hit your head, did you?"

"No."

"Then it's simple. We left a Drilion merchant in the water to pick you up. You and them." Weil's tanned thumb jerked toward the bow.

Borlund strangled a groan. He didn't want to be fussed over by Barbara Weil or the surgeons, wherever they ended up. What he wanted right now was to be aboard a ship outbound for some island so distant from Kertovan rule that everybody would have forgotten today's events by the time anyone learned where Sean Lincoln Borlund was.

A human officer with a Saadian crew had left a Drilion merchant in the water, possibly drowning, to rescue a human and a Saadian. If the Drilion actually had drowned, there would be a literally howling scandal.

Even if the Drilion had been hurt only in his dignity and purse, he would try to make a scandal. Sean Lincoln Borlund had lost his last hope of slipping quietly into a place in the Study Group and doing valuable work before anybody noticed him.

Instead, he'd managed to arrive under circumstances that would make a dozen drummers and drinkshop girls throwing wreathes at him superfluous. He'd thoroughly violated the principle of keeping one's head down and mouth shut, unwritten but almost as sacred to Kilmoyn's human refugees as the more formal "natural evolution."

He wasn't the first to do so, of course, But every other one he'd heard of in the last twenty years of the Study Group's existence had also ended in serious trouble!

Kilmoyn from that day until his body was slipped over
the side and his spirit set free to roam those seas forever.

However, he could at least ensure that no one followed him around, waiting for that day to come so that
they could step into his boots. He was fourth among the
Captains Over Captains in the whole Kertovan Fleet. If
he stayed fit for sea service he was likely in time to
become the first. Lord and Lady willing, he might then
have time to turn some of his dreams into realities.

He opened the pouch and sniffed. Krimo, cured in ale
but not oiled. He dropped a pinch of the ruddy leaf into
the bowl, then decided to add a drop of oil for easy lighting. He undid the pocket at the bottom of the pouch and
pulled out the carved eihn-tooth oil bottle. The spring-
loaded silver top let one drop of oil hang glimmering for
a moment, then slip softly down into the krimo.

Now the lighter. A spark, and the krimo flared yellow.
A little too much oil, but no harm done. I Hmilra puffed
several times to get the pipe well lit, then leaned back
again.

His spine had just touched the dreezan-hide when a
discreet cough floated past him from behind the chair.

"Captain-Born?"

The voice gave I Hmilra no reason to snarl at the
intruder, and a good many reasons not to. One was that
being rude to Nen Makhiri would be only slightly less
of an offense than setting fire to the House of Captains.
The other was that Makhiri would never have inter-
rupted a good bowl if the matter had not been urgent.

"Yes?"

"There is a message for you."

"Bring it in."

"Pardon. I meant, a messenger."

"Live and present in the flesh?"

Another slight cough, this time in reproof. "So it
appears, Captain-Born. A young commander, from Fort
Huomikki, with a mounted escort."

The only place to sit down in the grooming chamber turned out to be a bench facing the necessary pots. The commander looked at them sourly, then went to the door, hung the UNFIT FOR USE sign on the handle outside, closed the door, and locked it.

If you can't justify this carnival of secrecy, my young friend, I will have one of your ears decorating my cabin aboard Valor *and send the other to Alikili.*

"There has been an incident in the Bay."

"Not another case of public indecency aboard *Valor*, I trust? If someone has his bones rattling over that, they will rattle even louder when I'm done with them."

"No, Captain. It is a matter of possible negligence in lifesaving, involving a Saadian woman, a watch chief from *Valor*, and a Drilion passenger, among others."

"A Saadian woman?"

"Yes, and with a baby in arms."

I Hmilra noted that if one closed one's eyes, one could not tell that the commander had Drilion blood. His voice held as much outrage at unnecessary danger to a Saadian mother and child as if he were Saadian himself.

"Names?"

"The watch chief is Ehoma Tuomitti. The woman's name is—curse the writing—ah, I think it was Sikoe Yuurn, or something like that. They were in a ferry launch to the fort when—"

I Hmilra had turned into a statue at the two names. The commander did not notice. He sailed briefly through the remainder of the story, and only then saw that his listener was on his feet.

"What touches *Valor*'s name touches mine. Wait in the Vistors'. I will be garbed and with you as quickly as I can."

The commander's, "Yes, Captain" was addressed to I Hmilra's rapidly retreating back.

THE NEXT FEW MINUTES AFTER HE ROLLED INTO THE boat made Sean Borlund regret that his pistol was in his

the peace, by making her seem so hurt that even a Drilion merchant in a rage would not quarrel with her."

Weil looked eloquently at her rowers.

"So they are not mute slaves?" the woman said. "I did not think so. But they must have learned to be deaf to you and dumb to others, or they would not be rowing for you."

The rowers proved that by not missing a stroke or batting an eye. Borlund felt less calm. This was when he first wished for his pistol, if only to fire a shot in the air to interrupt the argument.

Interruption came nonetheless, as they pulled alongside the Drilion merchant and another live Kertovan, floating to either side of an uncommonly ugly corpse. The Kertovan woman, in boatcrew garb, swam lithely over to the boat, then peered at the bandaged Warfarer Tuomitti.

"Does she live?"

The other three all looked at one another, each daring the others to speak. The boatcrew—boat chief, from the earrings and lanyard—took the right cue and nodded.

"Pray to all." She turned toward the merchant. "Can you swim? Or just float like a—driftwood—until the tide carries you somewhere?"

The merchant replied with several tedious obscenities and a good deal of thrashing and splashing. Apparently he could swim well enough that there was no need for anyone to tow him to the boat. It took him long enough that Borlund began to be afraid the boat would have to move to avoid another collision, but the merchant finally floundered alongside.

It took Weil, Borlund, and the boat chief to haul the merchant over the side, with little help and not much more cooperation from the man. Either he'd exhausted himself swearing and splashing, or he was in an even worse temper than before. Twice Borlund wasn't sure they were going to be able to land this particular fish.

probably tougher than some of the Earth sea creatures
wiped out by pollution, but they still had a low tolerance
for raw sewage or toxic chemical wastes. Saadi Bay was
probably cleaner than a good many comparable bodies
on environmentally conscious, Gaaian, harmonious-
technology Esperanza.

The Drilion merchant lay back down again with a
melodramatic groan. Maybe he was good enough at
reading human faces, voices, and body language to realize that if he didn't lie down as if he were injured, he
would be lying down because he was injured.

Borlund was cold to the bone, drenched to the skin,
and feeling soggy inside as well. He was tolerating his
present and prospective situation only because he'd put
himself into it in a good cause.

He still wished Barbara Weil would moderate her
tongue. If you wished this kind of business to end tidily,
you did not publicly slash to ribbons the pride of Drilion
merchants.

But Weil, the boat chief, and the Saadian woman
seemed to be working almost as a trained team. The best
that a mere male could do in a situation like this was
keep quiet or at least out of the way.

Weil raised a hand and the stroke barked an order.
The Saadian rowers spun the boat around until Borlund could see Fort Huomikki over his shoulder, dead
ahead.

Jossu I Hmilra left the House of Captains as
quickly as he could without calling attention to himself,
which was not as quickly as he could have wished. The
young commander had brought his message and a
decent escort, but neither a spare riding dreezan, a
decent carrier, nor hire-fare to find one on the streets.

The man was young, perhaps too newly registered to
have faded the dye in his first dress kilt; he could not
appreciate I Hmilra's, "When I was your age, I did that
sort of thing too." The Captain discreetly counted coins

The driver pulled at his whiskers. A hundred Greats ago, he might have been fined or even (if unfree) flogged for insolence. The laws had been changed; the memories had outlasted them.

No surprise, really, when the cast of mind that made those laws has done the same.

"Jeh—yaaa!" the driver called, and the carrier rolled forward. One of the escort's mounts swayed nervously from side to side. The commander looked at the rider with an "If you dare to fall off . . ."expression.

Then they all stepped off downhill.

SEAN BORLUND SPENT MOST OF THE BOAT JOURNEY TO Fort Huomikki trying not to shiver, and the rest trying to read the signals now darting in all directions.

Lingvaas was signaling to *Aygsionan*. Both were signaling to the big *Valor*-class armorclad, and the warship was signaling to both of them and to Fort Huomikki as well. The fort seemed to be using both lantern and flag signals to talk to everybody at once, including the shore. Borlund thought he'd heard them firing signal guns as well, but that turned out to be only firing practice at the Kwinmouth Battery.

Borlund began to feel as if his arrival in Saadi could hardly be more conspicuous if he'd arrived wearing a glitterskin robe and a golden crown, in a ceremonial barge rowed by twelve silver-collared slaves. There were those in the human community who felt that perhaps humans ought to seek "higher visibility," but Borlund trusted neither their motives nor their political influence.

Certainly they wouldn't be too numerous in the Study Group, let alone its Directorate. There wasn't much they could do to punish him if they lacked either a case against him or the courage to raise a scandal by sending him home. However, they could see that he spent his first and only three-year term in Saadi working on petty details with little contact with any breed of Kilmoyan.

chapter 5

Jossu I Hmilra's progress to Fort Huomikki was slow enough to unsettle his temper, in spite of taking the quicker high road. There were long stretches of narrow street, the bricks or stones slick with the early morning's mist and the late morning's dreezan dung and spilled barrels. One crossing was completely blocked by an overturned charcoal burner's wagon; I Hmilra prayed briefly that the furnace wouldn't set anything afire before the Watch arrived. And always there was the din of the city—squealing axles, bellowing and whining dreezans and mustekkas, people cursing, complaining, or sometimes even being happy at the top of their lungs in half a dozen different languages.

I Hmilra could not shut himself away from the din with his own thoughts, nor could he say a single word to his escort without shouting. The only man he could reach was the hire-driver, who had long since proved that he was not being paid enough to be a conversational partner.

It was a weary journey, until they reached the high road which twisted down the bluffs above Kwinmouth. At the foot it joined the sea road, but on the way down it gave a fine view of Saadi Bay to the south and the city to the east.

Fort Huomikki and *Valor* were doing a fair bit of signaling, however, and two other ships also had lamps

one driving and the other clutching the rails for dear life. A swift conveyance moving even more swiftly—perhaps too much so for the wet sea road? Perhaps the commander was right in seeing meaning in those signals.

It was easy to say (as I Hmilra had done many times), "Don't take every Drylander fart as a portent of the next Skyfall." It would also be moderately easy to reach Fort Huomikki ahead of the Drylanders, or at least not far behind.

"Ten more slyn if we reach the Fort before those Drylanders," I Hmilra called.

"Aye. And if we go off the road?" the driver replied, unblinking.

I Hmilra laughed and passed a ten-slyn piece to the commander. "If we do, see that his family gets this as well as his fare."

"Just see that you don't ride off after your lord," the driver added. "Loyalty's loyalty, but a workingman's family needs a roof and a bed more."

Then the driver's whip cracked, and they were off again.

A BAND WAS PLAYING AS THE LAUNCH AND ITS TOW approached the Fort Huomikki boat landing. Practicing, rather—Sean Borlund didn't have much of an ear for music, but he could tell seasoned bandsmen of either race from novices. A bunch of novices today, it seemed—the brass section in particular sounded like some large barnyard animal having a difficult delivery, and no two drums were quite on the same beat.

The Saadian woman shifted her now-sleeping baby to the other shoulder and grinned. "Look at the clear sky, not the clouds. Noise is supposed to drive away evil spirits."

Borlund managed to return the smile. He couldn't tell from her tone whether she believed the old tale or not. The open boat was no place to ask when any answer was bound to offend someone.

before she did, she called over one bare shoulder to Borlund.

"This will be remembered, and others will learn of it."

Borlund was not so ungracious as to say the first thing that came into his mind, which was, "That's what I'm afraid of." Instead, he cupped his hands and shouted, "I was just the first one to see you. I wasn't the only one who would have helped."

The effort at modesty was lost in the din, and also because as Borlund spoke somebody threw the woman a second blanket and a cloak and she was too busy wrapping herself up to listen. She vanished, leaving Borlund hoping that he'd heard a promise, not a threat.

Barbara Weil stepped up behind him and said, "Come along."

"The next time somebody tells me to come along without telling me why or where, I may push them into the bay and jump on top of them until they sink."

Weil flushed under her tan for a moment, and her mouth tightened. Then she shrugged.

"If you don't need a doctor—"

"No. Maybe a healer and some hot hoeg. Make that a *lot* of hot hoeg, and I don't care what formula."

"Sweetened?"

"As I said, if it doesn't drink me first, I'll drink it. Then I think I want to lie down—"

"Better not count on that. The Study Group is sending down representatives, to interrogate—ah, interview you."

"Me?"

"Us, actually. So if you want to talk things over with me beforehand—"

"That sounds like plotting against the Group." As her face hardened again, he added hastily, "Or at least that's what the Directorate will call it. You may have nothing to lose from such a charge, but what about—?"

"You? How important are you?"

looked old enough that his children's children might already be seeking mates. Or could he be a veteran racer from the days before the railsteamers, when a crack carrier driver was written up in more than the leaf-scrap journals and his share of the wagers made on his runs could leave him a wealthy man?

I Hmilra had been a fair whip in his younger days and could recognize the embers of old fire still glowing in the driver. They shot down the road at a pace that always allowed them to swerve around or aside from other traffic and kept the wheels firmly on the pavement. But the margin between the carrier and disaster was always as thin as a drinkshop brawler's patience. Only his position and experience with a few such runs himself kept I Hmilra able to seem calm.

The commander had no such experience, and was too busy controlling his dreezan to have any strength left over for hiding his fear. His troopers clearly found this entertaining; I Hmilra found it all the more reason to keep his own face an impenetrable mask, which he vowed to maintain even as the water closed over his head. . .

They reached water level only a trifle behind the Drylanders, but on this last stretch before the turnoff to the fort, traffic was still heavier. I Hmilra stared glumly at the water curling over the beach, almost to the foot of the stone causeway. Between tide, wind, and probably a storm far offshore, the water was too high to allow passage along the beach.

I Hmilra had seen pictures of the early days of Fort Huomikki, twenty Greats before the Drylanders came to the Island Republic. It had been an island surrounded by water deep enough for the early harbor steamers. Now, often as not, a well-shod walker could pass at low water dryfooted from the mainland to the gate of the fort.

I Hmilra bent forward to call to the driver, then sat back, he hoped, before anyone noticed him. More slyn

without blocking the carrier. The commander's curses filled the air, so loud that I Hmilra couldn't have heard his own even if his mouth hadn't been suddenly dried into silence.

The driver's whip cracked like a rifle shot, and the Drylander's mount reared. I Hmilra had an unpleasantly good view of a discolored nail on a foretoe, and a brown patch across its belly from rear rib to male organ.

Then the dreezan lost its balance, skidding and toppling to the right. I Hmilra saw the Drylander in midair, wished him a landing with only painful injuries, then needed all his strength and every hand and foothold the carrier offered in order not to follow the Drylander.

The dreezans swung hard to the left; smoke rose as the driver locked the brakes on the left wheels. That kept the carrier from riding up and over the falling dreezan, perhaps even from overturning. As the team and carrier hit the edge of the road, the driver unlocked the brakes, cracked the whip, and sent the dreezans lunging ahead.

The Drylanders in the speeder had stopped to watch their comrade's fate. Now they were trying to get underway again. They were too late. The driver turned again, this time swinging the stoutly built carrier against the lighter speeder like a whiplash against a dreezan's flank.

The speeder came apart. Its two occupants were suddenly only two more pieces of debris flying through the air. One of them landed rolled up into a ball, and when he stopped moving, uncurled himself without apparent injury. I Hmilra thought it was the driver. The other flew like a rocket clean over the boulders, which would have cracked his bones to powder, and landed with a mighty splash in a weed-slimed tide pool. He also rose, sputtering and cursing in a way that no mortally hurt creature could have managed.

I Hmilra established that his legs would support him and that his teeth would not chatter. Then he rose, gripping the back of the driver's seat.

thought, that the incident had touched off violence among the various races of the fort's garrison.

Then he heard heavy guns firing. His thoughts turned to even worse possibilities, such as an attack by the Imperial Hask Squadron, at long last come out from behind its minefields—

"Damned recruits," the doctor muttered. "Even at drill, they can't get four guns off within a six-breath of one another."

"Oh, and when were you a gunner?" someone muttered, just loud enough to be heard.

"I helped defend Fort Kirja when the pirates attacked overland," the doctor snapped. "That was three days of battle. The only powder you've ever smelled is what you put in your hair."

The same or another someone made a rude noise but no other reply. The doctor stepped back from Borlund.

"All right, my young friend. To the best of my knowledge and belief, you're none the worse for your bath. Go take that hoeg for its heat, and some herb water and wafers to balance your fluids."

The idea of eating anything solid made Borlund's stomach shudder. To cover that, he looked at the clock on the wall. His nerves were *not* what they ought to be, if he thought the noise of firing practice and recruits going out to drill meant serious trouble.

Fort Huomikki was a key installation; a third of its garrison was picked Host regulars, half artillery and half infantry. It was also a major training camp for the Saadian Coastal Defense, whose recruits supplied a good part of the rest of the garrison.

Then an unmistakably human voice rose above the din:

"In the name of the Drylander Study Group, I demand entrance."

An unintelligible Kilmoyan reply.

"Very well. Then I *request* entrance, to speak to Sean Lincoln Borlund."

didate Borlund to the Group House," he said. "It was sufficient to both carry and guard him and his baggage. No, I don't know who we were supposed to guard him against—I was the junior member of the party."

Medvedev was not too junior to be free with accusations against a Kertovan or Kertovans unknown for assaulting the party on the high road just outside the fort. He was not so free with the names of the Kertovans. Barbara Weil 'finally lost what remained of her patience over that.

"The one you suggest may have assaulted you is Captain Over Captains Jossu I Hmilra. Very senior, very well-connected, and under the Fleet Reserve Law my superior and patron."

"I know all that, you garcik!" Medvedev snapped, using the most obscene form of the word for a sterile female. It implied that she was sterile due to vice or excess.

Weil's return look should have peeled paint off the walls. Borlund felt like throwing his cup at either of them, but decided not to waste the hoeg. Instead he stepped between them.

"Am I supposed to be quartered at the Group House or not?"

"Yes, as soon as we can take you there."

"When will that be?"

"Ah—as soon as I can gain access to a telephone."

The doctor, who'd managed to listen to the whole exchange in silence until now, laughed. "You can send word faster by walking, or hiring a recruit as messenger. We've only been on the wire-speaker net for two Greats, and the sea air puts it out half the time. Besides, it will take longer to get permission than to send the messenger. May I offer one of my orderlies, if they're all free?"

Refusing hospitality was a cardinal sin in Kertovan etiquette. Offending the doctor with that sin might make him willing to tell other Kertovans about the conversa-

chapter 6

"WAN'WA CROSSING! All out for Wan'wa Crossing!"
"I heard you the first time," Jossu I Hmilra muttered under his breath. The steward either didn't hear or thought a Captain Over Captains was beneath his notice. He tramped aft down the passage between the seats and vanished, still bawling, through the rear door into the next wagon.

I Hmilra was long since on his feet and heading for the front door, his attendant behind him. The man was really not needed for such a short journey, ending at the estate, but I Hmilra had not brought him for the work he was expected to do.

He had come out of town because the newsgatherers were on the prowl like Seakin on the flanks of a school of miuni. I Hmilra had never in ten Greats caught the man yielding to any temptation that a good servant was expected to resist, but why expose him to more? Slyn flowed like drinks, and drinks flowed like a broken feedwater pipe as newsgatherers sought to amuse themselves and perhaps even their readers by gathering fact, stories, rumors, and outright lies about today's unseemliness at Fort Huomikki.

There was such a thing as exposing a virtuous man to too great temptation. As the Watch made no objections (or at least no more than formal ones), the attendant boarded the fourth-twenty train with I Hmilra.

per, but the Fleet could live with her temper and she would see more with one eye than most did with two.

A pity that it will be hard to procure justice against those who hurt her. Perhaps favor to the Drylanders who saved her will be easier?

Several servants now climbed down to load the baggage and help I Hmilra up into the high-wheeler. He brushed them off and scrambled up beside the driver.

"After that train ride, I need fresh air more than invisibility," he said.

"Aye, those rail-riding things lock you up and then joggle you all about until you've less teeth than a new babe," the driver said. He was the last of the estate's original staff still on duty, and he'd come to the I Hmilra household even before then, a fisher lad with youth-tufts still covering half his face. All those Greats of service had earned him a free tongue, as little as I Hmilra felt like chatting.

"I once felt the same," the captain said. He grinned. "Particularly after hearing one of Othan's lectures on the future of railsteamers!"

"The lad did go on a bit, he did."

"Oh, he's put his money where his tongue wagged, and done well enough by it. Besides, there's more than money coming out of the rails. They're one way we can hope to build up the metalworking, for when we need more ships."

"Then you think it's coming to war, Captain-Born?"

The whistle of an approaching train saved I Hmilra from an embarrassing silence. By the time the twenty wagons of baled tasselroot, lumber, and canned oil had rolled by, he'd chosen words to the purpose.

"There's more than wars needing new ships," he said. "The Confederation will be many Greats buying ships before they can build them in their western provinces, and better they buy from us than from the Empire."

"Better still they stay ashore altogether," the driver

appealed more than it appalled. It would take the edge
off his curiosity about her, at least.

Not that he expected much to come of the curiosity;
at her age she doubtless had two or three children by as
many different sire-parents, as well as the responsibili-
ties of her position. Second-in-command of a Fleet vessel (even a shorehugger) was high Kertovan rank for a
human, and the negotiations for it might well have taken
longer than the gestation of a baby. (Would have, if any
Fleet priests put their hands into it!)

"Follow me," came another voice, this time with the
expected Saadian accent but the flavor of education as
well. Borlund followed.

He followed the Saadian accent across what seemed
like hundreds of meters of smooth, slick deck, coated
with dew over a light-toned varnish that made it just
possible to see where one was going. Oil lamps burned
in the standard positions at bow, stern, and along either
beam. Also as usual, they helped more with the navigation of other ships than with the navigation of *Lingvaas*'s own decks.

The journey couldn't have been that long—*Lingvaas*
was just over sixty meters from bow cap to banner
pole—but it was long enough for the sudden blaze of
light from below to dazzle Borlund. Carefully using both
hands and feet, he descended the ladder, then realized
that he'd forgotten his bag on the deck. He started back
up the ladder, and a familiar voice spoke behind him.

"Don't worry. I'll have one of the hands drop it in
your cabin. Come on around to mine for some hot
hoeg?"

Borlund would have accepted hot Seakin milk; he
was chilled and aching on top of his fatigue. He nodded,
and Weil gripped him by both shoulders and turned him
around, then squeezed hard.

"Welcome aboard," she said, then frowned. "Was that
doctor right, about you being fit?"

agreement with them not to do that. So keep your tongue between your teeth."

If you knew how many secrets I've been keeping since I was fourteen Standard, you wouldn't be fussing at me like Melissa the morning after our baby had the belly cramps!

"I'll keep my tongue anywhere you want it—"*not quite the way I wanted to say it* "—if I can thaw it out with that hoeg first."

"I can live with that bargain."

THE HIGH-WHEELER ROLLED UP TO THE GATE WITH THE mist turning TO rain that would hurt the crydo, and that the tasselleaf, already peeping over the lower fences, didn't need. The freight wagons turned off to the rear as the high-wheeler pulled to a stop. I Hmilra slid down from the seat, gripped a rump strap as his feet skidded on wet stone, then regained balance before he lost dignity.

"Many thanks, Pian."

"Pleasure's ours, Captain."

On the long walk through the entry hall, the reception hall, and the art gallery, I Hmilra caught the whiff of cooking, succulent if unidentifiable scents. So he was not surprised to find the study in order, with a fire in the hearth, his chair drawn up to it, gruuyan, biscuits, and the day's post on the brass tray on the sidetable, and Alikili nowhere in sight.

That meant she was back by (please, Lady, not *in*) the cookhall, and watching or at least listening to every move the cook made. He would be in a broth of injured vanity tomorrow, probably needing to be solaced with a raise or a banquet large enough to make him feel needed.

I Hmilra mentally composed the guest list for such a banquet as he sorted the post. A double sheaf of invitations to affairs given for no better or worse reasons than the one he'd considered. The day's journals—which he

driver; of the others who might qualify Ehoma Tuomitti was not fit to be moved and in no danger of legal trouble, and the other two were Drylanders. Kekaspa was not so fond of Drylanders that even for one in danger of serious legal attention she would use so many favors to take him safely out of town.

There was more room to wonder about the nature of the driver's "illness." Was he merely likely to be punished with unjust severity out of a desire to make an example and pacify the Drylanders? Or did Kekaspa know that the driver was active in some cave of Saadian rebels—and if she had learned that, how, and had she traded secrets that were not hers to give away?

Also—and I Hmilra looked at the letter's wrapper— the letter had come in the form of a regular posting, complete with the pay-seal, but it could not have come out from the city in time to be found in the post bin at the gate this day. Somebody had brought it and slipped it in with the rest of the post. Who?

Better not ask, I Hmilra realized. He had already been made sufficiently conspicuous by his own curiosity and the driver's—*let us call it bold initiative*. Making his own household even more aware than they already were, that he was at the center of irregular events, would be foolish.

One question he could ask, however, because it would be asked of one who already knew enough and more. Had Kekaspa given the driver's "attendants" (presumably among her trusted streetprowlers) instructions to kill the man if he was in danger of capture and interrogation?

A question that could be asked, but need not be. Kekaspa would know that her streetprowlers would not risk their freedom for the driver beyond a certain point—nor would she risk hers, or her husband's rank. She would leave that matter to their discretion—but had probably ordered them to take the driver so far upcountry that bandits were more dangerous than the Watch.

"I've known a few who were. That was one's favorite phrase."

"Don't slip like that when you face the Directorate."

"If I get a good night's sleep, I'll be awake when I do."

Weil looked embarrassed, annoyed, and amused all at the same time. Amusement won out. She winked.

"No, that's not an offer," Borlund added, managing not to be hasty. "I said a good night's *sleep*, not a good *night*."

"A useful distinction, I admit."

"One question. I can see this cult of doing nothing growing out of the cult of 'natural social evolution.' But I never heard any of this back on the Island."

"The old guard of the Study Group Directorate has too many friends on the Island Council, and you must know what they're like."

Borlund nodded. "They'll accuse you of wanting to turn rogue if you offer to teach a night-school course in engineering at a level the Kertovans reached fifty Greats ago. I suppose they give the Directorate a free hand. But what about the ones the Directors send down? Don't they talk? Or do they fall overboard?"

Weil's face showed that he'd gone beyond a joke. "I've never been willing to believe all the 'accidents.' Don't you believe them either. And watch your back."

That opened more questions than it answered, but dealing with a quarter of them *would* keep them up all night. Borlund also admitted that his curiosity now went beyond his own survival, into how Barbara Weil had ended up in as high a rank as any human held at sea among the Kertovans.

The humans ran part of the coastal traffic around their own island of Yproga, as well as fishing and research vessels. But the custom of a Kertovan monopoly of high-seas bottoms was almost as firm as law. There had been 'accidents' to humans who tried inter-island trade too.

Borlund lurched to his feet and kissed one hand to

Alone again, they threw off the furs and ate in bed, not clothing themselves. I Hmilra could be past desire without being past admiration.

"Thank you for keeping the peace with the cook," he said. "Unhappy cooks have led mutinies in times past."

"Uitso seems not the sort to mutiny," Alikili replied. "But I imagine that we will be doing more entertaining than before, if you are going to seek the High Captaincy."

"Am I?"

"You have said nothing to make me believe otherwise. Or rather, you have left unsaid everything that could do so."

"That could be from having my thoughts elsewhere."

"Not with you. I have spent too much time with you off the couch."

"And not enough time on it?"

"I did not say that or even mean it. I meant that one learns different things about one's beloved in each place."

"Indeed." Such frankness deserved to be repaid in kind. "Whether I am High Captain or not makes little difference to the course of the next few Greats. We need to strengthen our friendship with Eneh, if only to have allies behind the forts on the Hask."

"The City-States will not be enough?"

"Remember the map. Two-thirds of them are downriver from the forts. None of them have the strength to do more than defend their walls and storehouses, provided that they are not attacked by modern artillery. Few will offer a single hair to us, unless they are satisfied with our treatment of the Saadians."

"Have they the right to sit in judgment?"

"The Saadians do, but tell that to the first three folk you meet on the road—and be riding a fast mount when you do."

"Why do I feel that it's really neither war nor Saadians that is making you uneasy?"

the wrangling had not been made public outside the kin-borders.

This could easily change. Would change; because even if Othan and Elandra held their tongues, they could not turn aside the political ambitions of her brothers, who both saw themselves as future Councillors of the Republic. They would use any weapon that came to hand.

This prospect was something best contemplated after sleep, but it was too late in a busy day for more sleep, and indeed for much contemplation.

"Arrange another light meal tonight."

"By your command, Captain-Born." She rested a hand on his chest.

"Woman, consider that my wits also grow sluggish after too much—"

"Indeed, it has been said that the wits are more vital to happy joining than—"

I Hmilra gave something between a laugh and a cough, wrenched himself out of bed, tripped over the dislodged furs, and sprawled full-length on the floor.

He would have liked to sit down with Barbara Weil over anything drinkable, water included, to discuss the Directorate's anomalous behavior. Unfortunately, by the time the pressure increased, Weil would have needed to be twins to have time for anything but her ship.

Lingvaas was preparing for sea, and Weil had not only responsibility for her own work but for seeing that the rest of *Lingvaas*'s humans did theirs. Being senior over three other commanders (two deck and one engineering), nine watch chiefs, and thirty-one common Farers of every shipboard speciality except stoker, Weil had enough headaches of her own without listening to Borlund's.

But she kissed him good-bye when he climbed down into the shoreboat. The gathering sunfade didn't hide it that she was a sweaty, filthy mess after a day spent sending down the old mizzen topmast and sending up the new one, but Borlund did not care.

"When are you sailing?" he asked.

"Before you're done with the Directors or they with you, I suspect."

Borlund's determination grew firmer, to do or say nothing that would bring immediate action from the Directorate. With *Lingvaas* at sea, his only other line of retreat led all the way home—which was disgrace and rout, not honorable retreat.

Unless I want to throw myself on the mercy of I Hmilra the Inscrutable?

The Captain Over Captains had plainly interested himself in Barbara Weil's career and *Lingvaas*'s mixed crew. For Borlund to presume on his slight acquaintance with Weil to ask for similar favors from I Hmilra seemed injudicious, to put it mildly.

"Who knows? They may decide I can be disposed of without so much as delaying lunch."

Weil cocked her head. "You're picking up the right degree of cynicism. Just don't flaunt it in the wrong place, which is everywhere off *Lingvaas*."

Directorate was not rocking the boat, arguing politely that such a finding would do so might permeate even the thickest Directorial skull and reach the vestigial brain within.

And, of course, Barbara Weil could be wrong about the whole Directorate, thanks to some personal grievance she hadn't mentioned. That degree of paranoia gave Borlund no pleasure, but under the circumstances he couldn't abandon it either.

The journey ashore was much less disagreeable than Borlund had anticipated.

His first surprise was the boat. It was a regular hire-craft, with two rowers and a steersman, all Kertovan. It took him in to the closest landing stage, where a human waited on the boat pier.

The human might have been from Group Security. Certainly he was even taller than Borlund, and looked as if he lifted baby Seakin or wrestled sand-apes as his morning exercise. He was also singularly taciturn, whether by order or inclination.

If he was armed, however, the weapons were well hidden. His clothes were a prosperous Farer's shore-going kilt and tunic, modified for human anatomy, with only the brass-studded shoulder loop that was the Study Group's one concession to Kertovan uniform regulations for registered Watch members.

"Can you ride?" the man asked. "I have mustekkas waiting."

Borlund's first thought was that he had never seen a mustekka large enough to carry this man's weight; it should be an interesting sight. His next thought was wondering if his answer was part of his examination.

His third thought was that paranoia had gone far enough when it made him afraid to do anything. He nodded.

"What about my baggage?"

"I have a hire-cart coming."

"It's not here yet?"

Section two floors below. However, it was right next to the Security guardpost for its floor, and it might not be entirely his imagination that the Security people gave him particularly close scrutiny when he entered or left.

Trained to recognize signs of stress or impending "deviant behavior," the Security muikken could not be given the slightest opportunity to believe that they'd found it. Borlund had enough practice in deceiving less trained people who knew him much better that he was cautiously optimistic about able to veil Security's eyes.

He didn't know what to feel about the news. What he had expected to be an "eight-Tide wonder" had barely reached the evening editions on the fifth. Either he'd overestimated what the involvement of Drylanders and Jossu I Hmilra would do to an otherwise minor incident in Kertovan-Saadian relations, or somebody was trying to discourage public attention to the affair.

Probably the latter, with several somebodies putting their oars in, half of them for legitimate motives. Too much news coverage had been know to corrupt or confuse Security investigations, or even lead to riots, which did the same job even more thoroughly.

Borlund decided to go on reading the papers. Otherwise something vital to his own case might arise unexpectedly, to leap out and bite him at the examination.

He would not read them in his room, however, since he had the freedom of the public areas of Group House. He used that freedom to walk out whenever the weather allowed, with a jacket, canteen, and reading matter in an oilskin pouch. Sometimes he sat and read, sometimes he walked and watched the city and bay, sometimes he ran with no thought but to fill his lungs with smoky, salty air and push his muscles until they sent twinges of healthy pain up and down his body.

He certainly had plenty of room. Borlund had grown up with the joke that Group House should really be called "Group Castle." Actually being there instead of

half-turned, to avoid both vulnerability and confrontation, recognized even in the twilight with his peripheral vision his escort of three days ago, and saw that the man now wore a Security tunic with full insignia. Not to mention a pair of ostentatiously expensive and laboriously polished boots.

"Good day to you, Farer," Borlund said. It was an opening to which no one could possibly object, unless they were determined to find something to object to.

"It is a good enough day," the man replied. "Tomorrow may not be so good, at least for you."

"Do I see the Directorate or merely an Evaluation Committee?"

"The second, Farer," the man said. "I doubt that your actions loom so large that the whole Directorate will devote itself to them."

Borlund wasn't sure if this was meant to be encouraging or not. At least they were following standard procedure, and the Security man was definitely being polite, which was more good than bad.

Unless I'm being soothed in order to be caught off-guard tomorrow.

That was the paranoia rising too high again. "Is there anything I have to do tonight?"

"Most of the people you're likely to see are early risers. I suggest a bath, dinner, laying out your clean clothes, and retiring to bed early."

Borlund nodded. He could not read much into a Security man's giving him commonsense advice. It did seem to argue against any plans to throw him to the sand apes, to be pulled apart until his gnawed bones were good only for the cubs' playthings.

"Thank you." Borlund remembered just in time not to offer the man money or promise favors. Both would be considered bribes. Apart from the strict ethics of Security, the man was old enough to be his sire-parent.

"Good luck to you, Farer Borlund," the Security man said. He slipped away with that peculiar stance

he saw in corridors leading off the stair landings made it plain that the folk of the godhouse had once been friendlier to the Dark One than anyone cared to be now.

Of course, the humans of Kilmoyn had also used their share of caves and deep tunnels in their time on the planet. On the island, they'd even built an underground complex deeper than this one. It held the computers, classrooms for covert-knowledge training, machine shops and arsenals for the reserved weapons, and a hydroelectric plant driven off an underground river. All of it high value, if not outright irreplaceable, and all of it material that would produce not just cultural contamination but cultural chaos if spread generally across Kilmoyn.

Group House wasn't supposed to have anything like this, although there were rumors of an improvised computer and reserved weapons disguised as standard ones. The Study Group had to be more careful than most humans about keeping up the Drylander image, so that all the dire repercussions from the advent of "sky gods" would not bring Kilmoyn's natural cultural evolution to a sticky end.

Borlund wondered about the rumors. He wondered if "supposed to" wasn't the critical phase. Then he stopped wondering, as the fifteeth door opened on what at first glimpse seemed another endless corridor.

It ended after only six paces, in a trio of doors set into the far wall of a low, hemispherical chamber. The walls were bare stone, although ancient brickwork showed in the doorsills. This place had to be as old as the godhouse, if not older; it might even be pre-Skyfall. That could explain how it had come to be; pre-Skyfall societies had abundant labor, slave and free, that few of their successors had been able to emulate after the meteorite strikes, tsunamis, earthquakes, and "secondary kill" (what Bridget had called "the Four Horsemen of the Apocalypse") had done their work.

This setting looked right for a persecuting religion's torture chamber, but was probably only intended to discourage eavesdroppers—particularly eavesdroppers with holes in their pockets, who might listen to the clink of coins from leaf-scrap newsgatherers. Once upon a time it had been assumed that no human would deal with those, but the assumption had been plainly a fairy tale well before Sean Borlund was born.

The Examiners were seated at a long wooden table, with inkwells and papers in front of them, and a recording book in front of the junior member. Two from Security, their chests covered even if they did carry swords as well as holstered pistols. The swords were light dress weapons that would snap like fishbones if they ever met one of the heavy-bladed cutlasses in *Lingvaas*'s arsenal. All very orthodox.

So was the first part of the Evaluation. Borlund identified himself, verified that the documents submitted in his name were authentic, summarized his life and skills, and stated his intention to serve a full three years with the Study Group.

The second part was more orthodoxy in action. It was a series of questions, some of them more personal than Borlund cared for, others intended to test his ability to think on his feet or hold his tongue in the face of provocation. He'd already answered many of the questions for his qualifying tests or discussed them with veterans of service with the Study Group.

This last wasn't strictly legal, but only people who intended to go back for further terms fretted about the law. Borlund began to wish that he'd thought more about the implications of this before he came to Saadi. He might not have found Barbara Weil's suggestions so startling.

"Why is the Study Group in Saadi instead of Kehua?" the middle Councillor asked. It sounded like a low-pitched woman's voice, although it was hard to tell from the face.

"What about them?" was what Borlund did *not* say. He also rejected handing the Evaluators the answer they clearly wanted to hear. The simplest answer was always the safest. From the age of ten, he'd learned that authority figures didn't care to learn how easily you'd seen through their attempts to fool you.

Borlund took refuge in formality.

"Exactly how are the Saadians connected to this line of questioning?"

More exchanges of looks. This time the exchanges included the two Security guards. Borlund wondered if they were getting bored with the chase down a theoretical blind alley, or something more. Did Security have a different perspective on human-Kertovan relations, being at the sharp end of it more often than most other humans?

Something to bounce off Barbara Weil, if he ever had a chance to talk to her again.

"Would the position of the Saadians affect your loyalty to the present terms of our relations with the Island Republic?"

Borlund had to run that one through his mind twice before he understood it, and a third time before he could reply.

"I think the Kertovans and the Saadians are going to have to settle the future of their relationship themselves. We can't offer them much advice that they'd be willing to take, even if we were willing to risk our cover story."

"Then you think the relationship may be adjusted peacefully?"

"If it needs adjusting, and I'm not an expert on that, maybe. Even if it comes to a fight, we ought to stay as neutral as we can and be able to deal with both sides after peace breaks out. That will help more than anything else."

This time the nods were unmistakable. Borlund didn't allow himself to relax; he had the distinct feeling it wasn't over yet.

nobody noticed. The three Evaluators had their heads together and were whispering. The Security were exchanging looks that to Borlund showed infinite boredom. He sympathized.

The woman cleared her throat. "Candidate Borlund. Clearly you have caused a good deal of trouble without any intention of doing so. In fact, your motives were humanitarian and highly honorable.

"The trouble is just as real. Would you be prepared to take as your first assignment one that would keep you out of this city for the rest of the year at least? By that time, you will not be trailed by newsgatherers every step you take."

Borlund nodded. The speech didn't tell him what further response they expected.

"You don't feel that your parent-partners and offspring will be disgraced?"

This time Borlund wanted to laugh. Two of the women had thought it was almost supernatural that he had passed the tests at all!

"I seriously doubt it."

"Do you have a preference for assignment, within these limits?"

Time to start the game in earnest.

"Something as far inland as possible. I can do without seeing any more saltwater for a while."

This time it was headshakes. "Not possible, I'm afraid," the woman said. "The border areas are unstable, and the telegraph and railroads are in everywhere else. "No, we'll have to send you to sea. You've dealt with the humans aboard *Lingvaas*. Do you think assignment aboard her would work out—?"

Borlund's efforts to strangle a laugh nearly strangled him. The woman actually looked concerned.

"Did you have any problems you would care to discuss?" one of the men asked. "We know that ship's something of an experiment, and with a garcik running the human side of it . . ."

apologies sounded almost sincere as they wished him well in this challenging and unpleasant assignment.

Even the privacy of his room wasn't enough for Borlund. He stuffed his head under the pillow and two blankets before he let out half a Watch's pent-up laughter.

When he caught his breath, he realized that he'd naturally thought in Kertovan units of time. Maybe he did have "fur on the brain," but if so he was going to one of the few places where that was safe or even desirable!

Aygsionan, the purser would have let mother and child drown, possibly even smiling as they sank, certainly muttering, "Well, if the shtrug couldn't swim, why didn't she wait for a ferry?" He'd heard of Borlund's feat, hadn't been happy to see him turn to in the storm three commons ago without going overboard, and would be loudly unhappy about letting such a Saadi-lover contaminate his ship's decks any longer.

Igrinsaan was turning redward, but not hard enough to heel. The screw was slowing, however, and the topcrew were scrambling aloft, managing to look both quick and clumsy at the same time, as Kilmoyans so often did to the human eye. The foresail and fore topsail shrank, and soon *Igrinsaan* was ghosting in toward her anchorage with barely steerage way from her propeller.

Borlund was below decks when the anchor went down and the steam shot up the whistle, venting boilers and signaling the shore at the same time. It didn't take him long to finish packing, since he'd brought only a Farer's seabag and a hundred slyn in small bills and coin.

The balance of the letter of credit was on deposit at the Study Group Financial Cooperative. After some mental debate, he'd finally decided that implying he didn't trust them by depositing it elsewhere would be rudeness without good purpose, at least for now. (Which was a phrase he found himself using quite a bit lately.)

There was *Lingvaas*, close inshore, her after topmast missing and only shreds of sail on two yards on the mainmast. The storm had also scoured paint off her funnel, making it look fungus-splotched, and a repair party was over the side in two workboats.

Lingvaas had been to the wars, or at least through the same storm as *Igrinsaan*. With that much work to do aboard, they'd certainly not be quick to refuse able-bodied Farers, and if they had crew in the sick berth (not that Borlund wished any such bad luck)—

"Huh, Farer Borlund."

shiny-new. Hair short (the alternative to long enough to braid) and face clean-shaven (again, the alternative to a full beard).

"Permission to come aboard?" he asked, not sure which of the two Kilmoyans and three humans in sight was in charge—"had the deck," was the term he remembered.

"Permission granted," one of the humans said, in High Kertovan. "I'll inform Ladysoul—ah, Second Captain—Weil, that you've reported."

That seemed to settle any question of his being accepted, but where did that nickname come from? It was a high compliment, implying that someone's soul had been passed down from the time of the Lord and Lady creating water and land. A rare privilege, granted only to those who did well with each reincarnation.

Not to mention the other title. It was a title, not a rank—Barbara was no doubt still some level of watch commander. But as a title, it meant that she was now officially third-in-command of *Lingvaas*, next to Captain Viligas himself and a Kertovan Second Captain whose name Borlund could not for the moment remember.

No calling her "garcik" here! Borlund felt even more kindly toward *Lingvaas* than before.

But here came "Ladysoul" Weil herself—and Borlund had just time to salute the sternpost before he saluted her. (Again, the safest course. Fleet discipline wasn't strictly enforced aboard survey ships the size of *Lingvaas*, but he'd wait for someone to tell him that officially.)

"Welcome aboard, Farer Borlund." Weil returned the salute, then held out a hand. Borlund took it, as gently as if it had been made of glass.

He thought Weil was trying not to laugh, and he knew he saw her wink. Then she squeezed his hand and stepped back.

"Report to the steward for a bunk assignment. The Captain will want to see you before lights' out, but he's

cold-souled but most of whom would get away with anything (or anyone) they could.

Hence the armed guards on this picnic, four of the household's best, rifle-armed, vigilant, and carefully placed. Also two more, even more carefully placed, to be invisible to anyone who crept close enough to note the places of the first four.

But Alikili was holding out a plate loaded with smoked meat and salt fish, topped by sweetcrusts, and a full cup in the other hand. I Hmilra decided that he'd let the landscape take his attention long enough, and took the offerings.

This left him with nothing to hold the knife and fork, but Alikili's ingenuity came to their rescue. She popped both handle-first into I Hmilra's mouth, and watched while he tried to thrust them into the food.

With immoderate self-control, she didn't burst out laughing until I Hmilra had managed to impale the food without impaling himself. She was still giggling when he set everything down on the Hyolian-weave blanket.

"We are really too old for this," I Hmilra said. As an effort to subdue the lady, it was an abject failure. She laughed again, until she finally had to lie back on the blanket and pull her shawl over her face.

I Hmilra felt his own self-command slipping away. It would have departed entirely, except that he had a mouthful of pickled yoritsk and he was afraid of choking on the odd bone.

He finally swallowed. Then he swallowed again, as Alikili undid the top three thongs of her tunic. He wondered if the guards were looking their way.

"Lady, I'm an old man."

"Age is in the mind. I found none this morning."

I Hmilra remembered the morning, with the room sunwashed by the south windows, and how long it had been after they awoke before they left the bed. Perhaps she had the right of it.

He also remembered going back to sleep, then wak-

"Indeed. And where are they to come from?"

I Hmilra started to reply. She ran her fingers along his lips. He smiled and pretended to bite.

"No, hear me out. Where are they to come from, but from Saadi? And will they come from there, with relations between the Saadians and the Republic as they are now?"

"A good many Saadians will come forward, for a chance to learn warriors' skills."

Alikili replied with a silent but speaking look that mirrored I Hmilra's own thoughts. *The Saadians will come forward, to learn what they may someday use against us.*

"You doubt the value of the estates?"

"Their value seems to depend on how we and the Saadians go on with each other, over the next generation. Even if there is peace, in twenty Greats I will be too old to take much pleasure in wealth."

"Now it is my turn to remind you about age being in the mind."

"They say age is in the mind. They also say death is in a lonely bed."

He bent down and brushed her forehead with thumbs and lips. He wished he could do more. That was her plainest statement yet, that she did not really care to outlive him. The thought was flattering, but also a death sentence for someone so much younger. He swore himself to say or do nothing that anyone could imagine as encouraging her in that notion.

Instead he considered this new aspect of his old dilemma. He had begun to realize that he would decide between the High Captaincy and leading the expedition to Eneh mostly on the basis of profit.

High Captains wielded more power. But the leader of a larger expedition than any sent against the pirates of Luokkan would be no petty leader, and custom and distance from the Islands tolerated certain financial privileges for such. If he could not gather in a few hundred

motioned them to the other two chairs at the round table.

"Welcome aboard, Farer Borlund. Weil's sponsoring you says much. Your file says more."

Not half as much as I'm sure you'd like to know.

Viligas asked half a dozen questions, all intelligent, none idle, and most capable of being answered without revealing any secrets. However, the one exception needed all Borlund's tact and ingenuity.

"You are not being seriously punished for your actions, it seems," Viligas said. "Is your Directorate viewing the matter less seriously than we had expected?"

Borlund wondered, among many other questions, who "we" were. However, what he was expected to produce was answers, not questions. *Preferably without discussing a meeting the Directorate would prefer to keep secret from any Kilmoyan.*

Borlund cleared his throat, not only to delay his answer. His throat had been tickling since he came aboard and was beginning to hurt. He hoped his drenching in the storm hadn't finally caught up with him. Spending his first few commons aboard *Lingvaas* in the sick berth was for many reasons a dismal prospect.

"I don't have any access to recent information," Borlund said cautiously. "Not even the leaf-scrap ravings. The storm ruined them all before I had a chance to read them."

"I also imagine that aboard any ship with old Zaalpotz as purser, the cabin lighting was cavelike," Viligas said.

"That also," Borlund replied. He looked at the overhead and lined up his thoughts, forming a sequence that he hoped would be both informative and discreet.

"The more serious part of the day's incident was the confrontation with Captain Over Captains Jossu I Hmilra. I know nothing about that except what I read, and I'm not sure that is knowledge."

duties there, you will take instruction in deck seamanship, navigation, and engineering. As soon as we can do so without any protesting, you will be declared a Command-Candidate and allowed to sit for your Deck certificate. Is this fair enough?"

Borlund had not expected half of this, let alone being asked if it was enough. He decided that false modesty wouldn't go over well, and besides, right now he felt very little modesty of any kind.

It didn't hurt that Barbara Weil was grinning at him, with a complete disregard for what this might tell Captain Viligas.

"I hope I'm worthy of your trust, Captain."

Borlund didn't remember if he was offered a drink or not, or if he took it if offered. He did pocket a certificate for an impressive list of clothing and gear, all to be deducted from his next pay bag (or next three or four, from the likely cost).

Then he was climbing the ladder to the main deck, to be greeted by a large, stout Kertovan woman.

"You Borlund?" she asked. He couldn't place her accent, except that it made him wonder if she had a speech defect.

"Yes."

"That's aye-aye, Farer," the woman said.

"You must be the steward."

"Always that bright, are you? Let's see how bright you can make the pots. We've a few needing cleaning."

"Aye aye, ma'am."

At least that couldn't hurt. What did hurt was the laughter from farther forward, both human and Kilmoyan. Clearly the mixed crew was successful in one way—they all found that breaking in a new hand offered first-class entertainment.

Centuries passed. The Kilmoyans groped their way back to their previous level of civilization, then passed it. Three major power centers developed around the Western and Greater Seas: the Empire of Alobolir to the west, the Kertovans on the islands in the middle, and the Confederation of Dhandara on the continent to the east. A multitude of lesser powers, City-States, tribes, and other entities flourished or faltered.

But the upward urge continued. In the tenth century after the comet, a late Victorian Englishman dropped in a Kertovan city might have found much of the technology familiar. He also might have noticed a lack of noisome slums (preventive medicine was developed early, to hold down infant mortality), women laying out along the yards of ships, privately owned ironclads, domesticated killer whales (or their first cousins, anyway) used as coastal tugs, and much else to make him wonder if he had fallen asleep while reading one of H. G. Wells's tales.

If he had looked and listened long enough, he might have discovered that the Kertovans also had a streak of optimism. But it was not the complacent optimism of a Britannia that ruled the waves, it was the hard-won confidence of those who have taken the worst the seas of Kilmoyn could throw at them and wrested prosperity from the waters.

THE STARSHIP *RAMPART* WAS HALFWAY THROUGH A five-year, thousand-light-year voyage when she struck the dust cloud on the fringes of the Kilmoyn system. She survived; her ability to travel faster than light did not.

Most of the hundred crew and two thousand hibernators aboard survived. So did nearly all the eight thousand suspended embryos. With a reasonably large and carefully screened gene pool, if the Ramparters could get safely down on Kilmoyn they ought to survive.

By the skin of their teeth, they did. They'd hoped to leave the ship crewed (at least by hibernators) and in

technology, including medical research and a limited production of modern weapons and the stockpiling of their ammunition. In order to avoid inbreeding, they also worked out what amounted to a system of group marriages, with genealogical records rigorously kept pending the restoration of DNA typing. The social arrangements and taboos supporting this system were complex, including a near-ban on recreational sex.

In time, the Kertovans allowed a human settlement in their colonial capital of Saadi. Nobody on either side had illusions about generosity: this was an experimental laboratory that let each side study (and spy on) the other. But the benefits went both ways. Three generations after *Ramparts* entered orbit around Kilmoyn, it has become a high honor for a human to be chosen for the Study Group in Saadi.

day. With slyn, which we don't have enough of. I could feed this whole crew like Captain-Borns if I had enough slyn, which I don't and won't. So I have to throw myself on the mercy of fumblehands like you, who carve off half a kivirik trying to peel it!"

The cook brandished the ladle, until Borlund wanted to back away. He couldn't, or Belindouza would bully him even more than she did already.

He took a deep breath. "Give me a whetstone. I thought the peeler was sharp enough. Maybe I was wrong."

"No maybe about it. Sharpen it until you can split a hair with it, and keep it that way."

Borlund wanted to groan and knew he didn't dare. Peeling vegetables was either the last job at night or the first in the morning. Making it longer could only cut into his sleep or his study time.

It would have to be sleep, he decided. He couldn't let Barbara down—and he had the feeling that behind her were quite a few other people, some of them present only in spirit, whom he'd also be letting down if he didn't make himself into a proper Farer.

The whetstone clunked down on the deck at his feet. He picked it up without taking his eyes off Belindouza, and she favored him with a brief, teeth-baring sort of smile.

LINGVAAS WAS RIDING UNDER FORE AND MAIN TOPSAILS and a reefed aftermast lower. Not a way to get anywhere fast, but she was two commons ahead of schedule and Captain Viligas wanted to give the crew shore leave. So they were dumping ashes from cold boilers, painting the funnel, and so forth, while the winds pushed *Lingvaas* across the Osorikin Gulf as they had pushed her forerunners in the years when *Rampart* was still a file in a computer on Esperanza and no human now living on Kilmoyn was even a gleam in their parents' eyes.

The quartering sea still sprouted whitecaps and made

bucket, only dented instead of cracked. Then he lifted the broken pieces into the harness and stood up.

Or, rather, he tried. His leg joints seemed rusted, and he could have sworn *Lingvaas* was lying far over to both redside and greenside at once, which was impossible.

"You all right?" the Kertovan said.

"I think so."

"You might have hit your head," she added, taking his arm. After a moment, Bernsdorf came up on Borlund's other side.

"Sick berth?"

"Back to the galley."

That finally drew sympathy from Bernsdorf. "Send you back to Belindouza's mercy? When Seakin mate with jouti!"

"I'm on duty."

"After the healer sees you."

Borlund wanted to shake off both sets of hands and tell them that he was just tired. He didn't want anyone standing between him and Belindouza, and not just because the cook was a law unto herself and even Captain Viligas couldn't protect most of the crew from her wrath.

He could take it. He had to—and everyone had to see that he could. Particularly the ones who didn't know it already.

FARER STEWARD'S MATE BORLUND, ARE YOU LISTENING?

Borlund was ready to put the point of his knife under his chin if he could think of a way to do it without being noticed. Instead he jerked his head up and back. The pain in his neck and shoulders sharpened, then eased a little.

"Yes."

"What was the last passage we discussed?"

"Passage?" For a moment Borlund couldn't remember if Watch Chief Teacher Guundzousa was referring to a geographical feature or a part of a book.

Everyone had been working harder than usual, so Borlund was not the only one who'd gone short of sleep.

Except that he'd been short of sleep before the coastal excursion began, and not because he'd gone ashore to visit the drinkshops and pleasure halls. The cook wanted the gallery turned out and scoured before the fresh stores came, the teacher wanted seventeen navigational problems solved, both of them wanted the work done yesterday, and neither of them seemed to have ever heard of sleep deprivation, let alone Barbara Weil.

He didn't mind it that Weil might have been on another ship for all that she seemed to be doing for him. If she'd decided that he had to prove himself to her as well as everybody else, he could live with that. He'd rather live without her afterward, but that prospect certainly wouldn't affect Weil's judgment. She couldn't afford to be suspected of favoritism, and he had nothing to offer that could outweigh that risk.

He did mind being so tired that he might be scalded in the gallery, swept overboard, or fall from aloft before he took his deck qualifications. He'd already learned how little sleep he needed; now he was learning how to catch that minimum in naps even when his bunkmates were arguing or singing.

It was a race between fatigue and learning, and if he hadn't been able to sneak bowls of commander's chowder and fat-loaded biscuits from the gallery, he'd have bet on the fatigue. But extra calories really could substitute for sleep—up to a certain point, at least.

Hand over hand, Borlund climbed the aftermast shrouds. He did it properly, pulling himself up the vertical wires and only using the crosswires to brace himself. He was horribly tempted to go through the newlies' hole, in the top platform itself, instead of outside on the shrouds, but did it proper Farer-style.

There was a bad moment when *Lingvaas* heeled sharply to redside and one of Borlund's feet slipped out of the shrouds. But instinct aided fear, and two hands

Farers tossing lines over the side. Seakin sometimes drove schools of fish toward Kertovan ships. Other times, the remnants of their own meals brought scavengers who also made good eating after a final swim through cooks' pots.

Borlund remembered a particularly good fish stew, loaded with hotleaf that he'd minced and pickled himself, and bread that he'd baked that even Belindouza said was fit to eat. He was learning to cook; maybe he could find work in a waterfront cookshop if he had to leave the sea.

He didn't want to, though. He would miss the wide waters, and the Seakin blowing, and laying aloft when the wind was enough to be exciting rather than frightening, and listening to squeezepipes and five-strings on deck on a fine night.

He would miss—oh, he'd miss a hundred things that he hadn't really learned about from coasting voyages, things that were part of the Faring life such as you could only live aboard a deep-sea ship like *Lingvaas*.

Many more than a hundred. Borlund sat down, braced himself in a corner of the top, and began the list. He might have reached fifty—he could never remember— before he fell asleep.

LINGVAAS WOKE BORLUND BY TAKING ON A CORKSCREW roll that smelled of bad weather even to a sleeping Farer. He awoke, in rain blown by a gusty quartering wind that at least kept the top clear of smoke.

The next thing he noticed was that it was dark; he might have been at the bottom of an inkwell save for the masthead lights above and the riding lights below. It was only after counting the lights that Borlund realized he was not alone.

"Farer Steward's Mate Borlund, accepting relief," he said. He had to cough twice and try three times before he could get the words out intelligibly.

"I relieve you, Farer," the visitor said. Then a hand

and said quietly, "I suppose so." He wasn't going to talk about watching the Seakin, even to Weil.

"You are," she said. "Even Belindouza thinks so. She thinks you'll be a better one if you learn the way she did. Guundzousa doesn't agree. That's why he sent you to the aftertop. Not for listening to gossip, but to get you away from old Belindouza long enough for you to catch up on your sleep. If you were Farer enough to sleep in an aftertop at sea, that is."

"What if I couldn't sleep, or fell out of the top?"

"Then I suppose you wouldn't be a Farer."

"Cold comfort, Commander Weil." He didn't want to insult her with "ma'am," but he couldn't let that remark pass completely. He'd studied the concept of "survival of the fittest" in biology and in the history of science. It was the first time that he'd been the subject of an experiment in it, and he was not going to pretend that it was at all pleasant.

"Say that again when we return to Saadi. If you can say it with a straight face, I'll let you go ashore without prejudice."

"Aye aye, ma'am," Borlund said, but he said it so that Weil only muttered a mild obscenity. Then she added, "Are you going to drink that hoeg before it freezes, or let me drink it before I do?"

making the rounds of the big table, without doing more than raising an eyebrow or quirking an ear.

The paper with the complete attention of fourteen Captains and Captains Over Captains was a proposed list for the fleet sailing to the Bishak Gulf. On that gulf was the Kingdom of Eneh's only seacoast. Someday rails might pierce the mountains south of the Hask and provide a shorter route, but for now, if one was carrying any sort of burden, one voyaged to Eneh.

"A question, and not just out of curiosity," one Captain said. "Are you sure we need so many heavy ships? That means more coal, more provisions, more store-ships to escort."

"I thought the plan was to purchase anything we might need along those lines in Rinbao-Dar," another Captain put in.

The first speaker shook his head and pulled at one ear, which was no more than a stump thanks to a Luokkan pirate's blade. "I have problems with that. Or, rather, I have problems with relying on the goodwill of two cities where Imperial agents have been running openly down the street like stray fowl these past two Greats.

"Even if we can buy, the price is likely to be higher. Then it will be either ask the Halls for more slyn, or dip into our own bags, and I have even more problems with either course."

"All the more reason for a generous allowance of storeships," Jossu I Hmilra said. "If we have enough heavy ships, their escort will be no problem. We simply sail them in the same convoys as the transports, and we *must* provide a heavy escort for those. One hostile cruiser among the transports could be a massacre."

"How many 'hostile cruisers' do we need to guard against?" yet another Captain said. He was old for his rank, unlikely to receive further rank or honors, so had nothing to lose by being an earstinger. Certainly most of what he'd said was along such lines.

read. Convert packets into escort vessels and arm the storeships and transports.

"Two—I seem to recall a shipyard report a few years ago that mentioned a huge store of plates, frames, and engine components for the *Illiks*."

. Some of the other Captains looked as if I Hmilra had performed an elimination on the table in front of his associates. He tried not to smile at the reaction.

"I admit the floating turds have an evil reputation. But that's the harbor-defense model.

"Suppose we used those existing stores and a few more to build a more seaworthy version? Higher free-board, more deck space, more ventilation—"

"More hatches for the crew to escape when the Lord-forsaken things do capsize," was the latest mutter. "Or are we breeding a new race of Farers, with teeth to gnaw through iron plates and lungs to let them swim up from Seakin depths."

"—and all of it, in sum, more ships fit to stand up against heavy guns. We might have to lighten the arma-ment and even the gunhouses, but that's not likely to draw the wrath of either the Lord or the crews."

"I suppose we could do—what's that term the new school-trained engineers are using— a 'design study' for both," I Djurr said. "I've even seen a list of ships for conversion, although I think it was ten Greats old and not amended since it was written."

"Would you care to take command of finding the list and amending it from the surveys of new ships?" I Hmilra asked.

I Djurr tugged at his lower lip. "Only if I can have an associate. It is more work than I and my household could manage alone. If Captain Kwinzuzuurus is available—"

Kwinzuzuurus, the elderly "earstinger," looked bemused, as though he could not decide whether he had been rewarded or trapped. Finally he nodded, although his ears were twitching. That might be from uneasiness, or perhaps only from age.

hands helping the four engineer-designers with their study of the old harbor-defender, or at least to keep them from falling into the bilges or off the roundbacked foredeck. This gave her plenty of time to listen to the rude remarks all ranks were making about *Byubr* in particular and the *Illiks* in general. Compared with some of the terms she'd heard, the old "floating turds" was almost praise.

She vaguely understood that the plan was to make the *Illiks* more seaworthy, for some unspecified (or at least unspoken) purpose in the near future. The silence was not so much a concern for secrecy as universal knowledge that someone had the notion of taking the *Illiks* to the Bishak Gulf. No doubt they would do well enough there if they could survive the voyage; they had been designed for shallow or confined waters and the Gulf offered plenty of these.

But between planning and doing lay a great deal of rust, many loose rivets, bent frames, cracked plates, propeller shafts as twisted as a Drilion's ethics, and doubtless more horrors not yet discovered. And this was apart from the vices built into the *Illiks* from the time the moldings were laid out on the loft floors twenty Greats ago.

Tuomitti walked aft, thinking rude thoughts about hands who left so many loose lines and wires on deck. But most of them were newlies or gray, either with much to learn or with all forgotten.

Fresh-combed or gray and balding Farers were coming aboard Fleet ships every day. Nor were they turning only to the Fleet. Merchants were launching new and crew-hungry ships almost every day.

Near the chopped-off stern, Tuomitti leaned against the after-gunhouse and watched two engineers and two deck Farers measuring beam and other dimensions with long folding rules and string. They were silent except for calling out lengths and widths to a third Farer, a gray woman with a slate and stylus who was writing them

They were also close enough that the Captain Over Captains was painfully aware of how much better they rode than he.

Jossu I Hmilra had never been a good enough rider to enjoy it, and he thanked all who might be responsible that he had been born a Kertovan and not in the Empire or on the plains of Dhandara. In both lands, riding with pretentious skill (or at least the pretense of skill) was an essential mark of one born high enough to deserve social acceptance.

In the Island Republic to this day more tencasts were covered on foot and many more by ship, than on the back of any animal. There were still growing inland towns that could be reached from the coasts only by rail.

However, today Jossu I Hmilra was riding, where hundreds of eyes would fall upon him while he did. There was no riddle to this: he had to prove to all that he was fit to command the fleet being born for next Great's campaign.

He had presided over the meeting at the club, but there he had been among friends or at least those who respected his judgment and experience. In law, the expedition commander had not been chosen. Intrigue was in the wind, the water, and the rock itself; those seeking reasons to eliminate aspirants for the position would certainly use physical unfitness as one. Anyone of I Hmilra's age would certainly be suspect (testimonies to his health and vitality from Alikili would hardly weigh much in the official balance). It was up to him to prove otherwise.

Thus he rode, although gratified that today he could take a level route along wide, clean, and dry streets. Traffic was as thick as usual, more than he had ridden in for Greats, but he usually had room to maneuver. His dreezan was also a respectable middle-aged female, used to the city's hurly-burly and unlikely to do anything embarrassing, let alone dangerous.

They rattled across the Dzern River bridge, just as a

THE COMMON ROOM OF THE GREEN NET WAS ALMOST full by the time Ehoma Tuomitti entered. Most of the crowd was the usual Farers and dockworkers, getting outside hoeg or something stronger as fast as their gullets could deal with the servers' offerings. The servers were already looking harried.

Tuomitti waved to two or three old friends, as she pushed through to the counter with more determination than tact. On the way she noticed a few unusual guests, such as a quartet of Saadian Farers, all watch chiefs, in one corner table, and of all unlikely things a Daughter of the Rock with five children in two, in another corner.

Kappala Naytet slid the usual free first cup of hoeg down to Tuomitti, loaded a server's tray with five cups and two jugs of something else, and grinned at her friend.

"You look hungry. Even the sacred room has people in it, but there are seats left."

The "sacred room" was a small chamber off the common room, fit to accommodate eight friendly folk or four on more polite terms. It was also Naytet's private dining room, when she didn't have to eat off the serving counter or off the top of the stove (when the cook had his back turned).

"Blame it on yourself," Tuomitti retorted. "You didn't pack me enough lunch."

"Oh, I gave you all I thought you could carry in your weakened condition," was the reply. "Would I lay heavy burdens on an old woman who is also an old friend?"

Tuomitti regarded her host with the eye of one contemplating where the knife would hurt most as it went in, even before she twisted it. Then a voice came from behind.

"Old woman, my pubic hair!"

Tuomitti turned. "Zhohorosh!"

"So it seemed, the last time I looked in the mirror."

nearly dropped the tray. Zhohorosh fixed the server with an even colder look and gently took the tray.

"If you've a hand free, Ehomatsi," he said, nodding toward the server.

Zhohorosh was one of the few men allowed to use the diminutive of her name in public without getting at least a sharp rap across the nasal forebone. She grinned and fished in her pocket for a handful of coins, which she handed over without bothering to count them. She was on full pay even on light duty, doubtless arranged by old I Hmilra, and Naytet was not charging her anything like full fees for her board and lodging.

The sacred room had been occupied until moments before. Now only a server remained, hastily clearing the tables. The two Farers watched him leave with an armload of dishes that he could barely see over, and even more barely avoid a collision with the Daughter and her charges as the driver led them out.

"Am I getting old in truth, or are they hiring younger and more soft-green servers in every drinkshop in the Republic?" Zhohorosh asked.

"The second, I should say," Tuomitti replied. She gripped his upper arm and squeezed. The corded muscle under the hair was as firm to the touch as ever. Zhohorosh was a Gunnery watch chief these days, and probably above helping move ammunition, but he could certainly do it if he had to.

They sat and ate porridge well seasoned and laced with lumps of saltfish, an omelette of cliff-screamer eggs with diced snouter, and fruit soup. They washed it down with enough hoeg to float a life boat; Tuomitti was still on an abstinent diet and Zhohorosh was on one for life after an engine-room accident left him with half a normal stomach.

"So, how goes the work down at the yard?" Zhohorosh asked, when both had their mouths free for talking. "Are they sending you back to sea once it's done?"

"Your grandmother's blood also endowed you with a keen ear and a nimble tongue to repeat what that ear takes in," Tuomitti said. Her smile was even wider. "I should know."

"What vile rumor is this, that I babble secrets in bed? I am as close-mouthed as a scoopshell."

"Then you must have fallen far from your old standard, my friend."

"Are you asking for proof?" He looked sober. "If it will be hard for you, or cause tales to swim—?"

"I am well enough," Tuomitti said. "And no one has told me what to do ashore and still been heard politely, these last ten Greats. The engineers will be no exception to that rule."

"Then—shall we have some more hoeg sent up to your room? Or more?"

"Just the hoeg, my friend. I admit that an over full stomach no longer leaves me at my best."

THE RAIN CAME DOWN SO LONG AND SO HARD THAT BY the time Jossu I Hmilra left the train, the platform was three lines deep in water and everyone was huddled under the canopy. He himself was wet from feet to knees with just the short walk from the train. His kilt might have to be wrung out before it was hung up over the fire, lest it drown the blaze.

The journey from the station was no pleasure either. They had to take the longest of the three roads to the house, because water was knee-deep over the shortest and a bridge was closed on the second. Both master and driver reached home almost as wet as if they'd swum all the way, and I Hmilra refused to even drip on the post until he'd bathed, then let Alikili comb him in front of the bedroom hearth fire.

The post included several of the quarter-Great's share payments that he had requested now be forwarded as negotiable certificates to his home, instead of deposited directly into his pages. He intended to make them over

and to raise the payment I think you would beggar your household, your kin, and even me."

"Not you. Never you, Alika."

"So you say. You may even believe it. What I believe is that you plan to return a hero, prize-right or not, so that you can lead the Republic in the next war against the Empire."

"It would really be the first war. We haven't fought the lands on the Hask since before the Oompleenas started calling themselves Emperors."

"Names, names. The name you want is 'hero'—"

"As long as I deserve it."

"I think you will. I also think that many people will be surprised at what you do about our relations with the Drylanders and the Saadians, when you have the power to do so."

I Hmilra was silent for a long while, his arms around Alikili. Finally he discovered what seemed like the right words.

"I am selfish. I like to see everyone around me happy, even my tuunda and the Saadians."

"The Drylanders seem to go their own way, as to happiness or misery."

"They can continue to do so, for all of me. But they are a mystery. I would like the answer to that mystery before I die."

"You think they are dangerous?"

"They have not been, so far. But the rumors of those who remained behind in the Confederation make one wonder. The Drylanders could be the greatest blessing our folk have ever known. Or they could be a greater menace than a second Skyfall."

After that they held each other in silence, too tired and lost in sober thoughts to do more.

It was as well they were north of the island. South of
it, the reefs rose, fell, and thrust out fangs at random
intervals, few of them fully charted. The islands set
among the reefs like glass ornaments on a cheap brass
chain were inhospitable even when uninhabited. When
inhabited they usually held the sort of people who did
not extend a warm welcome to shipwreck victims.

None of this was relevant to what had brought Borlund out on the swaying, dancing yard in the rising
storm. That was a simple mechanical failure in a reefing
winch, and the advantage that Drylander physiology
gave Borlund in fixing it.

The short-legged Kilmoyans were not built for laying
out along yards to set or take in sail. In their earlier ships
the sails had been handled from the deck. In their later
ships they used winches mounted in the tops. These slid
the sails in and out laterally, rather than hoisting and
lowering them vertically, as Borlund had read sailing
ships used to do on Earth.

In the last generation of sailing vessels before steam
began driving them from the oceans, the Kertovans at
least used their compact auxiliary steam engines to
drive the winches. Large ships mounted the engines in
the tops, smaller ones on deck at the foot of the mast,
with the reefing and furling chains running inside the
hollow iron or steel masts and yards.

With two propellers, *Lingvaas* had not been much
dependent on sail for safety, more so when she needed
to turn a profit from fishing alone. Turned to Fleet service, she had not been allowed the kind of refit that
would have given her steam winches. With a mixed-
race crew, she was well toward the bottom of most lists
of ships on which to spend bulging sacks of slyn. The
Drylanders weren't sea-minded and few Kertovans
besides Jossu I Hmilra and his faction thought her more
than an interesting experiment that somebody else
could underwrite.

So she still had hand winches in her tops for Farers to

leaned over the top's railing to hand him the third tool belt. Suddenly *Lingvaas* took a perverse roll to redward. Amatai was off-balance, with one hand for the belt, one hand for the ship, and none to spare for himself. His full weight came against the railing.

Borlund was already reaching when he heard the railing crack. By the time Dat Amatai fell through the gap, Borlund had both hands free and extended. One snatched the tool belt out of a gray-furred hand that was within a heartbeat of letting it fall. The other gripped the back of the old Farer's jacket, until the Farer could get his own arms and legs around the yard.

"While you're visiting—" Borlund began.

Amatai laughed. It was not a very convincing laugh, but that might have been the wind. Was it still rising? Even if it wasn't, it was already making the sail crack like a drover's whip.

Borlund lifted the hand-candle and by its guttering yellow light examined the traveler. Nothing bent, nothing broken—as far as he could see. No, wait. A small gap in the track—the track displaced just enough to block the free passage of a rider (he guessed at the last, because he couldn't see it, but it made sense). . .

"Hand me a file," Borlund said. "Please," he added, since this was as much request as order. "No, just a moment. I have two—can you hold the candle?"

Amatai looked reluctant to move so much as a whisker, but after allowing himself a half-glare, half-grin, he took the candle. Borlund quickly filed the lip of the visible crack smooth, grateful that by chance he'd picked the hardest of the files.

"Now, push the traveler outboard."

"Out—?"

"Yes, curse you!" Amatai didn't look hurt, so Borlund didn't apologize. If the traveler slid outboard too fast, it stood a good chance of taking toes off Borlund's foot or Borlund off the yard.

The traveler squealed loud enough to be heard over

"Oh, they said they'd already sighted it," Rynko said petulantly. "They haven't said anything else. Now can I go down?"

"Oh, yes, you can go down, to the galley," Amatai said. He slapped Rynko on the shoulder. "Mr. Borlund's going to want somebody to help him, when it comes to tending the survivors."

Rynko's stunned look made both Amatai and Borlund laugh, just as well for Borlund. His voice would have shaken if he'd had to reply in words.

BORLUND DIDN'T NEED RYNKO'S HELP AND BELINdouza barely needed Borlund's. The lifeboat held no handful of survivors of an epic of Farers against the sea, but the passengers of a small freighter battling a fire in the cargo.

"Now if that cargo didn't contain twelve drums of disstul oil, we'd all be better off," the boat chief in charge of the lifeboat explained. "But that stuff's of an uneasy temper. Captain Suibaar, she reckoned she'd be better off with just folk who could take care of themselves if we had a leak and a flare-up. So we went off in the boat, and it's as well you came along with the sea kicking up, but I doubt we'll be presuming on your hospitality more than overnight."

In fact, it wasn't even that long. The steward's gang had barely time to provide dry clothes (with clean binders for the two children in the boat), hot towels, clean combs, and cups of hoeg or mklk, with sausage and pickled-vegetable soup for those who wanted it. Then the word came down from the deck that the freighter *Uillam* was in sight and wanted her people back, as soon as they'd finished drying, grooming, and eating.

Dat Amatai helped Borlund get the people up on deck and into *Lingvaas*'s steam launch, then vanished. Borlund was sure he was going to cajole Belindouza to give

woman was taking a personal interest in this process. But that had to be a fantasy spawned by exhaustion.

IF BORLUND HAD NEEDED ANYTHING BUT SLEEP AND food, he couldn't tell when he awoke. He was ravenously hungry, and Belindouza seemed ready to cater to his appetite as she never had before. There was even a hot gignel pie, which turned out to be the result of a little trading between Belindouza and *Uillam*'s cook, who had been in the boat and been much relieved to find his galley and stores nearly intact when he reboarded his ship. He'd sent wholemeal, canned and dried fruits, honey, and a large jar of preserved gignels back in the returning launch.

Gignels were a long way from Borlund's favorite food, in any form. Preserved, they were always too salty. But Belindouza looked as if it would break her heart and other organs if Borlund refused at least the first three slices she offered him. He also remembered that a heartbroken Belindouza was quite capable of breaking his head once the fit of generosity wore off.

So he stowed away a breakfast even bigger than his ferocious appetite demanded. Then he washed, shaved, and went on deck to take his place on watch.

Lingvaas was bound north again, with the highest of the islands north of Lesser Turha just peering over the western horizon. To the east, open sea stretched nearly a thousand kilometers to the nearest island of the Republic, the gray horizon unbroken except for a distant and unidentifiable masthead and a still more distant smoke trail.

Borlund went through the coming-on-watch routine. He recorded the depths read by the sounderman ("No bottom with this line," which was hardly a surprise since they were off-shelf and the charts showed a kilometer of water below *Lingvaas*'s keel). He noted in the deck log the set of the sails (both mainsails and the

rank. Borlund stared. He stared so long that Guund-zousa laughed.

"I suppose it would be best to end the suspense," the Farer said. He handed Borlund the package. "You may find it useful enough to open here, and you will not offend me if you do so."

Not opening gifts in front of their givers was such a rigid point of Kertovan etiquette that Borlund looked dubious. Then he saw the helmsman so carefully not smiling, and the messenger doing a little dance as if the deck made his feet itch, and decided that he might as well offend all of them to get back for whatever game they were playing.

The package was two books, *The Practical Farer and Commander* and a blank personal log. The first was the standard reference for registered commanders, and Barbara Weil had let him dip into her well-thumbed and gravy-stained copy a few times. This copy that he held was so new that the sea breeze couldn't blow away the scent of the binding.

The log was also brand-new, and seemed to have something inside it. Borlund opened it, then gaped and dropped both the logs and its contents.

"That is no way for a new commander to treat his certificate," Guundzousa said reprovingly. Or at least he tried to achieve that tone. His voice didn't entirely cooperate.

Borlund snatched up the elaborately engraved certificate and held it up. The words danced before his eyes until they blurred, and it wasn't entirely from the breeze.

He didn't need to read it all, however. He could make out the crossed ship, sword, and Seakin of the High Farer's Council of Delegates. He could make out the words "Certificate of Command Education." He could even make out his own name, although those were the hardest words to recognize. They were the ones he had least expected to see here, at least this soon.

what I am missing, and I won't be happy until I go to sea again."

"Damn," Barbara Weil said softly. Borlund didn't think she'd intended for him to overhear her, nor for him to notice that her eyes were wet.

Suddenly she gripped him by both shoulders, then hugged him hard.

"Welcome to the sea, Sean."

"The Lord of the Waves told you to greet me, of course?" he said.

Weil wiped her eyes and smiled. "He did not. But I've served him long enough, Drylander that I am. I should have a few privileges." The smile turned into a grin. "Aren't you going to open your present?"

It was a copy of *The Maritime Compendium*, as elegantly bound as the other two books and inscribed to him. (At least as far as he could tell. Barbara Weil had many virtues; legible handwriting wasn't one of them.)

"Don't flaunt this one ashore," Weil cautioned him. "It's not precisely banned like the Devotional List, but having a copy is nailing your flag to the masthead."

"What flag? It might be one I don't mind flying."

"No, I don't suppose you would. It's the flag of those who want the Drylanders to take their place on the seas of Kilmoyn. Not all of our friends are Drylanders, and many of our enemies are. But the enemies outnumber the friends, for now."

More words danced on her lips like the whitecaps overside, but the wind blew both away. Borlund wanted to hug her back, to show he understood, was grateful, would talk with her some other time when there was no one to hear.

Instead he saluted, the double palm of highest respect. He did it so awkwardly that Weil returned it with a smile.

Then Captain Viligas came on deck, and both commanders saluted him. It was time for the serious work of *Lingvaas*'s day to begin.

"Yes. A song-story that purports to tell the truth about how the Saadians felt at coming under the rule of the Republic. From the Saadian viewpoint, although this is hardly surprising. Both the composer and the writer are not only Saadian, but flaunt the fact."

"It is pleasant to know you are not walking blindly into this snarebed."

"I will be most unpleasant if you do not speak plainly."

"Very well," Alikili said. She took such a deep breath that I Hmilra had a moment's vague apprehension that she intended to bring on a self-induced faint.

"Every political Saadian in the Republic will be there. Every leaf-scrap newsgatherer will be there, watching the Saadians, the singers, and anyone else interesting they see in the audience. Your presence there will draw more attention than the affair at Fort Huomikki."

"They will probably revive that, too," I Hmilra said, musing aloud. "And all of this, less than ten commons before the vote on the command of the expedition to Eneh."

"I had not thought you were consulting the calender lately."

"You lack a talent for sarcasm, good lady. It is true and worthy to be remembered, that many folk of the Republic suspect me of sympathies for the Saadians. Add that to the fear of the Drylanders somehow allying themselves with the Saadians, and one can understand why harsh and thoughtless words are sometimes said."

"More of them may be said if you are at the Solvarsen Theater this afternoon than ever before."

"So be it. Or do you really think that, knowing I was cautious, even a coward, the Council for War would appoint me to the command?"

"Not seeming too friendly to the Saadians is wisdom, in some people's eyes."

"In my eyes, such people are fools, and I hope they

and now thought they were a quite extraordinarily beautiful hue.

"If you think that, then you have not been listening to the servants' gossip nearly as much as you wish me to think. They would defend you as they would me. Perhaps some of them will do it because they dislike Othan's kin by marriage rather than because they honor you, but—"

She laughed and dropped the gown, then came into his arms. Her hands roamed until he was able to stop them. Then he had more work, fighting the temptation to let his own hands roam.

"I suppose if we are driving rather than going by rail, we must make haste," she said at last. Her quick breathing and bright eyes told him that her regret in this matched his own.

However, once they had survived *Song*, the reception afterward, and whatever the newsgatherers might conjure up, they planned to escape to their hostel suite. There they would be their own master and mistress until sunbrighten.

SEAN BORLUND STOOD ON *LINGVAAS*'S BRIDGE AS SHE steamed into Saadi Bay. This was no particular honor, as all the other watch-standing commanders from the Captain on down were also there. The only exception was a Kertovan watch commander-second who was up on the foredeck, with the anchoring crew and the lookouts perched on either bow and on the bowsprit itself.

Captain Viligas had taken no pilot entering the Bay, as he had been sailing in and out of it for thirty Greats and knew every possible danger spot new and old, that could endanger a ship of *Lingvaas*'s shallow draft and high maneuverability. He also knew that even on a clear day like this, there was no such thing as too many lookouts watching for small craft.

Borlund wished that *Aygsionan*'s captain had been as cautious. But then, if she had been, then he might now

which had to be taking on stores and crewmen back from shore leave, judging from the number of small boats alongside. Borlund heard an order to the steersman to turn a trifle more greenward, in case one of the boats suddenly had urgent business elsewhere.

Then a signal lamp flashed from a wing of the guardship's piled-up bridgework. Borlund looked at that bridgework with an eye he had not known he would ever have, the last time he saw the guardship. There was one vessel that would never be voyaging to Eneh or anywhere else beyond Saadi Bay. Then reading *Lingvaas's* code numbers triggered another set of new reflexes.

"Signal from the guardship!" he called.

His voice was lost as two lookouts, the signaler, and three other commanders all saw the same thing and shouted almost the same words. They all looked at one another, then Captain Viligas laughed and raised his telescope.

When he turned back inboard, the smile was gone, and his face had the look of one who has bitten into an oversalted fish. "We are to anchor off the Englanti Mole," he said. "It seems our regular anchorage is full—with what, they did not say."

"That's right by the Solvarsen Theater, isn't it?" someone said.

"Yes, and at low tide we'll barely have a safe span of water under our keel."

"Oh well," another somebody said. "Perhaps we can watch the theater crowd, or even hear some of the music if the wind is right."

"I hope it blows dead toward the theater," Captain Viligas said with dignity. Borlund swallowed a laugh, remembering that the captain was completely tone-deaf.

THE BIG HIRE-CARRIAGE PULLED TO A STOP IN FRONT OF the Solvarsen Theater. I Hmilra's servants dismounted from the dreezans and the outside seats first. Their

struck heroic poses risked an arrow in his liver or a bullet through her brain.

"Beyond that, I have nothing to say worth anybody's attention. I would like to get to my seat in time to let the performance start as scheduled. When it is done I will answer questions for as long as they make sense, or maybe even a little longer. Until then, I am going to be very rude to anyone who bothers me, my lady, or anyone else for whom I am responsible."

He used his command voice for the last few sentences, which forced the hardy newsgatherer back. The crowd made a path, but made up for that by talking even louder. I Hmilra's ears were ringing as if he'd just left an engine room running at full speed, by the time they reached the forehall.

"At least we can listen to something more pleasant once the performance starts," he said, as he led Alikili up the stairs to the Presentation Boxes.

"I hope so," she said, making a gesture of aversion.

"How not?"

"I've heard that the music—at least some of it—is supposed to be an experiment. A special Saadian mode, or so they call it."

"I see. And we are to be experimented upon, rather as a healer-candidate dissects a live vruil?"

"I fear so."

"If that is the worst thing that happens today, I expect we shall all survive."

THE ANCHOR CHAIN RAN OUT SLOWLY, CLANKING steadily like the beat of a blacksmith with all the time in the world. *Lingvaas* had nearly come to a stop before the anchor went down. Captain Viligas was reluctant to risk any dragging this close to the Mole.

For good measure, the stern anchor went down as soon as the bow one had gripped the mud. By the time both anchor chains had drawn taut, *Lingvaas* was anchored securely enough to hold against a gale.

ber, your rank is legally the gift of the Republic. The Council has nothing to say about you keeping or losing it."

"Barbara—" Borlund said, hesitating over using her first name in public.

"Yes, Sean?"

"That doesn't mean I want to look foolish over political issues. I'll leave that to people like the anti-Saadians."

Weil smiled, then pointed at the paired chimneys just to the right of one of the theater's waterfront towers. "Look at that smoke. Somebody's going to catch it for burning trash now."

Borlund looked at the curling smoke. It was blacker and thicker than he usually associated with a disposal furnace, although he didn't know what might be burning in there.

Then smoke curled out of the turret, a window first darkened, then began to glow, and Borlund saw wisps of smoke seeping out from under the eaves.

"That's not the disposal," he said quietly. "The Solvarsen's on fire!"

JOSSU I HMILRA DID NOT FEEL QUITE AS IF HE WERE being dissected alive during the overture to *Songs of the House of Nilvan*. He did, however, feel that his ears were being aggressively bludgeoned.

He had been too close to too many large guns for too many Greats to have retained all of his hearing. He hoped to keep what was left for his remaining Greats, and doubted that too much listening to music like that of *Songs* would help.

He also resolved to give no watcher of any folk or political allegiance any cause to note his behavior. He would maintain the bearing of a Captain-Born if stinkworms began crawling up under his kilt and polluting his organs of generation!

The writer Shaarasti Ren's contribution to the pro-

the performance might be lavish, but would hardly be as delicious as his cook's work.

The intermission and the meal both passed so quickly that the lights were going down before I Hmilra had finished grooming his face and whiskers. Alikili ran a brush through his crest, then hers, just as the curtain rose. They settled back to watch the long-awaited scene of the Great Landing.

I Hmilra was so intent on comparing the song-speak passages with his readings in history and his grandsire's tales that he did not notice at first the glow from above the stage. He smelled the smoke first, then heard people calling out and saw them pointing.

He looked upward for the first time, just as the flames followed the smoke out of the vents above the stage. It was then that he heard the first scream, and saw the first swirl of panic in the seats closer to the stage.

FOR THE MOMENT, THERE WAS MORE SMOKE FROM THE Solvarsen Theater than there was steam in *Lingvaas*'s boilers. Fortunately, the fires hadn't been fully banked, let alone drawn. At a nod from Weil, stokers who'd come on deck for a breath of air dashed below again.

Meanwhile, the trumpet and drums sounded, "Ready fire and rescue party," so loudly that they must have heard it at Fort Huomikki. Everyone rushing on deck to collect axes and hoses and lower away the boats ran into the stokers rushing below, and for a few moments the scene aboard *Lingvaas* looked more like a panic than a crew preparing for action.

Eventually everybody reached their destination, about the time Captain Viligas decided to weigh anchor and put *Lingvaas* alongside the rear of the theater. The anchor detail put down their rescue gear and ran forward and aft, leaving the boat crews with steam to the boat booms but not enough hands to get the boats overside or crew them when this was done.

back alongside. It made a reasonable buoy until the full weight of the unshackled anchor chain came on it, when it promptly sank.

At least it didn't take anyone with it, and they had the registration number to help them find and compensate the owner if the boat was ruined. It was probably Saadian-owned, and if the fire was really sabotage intended to influence Saadian-Kertovan relations for the worse, the fewer Saadians who had grievances against the Kertovan Fleet, the better.

Also the sooner *Lingvaas* was alongside, the better for the people in the theater. As *Lingvaas* got underway, both rear doors opened, and both people and smoke poured out. Borlund ran forward to join his fire and rescue party, and reached the foredeck just as one of the fire escapes pulled loose from the building.

Not all of it—the section leading up to the roof still hung on its brackets. But the lower section was gone, ripped loose and fallen to the wharf, in a tangle of splintered wood, piled bricks, and twisted iron. The wharf itself was quivering, looking as if it might collapse next.

The balcony by the door had room for a few people, but even from *Lingvaas* Borlund could see many more crowding up behind them. Nor was the path to the roof a way to safety. Flames flickered and soared all along the upper rear of the theater, and the roof was beginning to smoulder. Borlund wondered how long before it fell in.

As *Lingvaas* came about to lay herself alongside the wharf, Borlund realized what offered the best hope for the trapped people.

"Do we have a rope ladder aboard?" he shouted, not caring who heard as long as someone answered and the answer was "Yes."

"Oh, aye," somebody said behind him, "Want it, Commander?"

Would I be shouting for it just to entertain people about to burn to death? was not Borlund's answer. The

chapter 13

HMILRA COULD tell confusion, doubt, and fear from the panic that turned a crowd of people into a mindless, clawing monster. So far he'd seen more of the first three than of the last. But the last would come; it would spread like a disease once it did, and if it infected the whole audience of the Solvarsen, many would die who might otherwise have lived.

I Hmilra did not intend to let anyone, mortal or otherwise, play such a ghastly joke on the Island Republic or its friends.

Fortunately the Solvarsen was only six Greats old and created according to the latest standards of both design and construction. For it to start so quickly and spread so fast, the fire must have started (or *been* started) close to a supply of flammables.

It was also going to reach a new and even larger supply very quickly. Tons of sets and scenery, mostly painted wood or canvas, were hung high above the stage, close to the fire. If those caught alight, heat and smoke would wreak havoc even among those well clear of the flames.

While all these thoughts paraded through I Hmilra's mind, his feet and voice seemed to act of themselves, like ship's repair parties cut off from the bridge by flooding or fire. He marched steadily down the broad stairs from the box, Alikili on his arm, two servants

I Hmilra contemplated the sight with brief but real pleasure. Either these people were ready to follow anyone who looked as if they knew what they were doing, or he was more recognizable than he had thought, even in the murky theater.

There were advantages to having your face in the leaf-scraps and even on the wall posters, he decided. There was also the disadvantage that a few hardheads (even on the Councils, perhaps) were going to believe he had done this to make himself known.

Less pleasant was the knowledge that Alikili was going to be right there with him, in fame or oblivion, life or death by fire. But there were other women in the newly enlarged band, and some of them were dressed as if they were both jouti and of bearing age. With these women risking their lives, Alikili would laugh in his face if he even thought too loudly of ordering her out of danger.

The front rows of the theater were almost empty as I Hmilra led his band toward the stage. The smoke was curling thickly along the ceiling, and the overhead gaslights were going out one by one, as fumes choked them or their lines burned through. I Hmilra wondered how many small gas-fed flames would be creeping through the storerooms between the ceiling of the theater and the roof.

The orchestra was down to half its strength, and half of those left were looking uneasily about them rather than at their music. The mentor was still on his stand, holding his staff as if it was a magical talisman.

Alikili sprang lightly up onto the stand beside the mentor.

"Get your people back a few rows, and then have them start playing."

"Who are you?" the mentor said, gaping.

He gaped wider when I Hmilra stepped forward and identified himself. "Captain-Born!"

"Yes. As my lady and second commander said, *Play*!"

money; but a potentially lethal one, not only to theatergoers trapped meters from a furnace, but to Sean Borlund if his feet slipped, and to *Lingvaas* and everybody aboard her if the rescue effort kept her alongside the Solvarsen Theater too long.

How long would be too long? Borlund would have given a few Greats off his life to know. The fire had to be eating away at the roof, and when it fell in, the walls might very well follow. If they fell inward, that was the end for everyone inside.

If they fell outward, it would not save the theatergoers, while *Lingvaas* sank under a red-hot rain of bricks and steel beams.

Borlund wondered briefly if Viligas and Weil really knew what they were doing, in assuming so blithely that *he* did.

Then it was back to work, as two Farers scrambled up to the top, carrying the rope ladder. Borlund took it, slung it across his back, and stepped back out on the yard.

At least he had the undivided attention of those Kertovans on the balcony who were still alive and conscious. He took a moment to look down, and was relieved to see that a party had scrambled ashore from *Lingvaas*, and was spreading a sail between the wharf and the ship to act as a net for anyone leaping from the balcony.

The Kertovans who had come down from the other balcony were helping, and there was no shortage of hands for the work to be done below. Borlund refused to think about their chances if the theater's rear wall collapsed, and instead estimated the distance to the balcony. Then he uncoiled the rope from around his waist, and tied one end to the bundled ladder. The other end was already tied into a loop, and he began swinging that end toward the balcony,

Somewhere around a half-Great later (actually on the fifth swing) somebody on the balcony realized what

would take a sudden turn for the worse when the roof supports burned through or the fire ate holes in the outer roof and could feed its hunger on fresh air.

I Hmilra had no idea where to find the cables for the fire curtain, but the guards spread out quickly in search of it. Alikili watched them go, and I Hmilra put an arm across her shoulders, knowing that she would want a living touch and that her pride would keep her from asking for it.

"Let's stand as far to one side as we can," he said.

"If the scenery falls, the heat will kill us even if we remain uncrushed," she said. "I would prefer not to end huddling in a dark corner."

So did I Hmilra, but he wondered if he would have dared say it. But then he was male as well as Captain-Born; he was supposed to be fearless without proving it by fine phrases. Alikili was a woman of mixed blood and uncertain rank; perhaps she felt he needed reminding.

He had just vowed to discuss that with her after they escaped, when the fire curtain suddenly dropped with a crash that made I Hmilra jump. Alikili laughed impudently.

"You look as if you would rather not end at all."

"So I would, but you will pay an obscene forfeit if you ever—"

I Hmilra broke off as two of the guards returned, both now openly wearing pistols and knives. One of them carried a fire axe, the other had a watch chief's disciplinary grip on one of the theater stage crew.

"Once we found him and told him we needed his help, it wasn't hard," the man said. "Now, Captain, wouldn't we be better off out of here?"

The fire curtain blocked the way back into the theater, but the stage attendant guided them swiftly to a spiral stairway on the right. Either the man was regaining his wits or didn't dare lose any more of what he had, surrounded by four large armed men.

I Hmilra's lungs and eyes had long been reminding

ing to call the Farers back to work and having about as
much success as he would have had trying to halt the
outgoing tide. With no commanders aboard (and
Tuomitti was carefully not going to look for them pier-
side), the two watch chiefs were the senior Farers
aboard. Not that Tuomitti considered someone who'd
not served aboard ship for twelve Greats a real Farer,
but he was on the Fleet roster and had as much claim
under Farer-law to make trouble for her as if he were a
Captain.

"This is not our work," the man exclaimed. "Keep
your people at—"

"*My* people? Are yours so lazy they can't keep this
ship afloat while we help at the fire? What good is the
dockyard for, then?" She refrained from the mortal
insult of wondering aloud if the dockyard hands were
brave enough for firefighting.

Short of a brawl, however, the other had no way of
stopping the Farers from manning the winch controls
and swinging out the launch. The launch was one of the
new models, with a steam engine so light that it was permanently installed, and a stoker was firing the boiler
even before the launch touched the water.

As the Farers started scrambling over the side and
dropping into the launch (even lightly loaded, *Byubr*
had no more than three heights of freeboard), it
occurred to Tuomitti to ask if anyone would be in the
theater.

Then her hands froze on the railings, as she remembered the notices for today's performance of *Songs of the
House of Nilvan*. She also remembered the lists of nota-
bles expected to attend—Jossu I Hmilra among them.

She could not see anything but disaster coming of a
fire in the Solvarsen today. Not with perhaps two thousand people in it.

"Ho, Chief! Coming w' us or no?"

The shout that broke into her bleak thoughts came
from alongside. The stokers must have done miracles—

off her gown as she did. I Hmilra did not fear for her modesty, which was protected by ample undergarments, but if she tripped over a swathe of the heavy cloth she would reach the bottom of the stairs on her head.

She reached the rope ladder and had it slung on her back before anyone except I Hmilra realized what she was planning. She had started climbing the dangling line before anyone was close enough to stop her. After that there was nothing anyone could do that would not endanger both her life and her mission.

So no one did anything, least of all I Hmilra. He did not even shout. Alikili would definitely not appreciate the distraction, and he himself would look like a fool or at least one lacking in self-command, in front of more witnesses than he had faced for his Captain's Oath.

Somebody—several somebodies—on the balcony had yet-unbaked wits. They reached over to pluck Alikili up the last half-span to the balcony, and one held her up while others tied the ladder in place. I Hmilra saw his companion grip the railing for a moment with one hand and shove her helper away with the other. He had to bite his lip now to keep from calling out. The thought that he had somehow *driven* her to this roared in his mind like breakers on a rocky shore.

Then he had to step lively, out of the path of a hose party from *Lingvaas* charging up the stairs without regard for the rank or indeed presence of anyone in their path. I Hmilra had the feeling that they would have trampled the Lord of the Waves flat if he'd been in their way, and knew that the time had come to make a dignified descent.

He did, after all, have also the right to embrace Alikili when she came down. He also had the right to say a few words to her, but that right he would only claim when they were alone.

SEAN BORLUND RESISTED THE TEMPTATION TO CLIMB down one of the stays to the deck. His hands were shak-

The cracks widened, then vanished in the smoke pouring out of them. Tongues of flame seared through the smoke, and debris began falling, with thuds and crashes now almost lost in the fire's roar.

Then the entire rear wall of the theater gave way in a moment, falling with thunder that drowned out the fire in the moments before the roof joined the wall. After the roof came the left wall, and after that Borlund could not see what was happening as dust joined the smoke to make a cloud that not only enveloped the ruins of the theater but nearly swallowed *Lingvaas*.

It was mostly dust and smoke that reached the ship. The flames tongued out briefly before the falling walls crushed them, and quite a few pieces of wreckage also made the leap. *Lingvaas* came away with scorched paint and rigging and hot lumps of wreckage smoldering all over her deck.

One bit smoldered on Sean Borlund's back as he crouched to shield three Kertovans, until someone dashed a bucket of water across it, him, and them. He grabbed the rest of the bucket to rinse his mouth, then handed it back to the Farer.

"What about the people from the other balcony?" he asked. He couldn't say "Jossu I Hmilra," and not only because he might have been mistaken about the man's identity. He was discovering that one could survive intending to be a hero but failing and then watching someone else succeed spectacularly. But the experience was still embarrassing enough to affect his voice.

The Farer pointed forward. A line of Kertovans was straggling out on to the Mole, now appearing, now disappearing as *Lingvaas*'s funnel and rigging blocked Borlund's view. He didn't recognize any of them, although two were standing so close that they might have been embracing.

Closer, a steam launch crowded with Farers in working garb was cutting in toward the pier. Borlund recognized Ehoma Tuomitti and gave a half-hearted wave.

chapter 14

SEAN BORLUND WAS writing in his journal by the light of a candle when Barbara Weil knocked on his cabin door. He could recognize her step and knock by now. His first thought was to tell her to go away.

But she was the last person on Kilmoyn whom he wanted to know that he was feeling sorry enough for himself to forget his manners. Sixty were dead from the fire, two hundred more in bed with burns and smoke-seared lungs, and his own grievance over not having been able to finish his own rescue work was trivial.

Now all he needed was to make himself believe it, which would have been easier alone, but at least Barbara wasn't going to make things worse—

"I can come back later if you want to be alone," she said, just loud enough to carry through the heavy wooden door.

Borlund couldn't even contemplate rewarding that courtesy with a "Go away" that would also come from his guts instead of his wits. He rose and opened the door.

Weil sat down on the bunk and looked at the overhead while he blotted the journal page and closed the book.

"You take that journal seriously," she said. "I wonder if I could look at a bit of it someday."

"Not today's bit, please."

"I already know you're feeling sorry for yourself, so I wouldn't learn anything I didn't already know."

Borlund forced a smile. "I suppose if you can read minds, you can tell if the Study Group is planning on bringing me ashore."

"The worst I can see is that they'll request it. You'll probably have the right to refuse, and certainly friends to support you, from both races."

"Which means making enemies among the Directorate."

"Do you care?"

"For myself, maybe I don't." Borlund considered that, decided that there was no "maybe" about it. "But I've got three bearer-partners and their children to think about."

"Are you the only one they've partnered?"

"No, fortunately."

"Then the Directorate will have to deal with all the other sire-partners as well. If they think they can afford that, maybe we'd better find *Rampart* and make a quick escape from Kilmoyn."

Borlund pointed at the door, to remind her that she'd been talking on forbidden matters not only aboard a Kertovan ship but loudly enough for eavesdroppers to hear. Probably they hadn't heard anything they could use to make trouble for the "Drylanders," but why borrow trouble when they were already getting so much thrust upon them?

Weil sat back on the bunk and crossed her legs, then rested her chin on her knees. "I think that journal of yours will help," she said. "If it has in it half of what I think it does. You wouldn't mind my reading one volume, from your training time?"

"If you can deal with my handwriting without going blind—"

"I'll come around and ask you to decipher anything I can't read," Weil said. She hopped off the bunk with the familiar briskness she showed when she'd decided on a course of action. "Pick a volume, and I'll be out of your cabin and your hair."

"By the highest command of the Fleet Farer File. Would you like to see my orders?"

Tuomitti nodded. Not that she thought Zhohorosh unqualified, or feared the problems that sometimes arose when bedmates became shipmates. But he had been a watch chief aboard a *Valor*-class armorclad. What had he done to make the Farer File assign him to *Byubr*?

Or what had *Byubr* become, to draw a Farer of such experience?

The orders had all the proper stamps and seals in all the right places. It even had Zhohorosh's family name—Lyd—which he never used aboard ship, for reasons which no one had ever been brave enough to ask him. The clerk's handwriting was no more legible than usual, and the paper smelled as if it had been steeped in flowerfowl droppings, but otherwise Tuomitti found neither irregularities nor answers to the mystery of Zhohorosh's presence here.

She sent her messenger for one of the steward's watch, to lead her friend to the chief's quarters, and meanwhile decided to get some good out of him while she could. She'd returned straight to *Byubr* with the launch, once they'd landed Jossu I Hmilra and the rest of his party at Fort Huomikki (more to hide them from the newsgatherers than for any other reason, she suspected). Half-expecting to see Saadi in flames and mobs storming the dockyard before dawn, she'd instead seen only the distant glow of torches and heard the (fortunately) still more distant din of streets full of drunken people trying to sing.

All of which left her sadly ignorant of what was going on in the wake of the Solvarsen Theater fire, and unable to even guess intelligently as to what the light of tomorrow might bring. This was not a situation that commended itself to her—or, she suspected, to anyone responsible for the safety of ships and Farers.

keep public attention shining on I Hmilra like a search-light on a floating mine for a good long while.

But that was hardly something to be talked of where others might hear. Also, Tuomitti remembered the conversation between the two lovers as the launch carried them to their landing. Conducted entirely with gestures and looks, it was still eloquent to one who saw most of it.

Tuomitti would have given all of her coming-ashore slyn to be able to listen to what I Hmilira and Alikili had said to each before they turned out the lights.

BARBARA WEIL RUBBED HER EYES, BLINKED, AND REAL-ized that the light really was dimming. The oil in the lamp must be just about down to the bottom.

One more day's entry, she said to herself, and turned the page.

At sea through midlight, then entering Tzigas harbor at six beats of the midlight watch. An easy two-common trip from Eltsisas, so the captain decided to coal ship immediately.

Coaled from lighters. Nothing much out of the ordinary, except that Tzigas is a harbor with a strong lighter folk Guild. They would not let our people into the lighters even to speed passing the coal.

Note: There ought to be a list of ports classified by Guild strength. There are some where it's worth your life to say a word against the Guilds. There are others where it's worth your life to try to organize a Guild. This makes a big difference to Captains, who certainly need to know, although it might not be wise to make the list public. The strong-Guild ports might be unhappy, to put it mildly.

Weil smiled. Word of mouth had done well enough in place of such a list for longer than she had been alive,

celibacy had been occurring to her lately, they remained notions. Even if she decided to turn them into realities, her friend on the Watch would remain exactly that. He was a man of sense and even some compassion, not a rebel as she'd been for Greats—or as Sean Borlund might become, with a little careful handling. . .

THE LAST MESSENGER WAS GONE WITH THE LAST WIRE-post, as was the last of the late supper from the tray on Jossu I Hmilra's desk. So, very nearly, was the last of his strength.

It had not been part of his plan to work so late after a day spent in a way that would have taxed a much younger Farer's strength. However, what he had seen and heard, and the wire-post waiting for him when he returned home, had convinced him that opportunity beckoned in the dark but would be gone like a seaflyer by sunbrighten.

Hence the work. Hence, in due course, the inevitable bills for the messengers and all the rest. I Hmilra decided that he would pay them himself, as the messenger services were seldom generous to their workers. Even if he could reconcile it with his conscience to send the bill to the Fleet Pay Office (and tonight's work would benefit the Fleet), reimbursement would be slow.

He closed his eyes, stretched, and found his right hand touching a familiar, slightly curved, comfortably textured surface.

"Is silent approaching another of your talents?"

"Not one I worked on as a girl, the way I did climbing. But bare feet and thick rugs make up for lack of practice."

"So I see." She was barefoot, and wearing a nightcap and an old chamber robe as she stood by the desk. I Hmilra stood up, began an embrace of welcome, and had to fight not to turn it into one of passion.

The thought of losing her was the thought of a darkness entering his life, which all the light in the world

Hmilra said. He began slowly, but as Alikili's smile widened the last words rushed out.

This time it was she embracing him. "Yes. I trust you. I even trust your kin. So—so this was not anything against you. It is just that a woman placed as I am—or any woman who has neither fertility nor profession—"

"Would you rather we of the Republic followed the Imperials or the Luokkan tribes, with their fertile women kept in strongholds and their infertile ones nearly slaves?"

"I do admit that being Principal Wife to an Imperial magistrate might have certain advantages—"

"Alikili!"

"Ask a question in jest, receive the same kind of answer." She was not completely jesting; her voice said that if her face did not.

"Forgive?"

"Forgiven," she said, with another brief embrace. "But remember that a woman is seldom allowed into a profession until after she has proved herself infertile. That gives the men a good few Greats' head start. We run the race with one weighted boot, against opponents in a pair of light shoes."

Kertovan life had always seemed fairer than that, to I Hmilra. But he had never doubted that those who were not Captain-Born males saw the world otherwise, and had several times been impatient with those who flattered him by pretending otherwise. He would *not* allow himself to be angry with Alikili over her offering the truth without being asked!

"Well, I do not think that you will have the chance to do this every third day," I Hmilra said. "I cannot afford to go to the theater that often, for one thing. For another, I sincerely hope that we do not have another such fire in my lifetime."

"What of the tales of the fire being set?"

"I have heard none such."

"Neither have I, but I have learned to hear your

added comfortably to his savings. But he never scanted in anything that would affect the safety of the ship or the health and comfort of his shipmates, so he was seldom afflicted with more supervision than he could readily evade.

Borlund found moorings at a waterfront drinkshop whose owner had enough confidence in the civil peace of Saadi to have not only opened but fired up the stove, broached a fresh case of hoeg, and set out tables on the lawn running down to the beach behind the shop. It was at one of those tables, halfway through his third cup of hoeg, that Barbara Weil found Borlund.

One look at her made him summon the attendant with a whole fresh pot of hoeg and a plate of biscuits. She looked as if she had not eaten for three commons and had either cried or been working all night.

By the time she'd emptied her first cup and demolished three biscuits, she was coherent if not cheerful.

"Those idiots of Directors have done it again!"

Borlund braced himself for bad news. "It" could cover what his Observant partners called "a multitude of sins," but from Weil's tone, this time the sins were larger or more numerous.

"Actually it's something they haven't done, or so the story goes," she added, reaching for another biscuit and refilling her cup. "It's no secret that we have a good deal of scientific detection technique available," she went on, lowering her voice, "but security and fear of cultural contamination have always kept us from releasing it. Innocent people have been executed or exiled because of this."

So far she hadn't told him anything either portentious or even surprising. Then insight struck—or at least tickled his mind.

"They won't help investigate the Solvarsen fire?"

"No. That would reveal too much of our knowledge, and raise suspicion. Of course, there's already enough

babbling but not quite making sense either. Something about a journal—*his* journal—

"What are you planning on doing with my journal?"

"Not all of it. Just parts. You see—"

"You drink." He refilled her cup, and pushed it and the biscuits at her. Eating brought silence, and silence bought Weil time to organize her thoughts.

"—you as my Third or Fourth," she concluded. "But you'll have a better chance at Third if you've done something that proves you're a true Farer by Kertovan standards. Which turning your journal into a manual of seamanship would do."

A whole fleet of questions sailed through Borlund's mind. What made her sure that she would be Captain of a Drylander-crewed ship? And what made her sure that the Kertovans, after allowing this break with tradition, would then turn around and dictate the crewing of the ship?

Most of all, how had she learned all this?

He stopped her in the middle of another cup of hoeg with that last question. The look she returned wasn't quite a glare, but definitely not a smile.

"Barbara, there are a good many worse things that could happen to me than going to sea under your command," he said. "In fact, most of them would be worse. But is this really a prospect? I don't want to neglect my duty to *Lingvaas* while chasing—"

"Suppose *Lingvaas* is the ship?" Weil asked. That silenced him. She went on.

"It's early to be sure of anything, but I do have a source close to the Directorate that lets me know what's at least being discussed. I shouldn't even be telling you this much, but if otherwise you're going to think I'm making it all up—"

This time insight was more like a gentle tap with a carpenter's maul. "Is your source in Security?" He swiftly described the man who'd been his shadow during his time in the Castle awaiting his examination.

interlude

FROM *THE FLEET COURIER*, FIFTEENTH FROSTTIDE:

When interviewed by our Special Gatherer, Captain Smeeyon Viligas allowed himself to be quoted about the new squadron of coastal-service vessels under his command.

The notion that having separate Drylander and Kertovan-crewed ships represents the failure of *Lingvaas*'s experiment in mixed crewing is an insult. It's also nonsense.

The seasoned Drylander Farers under Captain Weil are folk I would sail with at any time, on any voyage. But there are too few of them to take *Lingvaas* into battle unaided.

They will need to draw heavily on their kinfolk on Yproga Island. Some of these know the coastal waters, all are brave and strong, but most are not trained, let alone seasoned, Farers.

The task of training them properly is best left to their own folk. I am sure that they will do it well, and that *Lingvaas* will be honored in the Fleet when she joins it.

Our Gatherer further asked if Captain Viligas had any comments on the rumored influence of Expeditionary

"He's had three Greats to practice diplomacy with his mixed crew, not to mention its equally eager friends and enemies. He's avoided both mutiny and madness, which speaks well for his success.

"So those might very well be his own words. Remember that his mother became First Scribe to the House of the Lady in Vuisto before she died. That 'bluff old Farer' act of his is just that, more often than not."

Alikili leaned back and pillowed her head on his shoulder. "Are we getting up to dine or having a tray sent in?"

"Have you sorted the correspondence?"

"Yes."

"Nothing opened?"

"Nothing with a GUARDED grading on it."

"You're sure?"

"Being told that kind wire-posts from your family mean nothing to the Fleet is not something one forgets, particularly when you add a few words of the sort you do not commonly use."

Jossu I Hmilra felt blood rushing under his skin and his fur trying to stand up, at the memory of that quarrel. For a heartbeat he had almost been ready to sit down and draft his resignation from both his command and the Fleet, if the price would be Alikili. She had both forgiven him quickly and remembered thoroughly—her usual habit.

"Speaking of Scribes and Houses of the Lady," she went on, "our local one has visited me."

"More for the orphans and fosterlings? Not that she will not have it if they need it, but—"

"Not money, Joso. There are a number of the older girls, nearly women, who would like to join the expedition."

"The regulations are quite specific about what we can do with women before they are proved infertile."

"She wasn't thinking about having them go to sea for life before they've been tested. She's skeptical about the

Alikili now looked torn between tears and rage. After a moment she blinked, sighed, and rested a hand lightly on his forehead.

"My dear one, thank you. This war will be longer for those at home, if they have nothing to do but fear for those gone to Eneh."

TENTH LONGDARK:

For a moment, Ehoma Tuomitti thought that it was the swirling snow that distorted *Lingvaas*'s silhouette. Then the gusty wind curled the crests on the waves sliding past *Byubr.* At the same moment they blew aside the veil of snow.

Tuomitti thought many vulgar words and uttered a few.

"First time you've seen *Lingvaas* since they started her refit?" came Zhohorosh's voice from behind her.

Tuomitti nodded, unable to speak or look away from *Lingvaas*. Her masts were stripped bare, her funnel had vanished completely, something that looked like scaffolding was creeping aft from her forecastle, and sparks sputtered into the gray water from riveters at work in at least five places. Compared to what *Lingvaas* was enduring, what even the school-taught engineers had caused to be done to *Byubr* and the other four converted *Illiks* was a mere earbobbing, with perhaps a ring-piercing in the nose thrown in on the side.

At least the conversions had worked better than Tuomitti would have dared wager, even a single block. There'd been a few lively arguments when the engineers stubbornly insisted on rebuilding one *Illik* that really shouldn't have been put afloat again. The old cookpot had finally settled that matter by capsizing and going down one night, so slowly that the two shipwatchers aboard had been able to scramble over the side.

Otherwise, the best proof of the success of the con-

newlies as the Drylanders, there were enough to keep watch chiefs from wanton idleness or idle wantonness.

Lingvaas vanished into another swirl of snow, and *Byubr*'s whistle signaled her turn at the next buoy. It was a deep-toned, almost majestic whistle, easily worthy of a ship three times *Byubr*'s size and five times her fighting power. Tuomitti hoped there was steam for the auxiliary engines left after blowing it; she wouldn't trust some of the newlies not to kill themselves doing Farer's work by hand.

"What's this about a women's force, or maybe farce?" Zhohorosh asked.

"Oh, the Women's Squadron? Nothing much to it that I've heard. Just a few hundred volunteers to keep the bases running while everybody else sails off to Eneh."

"That's not what I've heard."

"What have you heard, besides your organs of generation?"

"I don't think with them, and—"

"At your age, Lord be merciful if you do."

"—I never did, as I was about to say before a certain sharp-tongued female assumed the worst about me."

She ventured to pat his shoulder, as he sounded genuinely hurt. "Pardon. I meant the number they'd likely have trained and ready by spring. There may be a deal more learning their way around a dockyard all through the war."

"Why didn't you volunteer? I'd wager that they'd make you a commander for the asking."

"You'd win that. I offered a wager, that I'd spend the next Great training rich merchants' daughters, and they said I'd win that one, too. I'd only just failed my Riisval when we went into Luokka, and I'll be too old and stiff for Faring if I miss out on this war."

"You'll be old and stiff three Greats before the next Skyfall." Then Zhohorosh hastily made a gesture of aversion.

Tuomitti hardly noticed. They were clear of the last

ing in front of McClintock and Sean Borlund had been enlisted long enough to know most of the basic commands. They put their hands behind their backs, relaxed their shoulders, twisted aches out of their necks, and set their feet wide apart.

Borlund contemplated the forty faces contemplating him. Men and women alike, most of them had lost the air of wondering what was going to happen next and suspecting that they wouldn't like it. The few who hadn't were mostly on a list for reassignment to the Directorate Fleet Base Unit.

Nobody who'd volunteered for *Lingvaas* was going to be sent all the way home. That would be a scandal and a disgrace; the political waves it would make could easily swamp a ship the size of *Valor*, not to mention any hope of Drylander participation in the Kertovan Fleet.

However, *Lingvaas*'s crew of seven commanders, thirty chiefs, and one hundred and ten Farers of one sort or another could not afford any dead weight. Not even in the stokehold, where humans would be working for the first time—that was an unwritten part of the agreement that had brought *Lingvaas*'s all-human crew into existence. (*Especially* not in the stokehold, where fire and steam waited in ambush to exact a deadly price for carelessness, and heat, fumes, and dehydration surrounded a stoker at every moment.)

It was safety, it was seamanship, it was common sense, and it was a political necessity. *Lingvaas*'s mixed crew had helped the Drylanders pass one test, in the eyes of most reasonable Kertovans (who seemed to have a slight majority for the moment). Her all-Drylander crew was an even more important test, one that might make the difference between humans staying on the fringes of Kertovan society for another century and their full integration into it within Sean Borlund's lifetime.

At least that was the theory, as Barbara Weil had quoted it with her tongue only slightly thrust into her cheek and her face almost straight. It had occurred to

But that sensation was part of being a commander. So was learning to live with it. Command was not courtship; consistency and justice counted for more than warm feelings on either side.

It seemed half a Tide before the last Farers buttoned up their bags and snapped to attention at McClintock's bellow.

"Very well," Borlund said. "Most of you passed admirably. A few of you did not. I expect that most of you know who you are, and your consciences are saying harsher things than even Chief McClintock could. However, just to make sure that you understand the importance of proper kit, he will—privately, of course—say those things.

"I will just say this, which I'm sure you've heard before but remains important no matter how often it's said—Not having a full kit before you sail can put you in three different situations, each one worse than the last.

"The first is having to borrow from your shipmates, which is disloyal to them and makes you enemies where you should have friends.

"The second is being unfit or unequipped for duty. That can spoil your record at best, at worst endanger your shipmates or ship. Your shipmates will not be grateful.

"The third and worst fate is being turned into a thief. That can put you in the confinement quarters afloat or ashore. Or it can put you over the side some dark night, far from land, if your shipmates detect you before your commanders do."

Borlund looked at the trickle of sunlight from the gaps in the clouds. "All right. We'll have PT when the chiefs join us."

McClintock again raised echoes from the barracks walls and the men stood easy. The wind was beginning to get up when the eleven men and women who were candidates for the rank of chief came jogging up behind the forty.

without making a big fuss about it. There was a family resemblance to the Watchman, too—nephew, maybe, or even son?

Borlund waved at the two the second time he went past. The third time he waved again—and this time the boy returned the greeting. His companion did not move; he did not even seem to be breathing. Borlund wondered if he'd frozen stiff in the rising wind, and looked at the clock on the barracks tower.

Then he tapped one of the leading runners, a rangy young woman with an Asian flavor to her features and complexion, on the shoulder. "You've proved you can do it. Pick a friend from the leaders and go fire up the baths. We'll all need to thaw out by the time we finish this run."

"Aye-aye, sir."

TWENTY-THIRD SALTSTOCK:

The hatch slid shut above Barbara Weil, cutting off the last of the watery morning light. From the buzz of voices ahead, everyone was already in her cabin, waiting for the briefing. Suddenly the portfolio of orders under her arm seemed to weigh fifty kilos, and with dagger-sharp points digging into her ribs as well.

Nobody shouted attention when Weil entered the cabin, because that was her standing order. Nobody even had to rise, because there was no room to sit. Seven commanders and the eight senior chiefs—two each from Deck, Engineering, Gunnery, and Stewardry—hardly left room to breathe in the cabin.

Opening a scuttle did something for the atmosphere, but it took judicious elbowing and a few rude words to clear a space for laying out the portfolio and spreading the map. It had HIGHLY GUARDED stamped all over it, in large red letters that seemed to impress everyone.

the crankguns, and everyone on deck with floatbelts on. A surprise attack—"

Weil nodded. They didn't have time for Maartens to show off his tactical notions, even if they seemed sound enough.

"Are we going to be attacked?" one of the Engineering Chiefs asked.

Weil recognized Adrianna Yoshino, one of a pair of twin sisters noted for their magic touch with machinery. She and her sister, Corinne, were partnered to twin brothers, irregular enough even if they hadn't also been suspected of being Observant or at least Believing. But the sisters had produced four children in five years, so there was no real cause not to let them join the Fleet.

"The assumption is that we will be, at some point," Weil said. "I can't give you the final strength lists, because I don't have them myself. But the talk is about a four-regiment landing force, each regiment with its own scout and gun detachments, supplies for several fights or sieges, and plenty of construction equipment for opening up the route to Eneh."

She turned back to the map. "The route is mostly water anyway. We'll have to do some dredging before heavy ships can ascend to Lake Bhir. The locks on the Shubirani are supposed to need repair, and of course we'll need to build rails over one of the lower passes in the Kayosi. I think they've all been surveyed, but which one will probably stay a secret for a while."

"And nobody around the Gulf is supposed to object to this?" Yoshino asked.

"I answer that if you'll tell me what you object to first."

Yoshino frowned. Weil tapped the map with the hilt of her dagger. Reasonable doubts were one thing, and she would allow them to be discussed openly. Insubordination based on militantly orthodox pacifism was another matter. Weil had long since decided that this

prosperous. They may not be grateful, but they could end up too busy making money to worry about whose fleet patrols the Gulf.

"And if the Kertovans cheat the local merchants, and we have a few hundred trained Farers to spare, what's to keep us from setting up our own shipping line?"

She didn't know which of several emotions was making everyone smile. As long as the smiles were real, she didn't particularly care.

in their use. Borlund still kept fingers mentally crossed for at least vital signals being seen and read in time.

The fingers of his body were otherwise occupied. The last shipload of stores for the fleet had only arrived from the islands last night. *Lingvaas* had sent ten Farers to join the emergency work party, then turned out all hands before sunbrighten to unload the lighter that a tug had brought alongside with *Lingvaas*'s share of the wealth.

Now the lighter was empty, and the slick decks almost so. Farers still had to maneuver around the guns, the boats, and the close-woven net of stanchions and wires holding up the flying deck. But the coils of wire, the cases of canned fish, the igniters in their double-layered red boxes—these were mostly stowed below now, no longer laying traps for Farers' shins and toes.

A horn blared, and Borlund heard the hiss of steam and the squeal of the boom winch. Another slingload— crates and sacks, anonymous at this distance, filling a net to bulging. Borlund watched the hoisting cable tighten, groaning as the weight of the net came on it. Somebody had loaded that net nearly to the limit, in their haste to get the loading done.

The net rose, now suspended two men's height above the deck, swinging slowly toward the midships hatch— hatches, now, one on each side of the flying deck. A working party with hooks held in gloved hands stood ready to ease it down the last meters.

One of those workers was the Security officer's nephew—or at least everyone aboard called him that— Roald Chaykin-Schmidt. Borlund had guessed right about his age, but he'd celebrated his fifteenth Naming-Day ten commons after his uncle brought him to the training depot. Now he was a Farer Junior, the youngest hand aboard *Lingvaas* and the particular pet of the Farer-Instructor Chiefs.

Borlund doubted that the boy's austere uncle wanted him made a pet by anyone, any more than he wanted

a very major one, or his name wouldn't have been invoked so publicly.

Unable to put a face to a voice he hadn't recognized either, Borlund knelt and took off his jacket to cover the dead man's head and shoulders. Fortunately it was the older of his two working jackets, and a few bloodstains or even more wouldn't do it any harm. But he realized he would have used his best dress tunic or kilt if there'd been nothing else at hand to hide the bloody horror that had been a Farer.

As Borlund straightened up, he heard the sound of a scuffle behind.

"Mindless Believer!" someone snarled.

"You cold-hearted—" a female voice began to reply.

Borlund whirled, saw Corinne Yoshino fending off the clenched fists of another woman, and stepped between them. He did this just as Yoshino counterattacked, and the edge of her flattened hand caught him across the side of his neck.

"Skyfall take your ancestors!" he snarled. "What's this about, if anything?"

The two women looked at each other, then at him.

"Well?"

The looks went farther, to the circle of shipmates who'd left off picking up crates and bags or their remains and stowing them below, to watch.

"This isn't a street and we're not entertainers," Borlund snapped, which at least got the hands as far as pretending to go back to work. Borlund remained conscious of attentive ears and an occasional head turned his way, but managed to ignore them enough to listen to the women.

"The first thing you can do is get a litter from the Healer and take your shipmate's body below. Both of you," he added. "If you cooperate that long, then go back to work, I may not say anything more about this."

"You want—?" both of them began at once.

something, but it seemed to consist mostly of brushing the seaweed dust off the shipmate he'd rescued. She was somewhat older than he, but not much, and she didn't seem to be minding his hands on her, or perhaps it was just human touch after her narrow escape.

"Farers," Borlund said. "Chaykin-Schmidt, go to the Arms Watcher and have him place Farers Yoshino and Yelm under arrest, then inform the Captain that we need a Judgment. Farer—"

"Reza." At least her voice was steady, although her hands weren't and there were tear tracks in the dust on her dark cheeks.

"Farer Reza, report to the Surgeon, and have him send up a couple of litter-bearers."

"Aye-aye, sir."

The two culprits looked at Borlund. He replied with a glare. "It's too late for either of you to get out of this easily. And I'm certainly not going to let you carry the body of a shipmate when you've dishonored his memory by a silly quarrel before he's grown cold!"

He knew that sounded pompous and might even be so. He also knew that he'd have to be careful about that when he was angry. Commanders who didn't ended up making themselves both ridiculous and ineffective.

Right now, however, he was too angry to care how he sounded, as long as what he *said* penetrated the thick skulls of Yoshino and Yelm.

BARBARA WEIL HAD SUSPECTED THERE WERE BAD times ahead as the list of last-moment preparations for sailing grew longer each time she looked at it. Suspicion turned into certainty when ten of her best people were pressed into a working party intended to correct somebody else's laziness or incompetence.

She went beyond certainty when she heard of the accident and its sequel. By the time Deck Chief Second Peller had been pronounced dead (a mere formality in his case) and the Arms Watcher had reported Yoshino

interrupt each other. If you do, any and all means necessary will be used to restrain the interrupter."

It loomed large in several sets of regulations and many books on leadership that a commander should never put him or herself into a physical confrontation with an offending Farer. Maybe this made sense for Kertovans or for drunken or drugged offenders.

Yoshino and Yelm, however, had made idiots of themselves while sane and sober. They had no excuse, and Barbara Weil realized that she would not much regret an opportunity to knock either of them even sillier than they already were.

Her eyes briefly met Sean Borlund's; she thought she read the same sentiments in them. Then she nodded to Yelm.

"Farer Yelm, you may begin."

BORLUND HAD NEVER BEFORE ADMIRED BARBARA WEIL so much as he did now, standing and watching her try to administer justice when she would as gladly have committed mayhem. He wondered if this urge came from more than fury at the utter pointlessness and wretched timing of the quarrel.

Was Barbara really Observant—possibly even an Observant Jew? Or was she more like him—not a Believer, not at all Observant, but knowing enough Believers and Observants to realize that the Rationalists had simply invented a new set of myths to intimidate those who held to the old ones?

He wondered. He also wondered how many more of that kind there might be, among the human exiles on Kilmoyn, and if they, the Believers and the Observants, might not add up to an unofficial, illegal, but very real majority of the exiles.

It hardly mattered for now, of course. The settlement in the Island Republic at least was no sort of democracy, and not much the worse for it. Dissidents who carried

subdued. It was as if not only the offenders but the whole ship was waiting.

Weil took a brief turn on deck after the testimony, which if anything deepened the silence. She didn't invite Borlund and he wouldn't have accepted if she had. The Arms Watcher had a mind more Security than Farer, and had once suggested that disciplinary cases like this could be handled by throwing the offender overboard and taking bets on how long they could stay afloat.

This was the first disciplinary case aboard *Lingvaas* that the politically minded would notice. Justice not only had to be done, it had to appear to be done.

Weil came below able to manage a thin smile. "Good news," she said. "It's clearing up, although the breeze may have a chop kicked up outside the Bay by the time we sail. Anybody who hasn't got their sea legs *or* memorized the location of the slop buckets may be in for a bad time."

She looked at Yelm and Yoshino. "You still wish to accept my Judge?"

Both nodded.

"More good news for me." Weil put her arms behind her back again. "Farer Yoshino. Your beliefs, observances, and faith are none of my concern, nor anybody else's, as long as you do your duty and help maintain discipline aboard this ship. To do anything else is failing your shipmates, a far more serious offense than reading religious books or attending a religious service.

"You have committed this offense. Trying to make an ordinary if tragic accident an omen is nonsense. Accidents in loading cargo, like people saying stupid things, are not omens. They are part of life, no more, no less. You could have undermined discipline if you'd gone on as you began.

"I do not accuse you, without evidence, of wishing to undermine discipline. That accusation might have been raised if you'd chosen a formal trial. However, I do

offenders go ashore, because I will not have them on my ship. I will also wash my hands of what may happen to them ashore.

"Since this is your first serious offense and both of you have pulled your weight until now, I will be lenient. You formally apologize to each other, here and now, swearing by what you believe in most strongly to keep the peace.

"You will also work one watch's extra duty every common for the next thirty. During that period you will also be fined half your pay."

"Do you accept this Judgment, on your Farer's oaths?"

Neither was slow to agree. Yelm had delivered her apology and Yoshino was beginning hers, when a messenger hurried in.

"The compliments of the officer of the deck, ma'am, and the flagship is flying 'Prepare to get underway.' "

"Thank him and say I'll be on deck directly," Weil replied. "Farer Yoshino, continue."

Yoshino practically gabbled the rest of her apology, and both she and Yelm seemed to fly out of the cabin when Weil dismissed them.

Borlund followed Weil on deck. He felt a weight lifting from his shoulders, although it was hard to tell how much of that was justice done and how much of that the sight of the fleet getting up steam.

Smoke was already curling from *Valor*'s funnels, and with his binoculars Borlund could make out not only the rainbow of signal flags but the crankguns and lookouts in her fighting tops. Seeming through the binoculars close enough to touch, an oceangoing tug was already underway, pulling three snugged-down barges in a line behind her.

Borlund jumped as *Lingvaas*'s whistle blew, the four short blasts for "Getting underway." Then more steam moaned and whistled as the capstan began its work

chapter 16

FLAG LOG OF KERTOVAN REPUBLIC EXPEDITIONARY
FLEET, FOURTH HARVEST:

Five beats of the sunbrighten watch, detached
first-class torpedo-carriers. Two making rounds of
fleet to collect mail. At five beats fourteen Boat
I/45 came alongside *Valor* to receive flag
despatches and mail.

At five beats twenty-one, Boat I/56 reported
unable to proceed and requiring tow. Detached
open-sea tug *Vayat* to tow I/56 either back to Saadi
or until able to proceed.

Vayat obliged to cast off tow of heavy lighter
(landing-stage type). Flag ordered armorclad *Azuuva* to tow lighter until further notice.

Six beats: lighter under tow by *Azuuva*. All other
vessels proceeding normally.

Jossu I Hmilra let his binoculars dangle from their
straps and turned inboard on the flag bridge. The torpedo craft and their lame cousin were now hull-down to
the west. Only their smoke was now visible from the
bridge, although any eyes studying the sea from Mount

porting torpedo craft would keep watch on the Empire and the City-States for a few days. Saadi's own defenses should stand off anything that came out of the Hask and slipped past the watchers inshore.

This "Fleet exercise" would raise the cost of the expedition's coal, stores, and spare parts to a still more formidable figure. By the time the Fleet had compensated the last Drilion Steward Chief whose mistress's shore quarters had been robbed in his unexpected absence, questions would not be asked in the Assembly. They would be shouted at the top of powerful lungs, possessed by Assembly folk also too powerful to ignore.

Unfortunately for both them and for Jossu I Hmilra, the "Fleet exercise" suggestion for solving the escort dilemma came from the High Captain. When the High Captain wanted to join some maritime enterprise, with any or all of the Fleet, it was not well done for a mere fourth-ranking Captain Over Captains to argue too loudly.

If he did, he could wave farewell to his chances of sitting in the High Captain's chair of state someday. He might even find his command of the expedition to Eneh dragging its anchor.

Waving farewell brought Alikili to I Hmilra's mind—and she was never that far from it. Had either of them been other than they were, I Hmilra was tolerably sure that at least the leaf-scrap rags would have cast him as an old man afflicted with senile lust. When he had been as young as some freshly hired newsgatherers and as wanting in experience of the world, he might have agreed with them.

But he and Alikili had finally achieved in the eyes of the world some of the dignity that they had so long held in each other's. That made for a restful darkness's sleep even in the narrow, solitary, and celibate bed of the flag cabin.

Steam hissed and metal squealed, followed by sharp-voiced commands that I Hmilra could practically recite

the same could be said about Sean Borlund—had been,
a few times, coupled with remarks about the possible
reasons for his promotion. (Borlund had reminded himself that punching out everyone who insulted Barbara
Weil would undoubtedly break both his hands and his
prospects, as well as reinforcing the rumors.)

Still, one of the big storms come up from the sub-
tropical seas off the Disputed Lands south of the Confederation would not be good news. The ships taking
the offshore route were all big and supposedly seaworthy, but some of them were half-crewed by newlies and
the stiff-jointed, and most ships were carrying heavier
loads than usual. Not to mention the crowded transports, which could turn into a Punishment World in half
a watch if the groundfighters started getting seasick in
really large numbers.

"Do you think we should rig for bad weather?"

Baer looked at the sky and shook his head. "The
light's almost gone, so all we'd do is wake up the night-
sleepers just when they've put their hammocks up and
their heads down."

That was the answer Borlund had been hoping to
hear. He had learned even before the thought of coming
to Saadi entered his mind, that a leader who makes
unreasonable demands on the led just to look good does
not lead well. He or she may lead for too long, but
never well.

As Borlund descended the ladder, he thought he
heard a shout of "Captain on deck." But he would be
seeing Barbara—seeing *Captain Weil*, he told himself
firmly—at the Commander's Conference tomorrow
morning. Tonight she was probably even less in the
mood for idle chat than he was.

At least Yoshino and Yelm had both been on the
working party that took the stove oil aboard and sanded
the spills, and managed to avoid either speaking to each
other or neglecting their duties. As progress, this was
like the swimming of a sloughfish, but sloughfish cov-

Fortunately I Hmilra's cabin had escaped with nothing much more than sodden rugs and smashed furniture, and the rest of the fleet had also suffered more lightly than anyone had been prepared to wager. Two lighters had to be cut loose, one was still missing, but a crew placed aboard the other at the last moment had cranked a flypump until the weather moderated, then burned signal flares to bring help.

Paint showed scars, deck planking rattled loose, water sluiced back and forth in bilges and passageways, and the inventorying of damaged deck cargo promised to be a long and tedious process. Also, most ships reeked of spilled food, vomit, and overflowing heads; cleaning parties had a busy few commons ahead.

But every ship was fighting-fit, every Farer and groundfighter soon would be, and even butting this west wind to the rendezvous would not fatally delay matters. I Hmilra made a mental note to visit *Valor*'s House of the Lord as soon as his duties allowed.

That would not be for a while. The launch from *Virgaadz* would be alongside before a Farer could recite the Three Prayers. I Hmilra lifted his binoculars and studied the courier ship.

Virgaadz had begun life as a fast packet on the Saadi-Kehua run, carrying three hundred passengers ready to endure vibration and small cabins in return for speed. Now she carried despatches, urgent reinforcements, and valuable stores for the Expeditionary Fleet.

She also carried a quartet of five-line guns and two heavy crank pieces. She was faster than any armorclad and most cruising vessels, although unarmored except for light plating around the guns and extra coal in the bunkers abreast her boiler room. So it had seemed a good idea to equip her to make a prize of any hostile vessel she could catch. If she or any other vessel of the expedition encountered such.

I Hmilra had begun to wonder if all the other Faring nations had left the seas to make room for the expedi-

Beloved friend Jossu,

I write more briefly than I intended, for darkness has come after a very long work session and I must finish this letter before I retire.

However, I can say that my work goes well, and my health likewise. I have several new friends besides the ones I named to you, and I have promised them hospitality in some neutral place that will not embarrass them, when you return.

Most notable to report is that I am to be made a commander in the Women's Squadron, one of eight being promoted from among the new volunteers. We number now some five hundred who have passed their training, and the commanders sent from the Fleet are too few to both continue the training of recruits and command actually on duty.

There will apparently be a new table of ranks within the Women's Squadron, with at least four grades of commander. I will be neither the highest nor the lowest.

I am satisfied that no one I know has procured this commandership for me to please you. The reports rendered upon me are sufficient to bring the blood to my face, although I believe I have at least been doing satisfactory work.

This scheme of new ranks gives me some pause, and rumor runs that some wish it to discourage fertile women from entering the Squadron. (Women holding one of the four special ranks will not have authority over anyone holding a regular rank.) However, I will not suffer personally from it, as far as I can see now, and would not take sides on the issue if it were to embarrass me.

        The reports from the northern lands . . .

I Hmilra smiled. He would have given his share in *Valor* to hold Alikili in his arms until sunbrighten. Ever conscientious, it had not occurred to her that the stew-

Twenty of thirdlight watch: armorclad *Byubr* moored to greenside of *Beszoiko*. Sent away coaling-assistance party to *Beszoiko*, Deck Commander Second S. L. Borlund in charge.

One beat fifteen: served hot soup to all hands.

Two beats ten: commenced coaling ship.

Sean Borlund tightened the damp handkerchief over his mouth. It didn't help much. Already he felt the grit of coal dust between his teeth.

Through the haze of dust he saw other ships presenting the same spectacle as *Lingvaas* and *Byubr* did, nestled up to either side of *Beszoiko*. It looked as if the whole Inner Roads was full of ships ablaze, as the coal dust rose in gray-brown clouds to scar the blue sky or drift out across the green water until it fell to make a scum on the pond-smooth surface.

In and out of the dust darted figures clad in very little or sometimes even less, both male and female alike. "Coaling modesty" had been a proverb in the Fleet since about a Great after it was discovered just what a filthy operation coaling ship was.

It wasn't as filthy and exhausting now as it had been twenty years ago, and Borlund had no shame in thanking Higher Powers for that (with the usual near-ritualistic mental reservation about their existence). About that time, metallurgy, factory capacity, and coal supplies all came together to make an all-steam Fleet practical. About that time several wise Farers also realized that there weren't enough folk in the Republic to crew such a Fleet if coaling ship needed a horde of strong backs every few days.

Hence the endless-chain bucket boom, a variant of a device already used in the boiler rooms of some of the larger ships to save Farers' sweat. Each coal-carrier that received a Fleet subsidy had two or four of the booms,

Halfway after, Borlund entered a particularly thick cloud of coal dust. Halfway through that, he bumped into somebody—two somebodies, and Kilmoyans from what he judged of their stature and skin in the murk.

They staggered out into comparatively clear air holding onto one another. Borlund stepped back and recognized Ehoma Tuomitti and a male Watch Chief. Both wore loinguards and sandals, headbands with their ship and rank badges attached, and nothing else.

"Farer—no, Commander Borlund," Tuomitti said, grinning. Her teeth were the only visible white on her. "How flows your world?"

"Well enough," Borlund said. "May I have the honor of an introduction?"

"Zhohorosh," the man said, saluting. "I am reminded that I owe you much for Ehma."

The look he threw his shipmate told Borlund all he needed about Zhohorosh's relationship with Tuomitti. His first thought was: *Aren't they too old?* His second was to realize that Tuomitti was no farther along her life-course than Bridget was along hers; if she had been fertile, Tuomitti would still have been of child-bearing age. It was unlikely that she needed a winch and cable to find a bed partner.

"I will do the same for you if fate calls me," Borlund said, "but let us hope that it does not. If I want to join a bathing party, the Inner Roads of Skirmana Bay is not my favorite place for it."

The others laughed. Borlund squinted against sun and coal dust and tried to get a good look at *Byubr*. It was hard to tell under the coal dust and salt-smeared paint, but the old "floating turd" looked a trifle more efficient than she had before her refit. Her main gun still looked impotent against anything faster than a log raft, but her upperworks bristled with two-line and crankgun mountings that would certainly stand off torpedo-carriers.

Certainly a refit and modernization had improved *Byubr*'s looks more than *Lingvaas*'s. Without her masts

"Everyone who hasn't taken their rest, take it now," he called. "Then back to work for everyone!"

FLAG LOG OF KERTOVAN REPUBLIC EXPEDITIONARY FLEET, FIF-TEENTH HARVEST:

Three beats fourteen of sunbrighten watch, launch lowered to take Captain Over Captains Jossu I Hmilra to highship for conference with High Captain.

Five beats six of sunglow watch: highship made signal that Captain Over Captains was returning. Fleet also raising steam.

Five beats twenty of sunglow: *Valor*'s launch in sight from the bridge.

The launch was butting into a light chop thrown up by the rising west wind, and spray had already come over the bow several times. Jossu I Hmilra pulled the hood of his waterproof up and hooked one arm through a grab-iron, but otherwise left matters to the boat chief. She was an old, short-tempered, and thoroughly reliable Farer who would have the steering gear, engine, and if need be pumps and lifesaving gear in the best possible shape.

Off to redside a small clan of Seakin was raising breath-sprays, preparing to dive deep for feeding. The High Captain had said nothing about the attitude of the Seakin toward this expedition and the war it might lead to, which left I Hmilra hoping that this meant nothing had changed.

When they last expressed themselves on the subject, the Seakin had said (or rather, the Lordspeakers had said they said) that they passed no judgment on the cause of Kertova, friendly or unfriendly. They would hope that

the passes and begin eating the land bare to supply it. The rails over Redrock Pass are at least two Greats short of complete. Without them, an Imperial army will have to live off the land or be supplied by sea."

Unspoken was the implication that preventing resupply of an Imperial army by sea might be one task falling to the Expeditionary Fleet. Not even wisely thought about was the implication that the Republic was indeed prepared for war with the Empire if necessary—and the commander on the spot, who had no power to judge the necessity, would have the responsibility for fighting the first campaign of the war.

At least the Republic had the power to reinforce him if he needed it. I Hmilra watched the sky turning gray-brown over the main Fleet as its ships raised steam, and long plumes of coal smoke trailed away on the wind. The launch had come far enough so that individual ships were beginning to overlap, even blur. The Fleet now looked rather as if the Fortress on the Hask had dispersed into its individual bastions and gone afloat for a breath of sea air.

Now signal guns began firing, adding their flat, distant thudding to the thump of the launch's engines and the slap of water at the prow. A breath of sea that held more than air showered over I Hmilra, and the chief hand-signaled a small course change to the boatsteerer.

Guns reminded I Hmilra of another matter still more uncertain than he cared for.

"What about the fortifications of Rinbao-Dar?"

The largest city on the eastern shore of the Bishak Gulf was by law the capital of an independent republic extending along the shore north to an area long in dispute with the Regality of Eneh. The republic's actual control over anything more than two commons' dreezan-ride from its massive walls was nominal, but even that modest territory produced wealth sufficient to make the city a notable stronghold.

"What about them?" the High Captain asked. I

corps of commander-planners, as the groundfighters already had in spite of their lesser strength and duties.

"I could almost wish this expedition provokes the Empire to a fight," the High Captain said.

Now he seemed to be speaking to himself, the walls, his old commander, perhaps his ancestors—anybody except the living Jossu I Hmilra across the table from him.

"That fight must come," he went on. "I would not mind if it came while I can still take a ship out to sea. I fear that the battle will not come until it is your responsibility to face it."

The words might have been taken as a subtle criticism, but the tone said otherwise. I Hmilra smiled at the older Farer.

"If I command against the Empire, and you are still fit to come aboard, you will have a place in that war. Don't be too hasty to lose your sealegs and let your seaclothes molder!"

"I swear it," the other said, returning the smile.

From ahead came a hail, bringing Jossu I Hmilra's mind back to the present.

"Launch ahoy!"

The boat steerer replied.

"Expedition!" Meaning that the launch had the Expedition's commander aboard.

Above the smoke clouds, something small, silvery, and round now floated in the sky. I Hmilra had to look at it twice before he realized that it was not the Lesser Moon making an out-of-season appearance, but the balloon rising from inland.

Quick work by the detachment ashore. I Hmilra spared a moment's thought for the groundfighters, patroling the forest to keep possible enemies from slipping within rifle shot of the balloon base. One bullet into the gas generator could produce an explosion as violent, if not as deadly, as one aboard a powder hulk.

Then he stood up, unhooked his arm from the grab-

radio (at least the old-fashioned code-using "wireless") and knew that would be a mixed blessing. Faster communications would help everyone—including those trying to penetrate the secret of the Drylanders.

Soon *Minguuso* had faded into the dusk astern, and Borlund turned his eyes forward. With less rigging blocking the view, not only gunners could clearly see what lay ahead. In this case, it was *Byubr*.

Byubr was going with the Vanguard to add some heavy gunpower and anti-torpedo protection. One or the other would almost certainly be needed before the rest of the Expedition came up. Another *Illik* steamed in the redside column, and both seemed to be having a fairly easy time butting into the chop. Their long rams still scooped green water over their foredecks at intervals, but the upperworks remained dry and the gunners could have cast loose their weapons without being drenched to the chin or flooding the magazines.

They'd done good work on the "floating turds." Borlund had heard how Farer gossip had turned from predicting doom for everyone aboard them to mild envy at the amount of armor between their crews and enemy guns. He could appreciate that, as his station in battle would be out on the deck with at most sandbags between him and the enemy.

The drum beat a familiar signal that Borlund recognized even before he heard the cry of "Captain on deck!" He stood with a deliberately stern expression by the binnacle, until he heard footsteps and sensed Barbara Weil's presence beside him.

"All well, Farer Borlund?"

"I think we really ought to sink this ship, let the ocean wash around in her for a few commons, then bring her up and rinse her out with fresh water. That *should* see off the last of the coal dust."

He heard laughter, then in a more sober tone:

"Anything else to report?"

Borlund swallowed and decided to gamble.

the ladder to the main deck. It gave him no clues about hidden meanings in those last words. At last he decided that there hadn't really been any, except in his imagination.

Which he did not need to have working overtime, as commander of the deck on a warship steaming toward battle.

houses with a few public buildings, the whole trailing off toward the north along another railroad that linked it to the docks above the bridge.

No fortifications; Dar had needed none even in the days when it had no weapons against ships in the river below except stones hurled over the cliff. Borlund thought he saw a few of the pre-dug gun emplacements, which could be equipped from the arsenal on half a common's notice. He couldn't make out any guns in them, which meant that either the city Matriarchs didn't think the Kertovans a threat, that they had the guns hidden too thoroughly for any casual observer to find, or that they had some other plan for dealing with any possible danger from the Expeditionary Fleet.

Borlund decided that half of a commander's job was listing what he didn't know and devising ways to fill in the gaps. Establishing the location of those guns—which could clearly sweep the whole Outer Harbor as far as Yatago Island, if they were eight-liners or bigger—was clearly a high priority.

Fortunately, it was also somebody else's responsibility.

"Flagship done signaling," the signaler said. "Nothing particular to us, but a general signal about preparing boats for the shore parties."

"That's particular enough for me," Borlund said. He turned, and cracked his elbow painfully on the breech of the foretop's crankgun. The signaler carefully looked elsewhere until Borlund had fought down the urge to curse.

Climbing down to the deck, Borlund once more had to fight mild vertigo. He still wasn't use to climbing down a naked mast surrounded by nothing but empty air, instead of by the vertical labyrinth of spars and rigging that the refit had removed.

By the time he reached the deck, Captain Weil was up from below. *Valor* had also finally sent *Lingvaas* a particular signal.

She saw nothing—well, maybe one or two suspicious bulges, and definitely a couple of Farers who needed more help standing up than they should have. But the bulges could be snacks from the vendors who'd already rolled their carts up to the waiting Farers, and the heat could have even a sober Farer needing a helping hand.

She was about to commend everyone on their discipline, when the shriek of a railsteamer whistle made speech impossible. She closed her mouth, to preserve dignity and keep out the swarming insects, and watched the train up to Dar pull out. Commanders and Farers of the Purchasing Division of the shore party hung out of the windows of the rear coach. She recognized Sean Borlund from *Lingvaas*, and knew that Zhohorosh would be in there, too.

Sending only a small party into the city itself and leaving the rest of the shoregoers close to the water, ready to load the boats, had been a decision signaled from the flagship. Aboard *Valor*, they hadn't wanted too many from the Fleet in the city, with the tribesfolk between them and the water.

On shore, facing the tent-city of the tribes, Ehoma Tuomitti thought that old I Hmilra had the right idea.

"Heads up," she called. "We'll be one-third on duty and the rest off until the supplies come down. Duty Farers to be armed at all times. Off-duty can disarm inside our lines, but go armed if you leave them.

"Also go in parties of four at least, go easy on the fruit-ales, and watch your backs and purses. There's five thousand tribesfolk in town at least, selling hides, furs, pottery, silverwork—all their best goods. They've also got enough rifles and ammunition to fight a small war, so don't make them think you're the enemy."

"What can they do with single-shot rifles?" someone asked, obviously trying not to laugh.

"One shot can kill you if it hits, and I've heard tales about tribal marksmanship," Tuomitti replied. No cause

tribe, I Hmilra couldn't remember—he hadn't studied the tribes of Rinbao-Dar, not expecting to have to deal with them.

So much for not studying the Rinbao-Dar calendar, I Hmilra thought.

He sipped from his own drink. "I rejoice that my hospitality pleases you. How do you propose to repay the debt I have thereby imposed on you?"

Drojin contemplated the overhead, as if he was trying to decipher obscure runes on the steel beam. Then he shrugged.

"I offer you a choice of many ways. But the best way, I think, is one that requires you to answer a further question of mine."

"You cannot require me to answer any question of yours, not without the orders of your superiors *and* mine," I Hmilra said, more politely than he felt. This was not the first time he had found Kertovans of the Rinbao-Dar mission believing they were outside the law, almost a sovereign republic of their own, bound as tightly to their hosts as to their native land.

It gave him more sympathy with the Drylanders of Yproga in their sometimes-strained relations with their Study Group in Saadi. It too seemed to feel that it knew best the interests of all Drylanders, even if they were barely one in fifty of their folk.

"That was perhaps a stronger word than circumstances justify," Drojin replied. "May I at least ask the question, without any obligation on your part to do more than listen?"

"An old Farer like me will listen to almost anything," I Hmilra said, with a smile. "But because of my Greats spent Faring, I doubt you will say anything that I have not heard before."

Drojin shrugged. "Perhaps. How well are the Drylanders, aboard their ship *Lingvaas*?"

I Hmilra chose to make a literal answer to that question his own opening move.

story, but the matter was not one on which speculation was encouraged.

At least this saved I Hmilra the trouble of finding a school of fangjaws into which he could throw Vuikmar Drojin. The Expedition commander thought he might still heave someone over the side, probably whoever had decided to make this a surprise, but would omit the fangjaws.

"There are no women aboard this ship with whom you could make free without their consent," I Hmilra said. "My valuables are locked up. So we do our work quickly, I trust."

"So it would seem." Drojin sighed and poured his cup full again. "I suggest that you open the inner pouch."

How THE RIOT STARTED WAS A MATTER ON WHICH there was never real agreement. The best that anyone was able to do was annoy enough witnesses to piece together an account that satisfied them. Arguments over whether the riot was provoked or not went on until the last witness was dead, and afterward among historians of every folk and tribe involved.

Ehoma Tuomitti was a witness, and she remembered it this way.

"A Gurthagi rider on an ariyom—that's the southland riding beast, looks like a dreezan that's been starved for half a Great—he brushed against a walker.

"The walker fell over and hit a vendor's table. The vendor was selling fire-sticks of smoked fish and vegetables. His brazier went down with the table and landed on the next tent over.

"The people in the tent came out in a hurry. They didn't have anything on, and from the way they looked it was pretty plain what they'd been doing. The man hit out at the vendor. The vendor drew a knife, and the woman grabbed up a pistol and shot him.

"Then they noticed that the tent was on fire. They

naling and getting up steam. So we knew they'd learned about what was going on, and maybe even knew more than we did. The whole tent city was dust and smoke, and it might have been in a fogbank for all we could make out.

"The Fleet might know what was happening and where we were. What I wondered was, what could they do to help us if we needed it?

"It felt a lot lonelier than I enjoyed, being out there by the bridge that day."

I HMILRA'S LUCK WAS IN. THE INNER POUCH HELD A map that he could take in at a glance, and a stack of documents that would need several watches to read, let alone digest. He was able to finish the map before word of the tribal riot came from shore, and had his response firmly in mind already.

"Signal to the shore party: 'Take all measures for protecting Farer lives. Reinforcements will be sent as necessary for that purpose. Otherwise avoid taking sides.'"

When the messenger was off to the bridge again, I Hmilra could see that Drojin was less than happy. No doubt he had profitable business dealings with the tribes—the tattoo made that plain—and they were in danger. Or could his motives be more respectable?

Never mind Drojin's motives for now. "I see the map shows a fairly extensive network of Drylander sightings in the Bishak Gulf area. More on the west side, in Imperial territory, but some elsewhere. Is that what it was intended to tell me?"

Drojin nodded. "The—we can call him the Red Windflower, if you wish—"

"I do."

"The Red Windflower did not write this, but asked me to speak with his voice if you did not have time to weigh all the evidence. In the documents," Drojin added, then coughed at I Hmilra's glare. The commander expected

"Good. Then I think I will ask you to remain aboard while I read through—"

I Hmilra had not finished the sentence when Drojin's hand darted inside his tunic. The commander acted with the instincts sharpened in the wrestling bouts of his youth and not quite blunted by the passing Greats.

He punched Drojin as hard as he could in the easiest part of his body to reach, which happened to be his chest. Then he hurled himself against the table.

It was light enough to topple from such an impact, and heavy enough to pin Drojin briefly. Long enough, anyway, for I Hmilra to snatch up the nearest heavy object, the empty jug.

He smashed it hard against Drojin's chest, hitting him there to keep him alive and maybe even conscious for a hasty interrogation. Unless Drojin turned out to have been simply suffering from a fever-induced fit, he would need that interrogation—plus several others, longer and as rigorous as necessary to learn what he knew.

Drojin screamed, and now his hand lunged inside his waistband. I Hmilra struck again as the hand emerged, and bone crunched. Fingers dangled limp, and a small two-shot pistol clattered to the deck. Then the door burst open, and for a moment I Hmilra was in more danger from being trampled to death by would-be rescuers than he'd been from Drojin.

It was then that I Hmilra realized that he'd never thought of calling for help. He hoped Alikili would never learn that—what she would say to his wrestling would-be murderers barehanded hardly bore thinking about.

Then he stood up, elbowed a clear space around him, and realized that he wasn't barehanded, either. He'd completely forgotten to draw his own pistol, a rather more potent weapon than Drojin's.

He pretended that the pistol needed examining, while the guards bound and gagged Drojin. By the he'd finished, his hands no longer threatened to betray him by

Great Gates, each equipped with a fixed bridge and a pair of massive gates. The gates themselves would be vulnerable to medium artillery, but every one of them was commanded by two or three well-armed bastions. As for knocking down the walls themselves, the only way to do that without a regular siege would be heavy naval gunfire from the river—and there was no deepwater anchorage in the river out of range of the batteries of Dar.

As long as the two cities were nominally under a single reasonably competent government and their people remained loyal, nobody but the Empire of Alobolir could seriously contemplate taking them. Even the Empire could not readily afford the price in lives, matériel, and time.

Borlund was surprised at how quickly he reached this conclusion. Two Greats ago, he would have called himself a total innocent on tactics, strategy, and weaponry. He might even have exhibited that ignorance with a trifle of self-righteousness, in front of the right audience.

No more. The last two Greats had administered a heroic dose of reality, curing him of a great many conditions from which he had not known that he was suffering. While he served with the Fleet, he would no more give up his warrior's eye than he would resume going clean-shaven.

Borlund stopped in front of a set of six stalls selling rawhide (very raw, from the smell) and scratched his chin. Then he corrected himself. He would shave off his beard if he was going to spend much time in tropical climes. The itching under it had gone from irritating to unpleasant and he could already foresee its going on to unhealthy.

Ahead were the factors' tents, almost a small town in themselves. Anything not on display in the market (and the tribes had a reputation for being light-fingered, so quite a lot wasn't) could be ordered in any quantity available from one of the factors—for a price.

Borlund was profoundly glad that he had nothing to

Right now he needed the tinkers' and brassworkers' area. The second item on his list was something as mundane as a dozen new chamberpots. *Lingvaas* had received a crate of necessary vessels either rejected by or retired from the Fleet. Most of them had not survived the voyage south, and the sick berths were housing the survivors.

Borlund's next thought was that the tinkers had come to him. The clattering and clanging certainly sounded like metalworkers hard at it. Then he saw the four-dilgao team swing around the factors' tents and on to the main road south.

The quasi-bovine dilgao needed a high-sugar diet that could only be easily supplied in the south, so Kertovans only saw it in zoos. But properly fed and with a trained driver, a four-dilgao span was the most efficient draft animals on Kilmoyn.

What these were efficient hauling was a fieldgun, one of the old models without recoil cylinders, but a five-liner at least. Two more spans of dilgaos followed, one with a wagonload of gunners and tools, the other with what had to be an ammunition cart.

Two more three-span gun teams followed, a full battery from what Borlund remembered. As the last one passed, a mounted messenger with half a dozen escorts cantered past, raising a storm of dust. As the dust settled a column of groundfighters came trampling along in the wake of the guns, high-peaked helmets pulled low over dusty faces and plumes already sagging from the heat. But their equally dusty jackets also sagged with ammunition, and the bayonets on their single-shot breechloaders were fixed.

Somebody was about to shoot and somebody else was about to be shot at. Or at least the Matriarchy intended everyone who watched to think so. Borlund wondered whose minds were the Matriarchy's targets, if they were not planning to shoot at bodies.

He stopped wondering when he heard the crackle of

chapter 18

THE FARERS WHO had been ordered or at least thought they had been ordered to defend the railroad bridge had to run most of the way. This was no easy work under the southern sun and carrying their weapons ready for action instead of slung for convenient carrying.

Even Ehoma Tuomitti had her doubts before they were halfway to their destination. Whatever was boiling over in the tribal camp and fair, the tribesfolk seemed to have the sense not to let it scald Kertovans. Stray bullets kicked up dust within pistol shot of the marching Farers, and occasionally a blood-freezing scream would make some younger Farer shudder and claw at ear-tufts, but that was all at first.

By the time they reached the station, however, all thought the caution justified. A mass of tribesmen seemed agreed on one goal: marching on the station. A handful of Rinbao-Daran Patrol and second-line soldiers seemed agreed on another: defending the station.

"Stay here and help us!" someone shouted from the ranks of the Patrol.

A Kertovan commander (Tuomitti couldn't tell identity, let alone seniority, but hoped that the voice had the second) shouted an impatient reply:

"We have to move to the bridge. Our orders are not to take sides."

Tuomitti thought then and long afterward that the

would be put to work doing *something* until wisdom came—or vanished entirely?

Tuomitti rather hoped this was not so. Dying to do something useful could hurt just as much as dying to no purpose, but afterward you felt less foolish when you faced Lord or Lady.

She was almost asleep when she heard, far off, whips cracking, drums beating, and even the bugling cries of dilgaos.

JOSSU I HMILRA HAD COME STRAIGHT FROM THE MEET-ing with *VALOR*'s senior commanders to *Lingvaas*. What he saw (or rather, could not see) from *Lingvaas*'s deck persuaded him to hurry straight from her deck to the foretop.

Now he braced himself with one hand on the crank-gun mount and held his binoculars to his eyes with the other. He could look over the dust cloud now shrouding the tribal camp, and if someone had been signaling from the walls of Rinbao he could have read their message.

As it was, he could see enough to confirm the shore commander's wisdom. At first he'd wondered what defending the bridge could do except perhaps involve the defenders in a fight with the tribes. Now he could see that the tribes were nowhere near the bridge—weren't yet doing more than glowering at the station—and trouble wasn't going to come from tribes fighting the Kertovan shore party.

Not unless those retreating from the city had to swing well to the east, between the city and the camp. They wouldn't need to do that if they could use the bridge.

But to the west of the rails, Rinbao-Dar's ground-fighters were deploying. Guns—more than one bat-tery—and infantry to defend them while they swept the camp with sprayshot and explosives, then follow up with a charge to close quarters.

Assuming somebody wanted a massacre of the tribes,

Weil is bearing the same burden of command as I did and *a mighty weight of responsibility for the future of her folk.*

I Hmilra's guards came up just in time for him to send them to get steam up in the launch. Weil looked a question.

"I'm going ashore," he said. "That's why I was concerned about your gunnery."

"Oh," she said. He saw no flinching, but heard it in her voice.

SEAN BORLUND WAS THE FIRST COMMANDER TO DECIDE that the Rinbao-Daran troop movements were cause for rallying the Kertovan shore party. The others, however, were only moments behind him.

In a great flurry of shouted orders, beaten drums, and people running as if they had neither plan nor purpose, the shore party drew itself together. By the time the last gun was out of sight, some four hundred Farers, a hundred pack animals, and fifty-odd loaded carts and wagons had assembled by a grove of trees just under a thousand paces from the walls.

Less pleasant for Borlund was the discovery that he was second in command of the whole motley flock. Three of the four commanders senior to him, along with some forty armed Farers, had gone into Rinbao a watch ago, to visit Trade House, the Matriarchy's Delegate, and a few other places required by protocol. They were also supposed to be arranging for a state visit by Jossu I Hmilra and shore-leave privileges for less exalted Farers.

Whatever they might be doing, they were not coming out of the city. Borlund learned this moments before some gunners on the walls further ruined what little appetite he had left by opening fire in the direction of the tribal camp.

A good many Farers yelled that they were under attack, others dove for cover in ditches (usually damp

"Good. Now, one of us had better go and find if we have any teamsters among our Farers. All the locals seem to have run off, and I'd hate to abandon all the wagonloads."

What they really needed, Borlund thought, was a drenching rain, to dampen everyone's ardor for fighting, reduce visibility for the trigger-happy, and make everything except hard-surfaced roads impassable to cavalry and artillery. Looking up, he saw that the sky promised no such gift, saluted, and went off to round up wagon drivers.

THE SHOTS BROUGHT EHOMA TUOMITTI RUSHING UP from under the bridge, pistol in hand. She measured the distance of burst with a practiced eye, then decided that nobody but the tribal brawlers and maybe not even they were the targets.

She was less sure about the guns to the west of the road. From where they were going into position, they could strike anywhere from the city walls to the shore, although not too accurately in the second direction. Even if they were aimed at the tribes, they were going to be firing over the road and the bridge, with Kertovans already where the shots would land, and more to come if the people who'd gone to market came out, as Tuomitti sincerely hoped they would—and soon.

Tuomitti also hoped that the tribes would know who was shooting at them if it came to that, and attack their real enemies. She suspected that was a vain hope, because the tribes would come boiling out of their camp in no mood to spare anyone in their path.

Against a mob of enraged tribesmen, Tuomitti had a pistol and twenty rounds, a boarding sword and clasp knife, a sun helmet, canteen, and bread pouch, and two whole field-dressings already impregnated with wound-cleaner. Also her hopes, and whatever favor her prayers and offerings at godhouses had given her.

Enough for a valiant last stand, of the sort thrilling to

less likely the second Farer had spoken up to advance a feud.

I Hmilra ran out of colorful phrases about the commander's ancestors and took a deep breath. "Where is the farthest sun-mirror, and do you have another mobile one?"

"At the bridge, and no."

The commander's stern face made it plain that he would not accept blame for the missing sun-mirror. Perhaps he didn't even deserve it; that could, in any case, be settled later.

The heavy thump of a naval gun forestalled a further explosive reply from I Hmilra. A moment later the tearing-canvas cry of the flying projectile clawed a path across the sky, ending in another, more subdued thump.

I Hmilra started for the watchtower, but the lookouts were as alert as their duty required. One shouted down to the commanders:

"Some of the tribals were pushing over toward the railroad station. *Lingvaas* fired a shell, but it didn't explode."

That was probably just the way Captain Weil had planned it. Pulling the fuse from a shell before firing it made for a good, harmless warning shot, since the conical shells would dig in instead of rolling like the round solid shot.

"*Lingvaas*?" the commander asked. His eyebrows rose and his crest seemed to be twitching.

I Hmilra wanted to reach out and smooth the twitching crest, as he had with his children when they were no taller than his waist. The commander seemed as far beyond his limits as a child alone in the dark.

"Does that make you uneasy?" I Hmilra asked, softly. He himself was uneasy over the commander's not noticing what ship was assigned to direct support of the camp, but that was yet another matter for later discussion.

"It is hard to feel otherwise, with the rumors—"

were too heavily loaded to handle weapons, so they left these in the carts and distributed the ammunition among the guards on the flanks.

This left forty or fifty people nearly helpless if somebody *did* get inside the column with as much as a Gurtagi skinning knife, but Borlund had long since given up hope of guarding against every danger. He was only trying to pick the most critical ones, instead of leaving matters to chance.

There'd been no rain, and the day seemed to have grown hotter as it dragged on toward evening. Certainly the last trace of breeze from the water had died, and every step by Farer or beast raised dust that seemed to hang in the stifling air until someone came along to breathe it in and add another layer to the hair of nose, mouth, lungs, and eyes.

Borlund used the last of his water to moisten his kerchief and wipe the dust out of his eyes, then looked south toward the cliff-crowning fortresses of Dar. Was it just his imagination, or were figures moving on housetops and—much more disquieting—around the gun pits?

Another moment's standing and staring into what in a decent land would already be twilight told Borlund nothing. He shrugged and quickened his pace, relentlessly putting one foot in front of another, passing sagging bearers and pack animals with their dust-yellowed tongues hanging out and saliva dripping onto the road, until he was back at the head of the column.

The bridge was in sight now, barely a kilometer away, and the road to it was clear. Not clean—discarded clothing, the odd glinting cartridge, and even a body showed where the tribal fighting had briefly spread onto the road. But no obstacles, and figures in Kertovan garb standing on the bridge already waving—

A Rinbao-Daran trumpet let out its high-pitched cry and found echoes. Borlund jerked his head right and saw some of the troops he'd seen earlier coming out of

was docile enough to need no saddle, but so sway-backed that Borlund's boots nearly reached the ground.

He'd just persuaded the beast that lying down and rolling to crush him would accomplish nothing when the first Farer returned.

"Commander's orders—we are to proceed as before. Halting would make it look like we were cooperating with the local grounders against the tribes."

Borlund looked and saw that where it was the column gave the Rinbao-Daran artillery a clear field of fire against the tribes. He realized that he must have spoken aloud when the Farer replied.

"Don't know, commander. But Old Lady Skobeen was really stiff about it."

Walking onto ground beaten by that much firepower might make a lot of other people of both races even stiffer, as they lay dead, mingling their blood in the dust. Borlund agreed with the commander in principle, as he'd grown even more suspicious of what might lie behind this oddly timed tribal riot or whatever you wanted to call it.

He did not agree that a wholesale slaughter of his people was a necessary mark of neutrality and good faith. If somebody was going to be slaughtered, it ought to be a single person, far enough ahead of the rest so that his or her death would be a timely warning.

Borlund realized that he'd been thinking of this move ever since he ordered up a mount. He'd even decided on the single person. It had to be a commander, and that meant him or Skobeen. Being a Drylander would earn him more attention, apart from his being able to reach the spot more quickly.

If the Rinbao-Darans did kill him it would prove the Drylanders' good faith and loyalty to the Fleet. If they didn't, he stood a better chance of learning about human activities in the south—not that he knew the local language, but he could always keep his ears open, listening for Kertovan speakers or reliable translators.

knew when to slaughter and when to scare, and hoped that the commander's words put no doubts in minds where there'd been none before. Sometimes, though not often, the best way to deal with a mystery was to treat it as a simple, common matter until people grew bored with trying to find something complicated or unusual in it.

A watch chief Tuomitti didn't know spoke up.

"The tribesfolk did seem to be getting on their bold shirts," he said, "but the shot changed that right off. Some of them didn't run right away and we thought they might have taken rocks or dust where it hurt. But they all got up in time and ran back to their friends."

"We owe *Lingvaas*'s gun crew a few gifts for that," I Hmilra said. "My orders are for you to hold the bridge until our people from the markets join you. We will then be out of the way of the local groundfighters and too strong for the tribes to attack, and can return safely to the camp."

"What about our people in the—?" a commander began. He broke off as I Hmilra stiffened in his saddle, nearly sliding out of it. The commander raised his binoculars, and Tuomitti would have given a foot for a half-height's better vantage to let her see it as well.

I Hmilra dropped his binoculars, drew his pistol with one hand, and gripped the reins of his mount with the other. Tuomitti supposed he didn't ride much worse with one hand than with two, and perhaps some of those tribal bodies weren't as dead as they looked.

"Our people from the market are coming on, the local forces look ready to fire on the tribes over or through our ranks, and someone is riding out from the column." He dropped the reins and raised his binoculars again.

"The one riding out is a Drylander."

"Damned fool," came from several throats, but not loudly, and even straining her ears Tuomitti didn't hear anyone doubting the Drylander's loyalty. She wondered if it was Sean Borlund—the Lord of the Waves seemed

single-shot breechloaders and new and filthy boots, but their uniforms were as ragged as their discipline.

Their commanders called them to order quickly, with explosions of oaths that would have made Ehoma Tuomitti envious, and blows with fist and stick that would have appalled her. Borlund was making such copious mental notes of the state of the local army that it was some time before he realized that one of the commanders was standing beside his mount, trying to get Borlund's attention.

"Who in the name of the River Spirits sent you?" the commander asked, in heavily accented Kertovan. The commander appeared to be male, and he wore a modern uniform tunic over more traditional southern-style short, baggy trousers. He also wore boots and a belt with not only a sword but two pistols.

Borlund saluted. "Honored commander, I come on an affair of peace."

He spoke as formally as he could, slowly enough to be understood but (he hoped) not so slowly that he would seem to be condescending to the uncouth southerner. The Kertovans had bad habits in that direction, one reason why Imperial sympathies had been gaining ground in the south during the last generation—or so rumors ran.

Two things seem to run in war, Borlund decided. *Bowels and rumors.*

He explained the desire of his people to leave the area without harm to either side, as they had no quarrel with either. Also, they did not wish to endanger the negotiations now in progress within the city between the commanders of the Fleet and the representatives of the Matriarchy. (Borlund puffed up the phrasing of that last point like an observation balloon, until a listener might have thought half the Matriarchs and half the Republic's Senate were meeting in the holiest of the Mother's temples to devise a way to universal peace for the next ten generations.)

brought him down on top of the commander. The man gave a half-stifled yell of protest mixed with pain, then quieted as another bullet whipped overhead. The third time, Borlund listened for the shot, heard it, and heard instead the solid *chunk* of the bullet sinking into flesh.

Ariyom blood sprayed over him, as his mount reared with a bubbling scream. It reared again, spraying more blood from its gaping throat, then collapsed on its side and very nearly on Borlund. He rolled clear, then roughly pulled the commander after him.

By now enough city groundfighters had realized, however dimly, that somebody was shooting at them. Fortunately, the artillerymen (who seemed a good deal better trained) kept their eyes and their muzzles pointed front. But from every infantry unit, bullets began to fly.

Borlund raised his head, tried to peer over the fallen animal and the half-panicked groundfighters to see if any of the bullets were hitting his comrades, but couldn't make out any details. At least the column was still marching, although he thought some of the guards on the near flank had unslung their rifles.

A long burst of firing, a score of rifles shooting so close together that they sounded like a crankgun in action, made Borlund flatten himself again. If he could have dug a firing pit with his nose, he would have done so. He was frightened, frustrated at the apparent failure of his mission, embarrassed at the thought of dying while looking like a fool, and eager to get his hands around the throat of that unseen rifleman.

Not to kill him outright, of course—he had secrets to reveal first. Just to remind him not to make a fool of peacemakers.

It was then that shouts joined the shooting and made Borlund raise his head again. It was a moment before he believed that what he saw was real, and decided that five mounted Fleet Kertovans really were riding toward the column.

One of them even had a sword in his hand.

hand yet, but it was easy to see that placed where they were, the tribes had only three choices.

One was a parley with the Matriarchy. Some among the tribes would rather die—enough to bring on a fight. A second was a death-or-freedom charge, certain to bring death rather than freedom even if it didn't involve the Fleet column and force it to fight on the side of the Matriarchy in self-defense.

The third was for the tribes to swiftly and thoroughly learn the art of swimming.

I Hmilra flicked his sword again. One of the guards raised the truce flag, a golden harp on a black field, and began waving it. The sacred truce flag implied conceding superiority to the people one was approaching, but it also imposed on them a rigorous obligation to stop shooting at those under the truce flag.

The first response to the flag was further scattered shots in all directions. One of them plucked a guard out of his saddle like a small child snatching a cake. He landed on his back, rose with one arm dangling bloody and useless, but cursed too fluently to be mortally hurt.

The truce violation was enough to send the Matriarchy's commanders running about among their people, urgently trying to restore discipline. They knocked up rifle barrels with swords and halberds, snatched weapons from stubborn hands, and generally threw their own ranks into such confusion that if I Hmilra had been leading five hundred mounted fighters instead of five he could have broken the Matriarchy's infantry in moments.

He would also have died soon afterward as the guns swung about and opened fire. On the walls or in the field, the Matriarchy's gunners had stood between their cities and disaster at least seven times that I Hmilra had read of. They took pride in their craft, and knocked that pride into any laggard who remained in their ranks more than a single Great.

To diminish both the confusion and the target he pre-

without much chance of finding even a trace of the snipers. Or so the commander said, and from the maps and I Hmilra's memories, they probably told the truth.

"Very well," I Hmilra said. "As Fleet Commander, I declare that we have no serious grievance with the Matriarchy over these shots. We will accept blood-money for the Farer wounded by the wild firing."

The commanders had just time to look relieved before I Hmilra continued.

"This is, however, on condition that we receive unmolested passage for the column to our camp on the shore. Also, that the Matriarchy guarantees the safety of our folk within the city of Rinbao, which they entered lawfully, with full diplomatic rights, and by written agreement sworn and signed in the sight of all gods and holy ones by those having the right to swear and sign for both sides."

I Hmilra contrived not to yield to a coughing fit after uttering the entire last sentence without taking a breath. Borlund and the guards looked as if they wished to applaud.

The Matriarchy's commanders looked less pleased.

"We can hardly halt everything else we have in hand to bring your people out of the city!" the commander who appeared senior growled. He (or maybe she, inside a shapeless tunic but with elaborate earrings and a fertility tattoo on one cheek). "Could you promise the same, in our situation?"

I Hmilra made an emphatically negative gesture. "No, nor are we asking it. We only ask that none of our people be put in danger by the crisis in the Matriarchy's relations with the tribes."

"Are you breaking off negotiations, then?" a younger commander snarled, drawing glares from his (definitely his) associates.

"What are we negotiating, besides the amount of time spent on ceremonial?" I Hmilra asked. "If you wish our people to continue these discussions in a city about to

the weapon the sniper (if it had been the sniper) was carrying hadn't been more than half the right size.

"Looked like a toy, the fellow was that tall," the fighter said, in a burst of clear speech. "I think—ahhhh—think—it—he could have been—one of his folk."

The fighter jerked a thumb at Sean Borlund, and lost consciousness. I Hmilra was too busy ordering his churning thoughts to notice when life followed consciousness.

A Drylander, with a rifle shooting farther than any comparable weapon known to any of the three northern nations? Either one created interesting possibilities. Together they created real danger—possibly great danger, if added to intrigues among the Kertovan community in Rinbao-Dar and Imperial plots. None of which could be averted by anything done or said here today.

The primary task, the safety of his people, remained firmly before I Hmilra's eyes.

"I suggest that this makes it even more important for our Farers to leave the battle area," I Hmilra said, addressing the commander. "I would wish upon no one, not even a declared enemy, the burden of fighting with foes to the front and treachery to the rear."

"What will you do if we don't give safe passage?" the loud-mouthed commander said.

The senior (definitely female, I Hmilra decided) shot him a look which said that *he* might get safe passage to a prison cell if he opened his mouth again without orders. I Hmilra thought, however, that the question gave him an opportunity.

"We will leave the area regardless. Our Farers in the city will find a defensible house and remain within it until peace returns or they are overcome by sheer weight of numbers. Neither body will yield without resistance.

"If you open fire while we pass before you, then we may decide you are attacking us. Then we will have the right to extract our people from Rinbao by force.

All during the fading daylight, Farers had been leading pack animals up to the bridge and unloading heavy
sacks, which they placed in pits dug under its supports.
Then they filled in the pits—and all the while, anybody
who wandered too close was sent scurrying away, and
anybody who asked questions met tight-lipped silence.

Even an old friend and bedmate, a gunner watch chief
from *Valor*, refused to answer Tuomitti. She then
thought briefly of asking Sean Borlund, who had
remained with a handful of Drylanders on watch over
the bridge.

If his look was that of a hero, Tuomitti hoped she
would be forever spared that splendid ordeal. Borlund
had the look of someone who could barely answer to his
own name, let alone any more complex question.

At last light and the work below the bridge were both
done. Urgent signals, passed along silently with hands
and shielded lanterns, pulled the last defenders from the
bridge.

The nearest was three hundred paces from the bridge
when firing broke out inland all along the tribal front
and all along the Matriarchy's position as well. Tuomitti
saw a commander she didn't recognize watching the
darkness, binoculars raised and head cocked to one side
as if listening.

Then Tuomitti heard it as well. Firing well out to the
Matriarchal flank. Tribes, the horde of Drylanders
rumor had placed in the scrub and hills, the lost
Marines of Captain Tuusivi? A problem for both Matriarchy and Fleet, if the fighting spilled over toward the
shore.

A problem, however, for which there was already a
solution. Tuomitti saw the commander nod—then saw
nothing for quite a while, as blazing white-orange light
snatched away her night vision like a gale shredding a
topsail.

The bridge heaved and the roadway bowed upward,
twisting itself apart as it rose. Fragments of iron min-

chapter 19

THE COMMANDERS' HALL aboard *Valor* was below decks and behind armor. The rain and the whine of the ventilating fans (about all that kept the cabin habitable, on this close hot night) fought off most other outside sounds. The speakers finished the work of making it impossible to tell how the battle ashore was going.

Not that the battle ashore was Barbara Weil's greatest concern. All of her people were safe, and Sean Borlund was even rumored to be due for a commendation—which she thought he richly deserved. The camp would hold, and the only shooting its garrison might have to do would be in self-defense—a right that reasonable folk on all sides would certainly concede them.

But not all folk were reasonable, and there was also the matter of what to do with the Fleet and the ground-fighters whom the Island Republic had sent so far, to what seemed at the moment little purpose. It might be a sign of doubt in Jossu I Hmilra that the Fleet Commander had called this Council of Captains, but if so, he was not the only doubter afloat or ashore.

In such a Council, it was required that the Fleet Commander hear the voice of every Captain or the Captain's authorized representative. It was further required that each Captain or representative speak. Finally, it was required that after all Captains had spoken, they obey

Weil realized that she should have been listening more closely, even while she was trying to come up with a sensible suggestion. Muisk was not much of a speaker, and that was a soggy peroration, but it was one nonetheless.

My turn now.

Fortunately I Hmilra chose to call a halt in the speaking, to allow the stewards to refill the water jugs and clear away the plates. Most of the biscuits and cakes departed uneaten; between heat and tension few had much appetite. Weil was one of the few who turned in an empty plate.

As she did, she realized that she hadn't worked so hard and sailed so far just to tamely turn and go home. She also hadn't worked and sailed to become involved in a local war—for all practical purposes, a civil war.

Either would raise a good many questions among the Drylanders, and perhaps ignite that long-stifled brawl between the Study Group Directorate and its supporters and the rest of the Drylanders. That brawl would answer no questions and do little else, but it would surely leak many secrets—too many, with someone like I Hmilra watching. Not to mention other humans, with fewer resources but more knowledge of what to look for.

Those humans would also, most probably, have fewer scruples about playing Gods from the Sky. Or, situated as many of them were, aiding the Island Republic's enemies.

So what offered a middle course?

The Expeditionary Fleet itself was not of much consequence. This war would be settled on land. But the eight thousand Eneh-bound groundfighters the Fleet escorted could play a potent role in that land settlement.

Suppose the groundfighters were somewhere else? Back home would be much too far. If they were thoroughly occupied, somewhere else closer—as indeed

crumbling building of an old villa. On the soundest portion of the roof, a crankgun squatted behind sandbags. More sandbags hid riflemen, a mixture of Farers and groundfighters from the Seventh Bohoians.

In spite of her Farer's conviction that groundfighters were drawn from the weak-stomached and the palsy-fingered, she was glad to have at her side people who'd spent more time than the average Farer with a rifle in their hands.

By the time Tuomitti was half around the trenches (and from alternately wading and falling, wholly covered with mud), the rain had stopped completely. It was only a few breaths after this that she heard a voice calling from the darkness beyond.

At first it sounded like the dying bleat of a gyurok, sound without sense, and no telling what folk it might be. Then she heard what sounded like a Kertovan cry for mother, and a moment later an unmistakably Kertovan:

"Wounded—help. Hellllp—"

—mixed with gasps and moans.

Trap? Not necessarily. Half a score of Farers were still unaccounted for. Everyone hoped they would lie low until the fighting was done, then come in. Here, however, might be someone who had rushed matters.

No reason for her to do the same, however. Tuomitti made her way to the two sentries at the next bend of the trench.

"There's someone coming in—one of our missing, sounds wounded. I'm going out. One of you go and alert the crankgun crew. The other stay here, and be ready to cover me. Do you have a flare?"

The two sentries were groundfighters but not reluctant to obey a Farer who knew her business, which was more than could be said for some. One of them held up a hand-thrown stick-flare, with the igniter cord already hanging free, ready to pull.

"Good."

Tuomitti undid her boots and dropped her raincloak

she took much attention away from organizing her thoughts to deal with the inevitable questions.

She had spoken more or less off the top of her head. Many details remained to be filled in. If God (or some other source of power) was not in the details, her chance of carrying the debate certainly was.

Muisk finally sat down, as I Hmilra seemed to approach the moment of ordering him to do so. The last four Captains spoke, only one openly in favor of Weil's suggestion, but none of the others openly against it.

By then everyone else had their questions ready—and Weil was equally prepared with her answers.

Would the troops be safe, on the eastern bank of the Bhir River?

Unless the Empire wished a war, yes. The territory was claimed if not settled or held by Eneh. The Empire had never made any claim on it. Their marching into it in force would be a simple invasion.

Would Eneh consider the troops so far south a real means of support?

Probably. Certainly they would understand that the landing force could not sail up the Bhir, past the rapids and all the other obstacles, with the situation in the Gulf so unsettled. The groundfighters and the Fleet would have to be much more careful about locking shields and guarding each other's backs than the original plan had intended.

This might well be true. But what if the Empire had, as some said, shipping and men to seize the islands off the coast of the Matriarchy?

A force of groundfighters could stay behind to build and guard a base for a squadron of shallow-draft ships. From that base, launches, torpedo-carriers, and chartered local steamers could patrol the islands and warn of any hostile moves in time to bring the Fleet south again.

Why shallow-draft ships?

ster, as the Study Group Directors and their allies might put it?

That question could wait until later. In the corner, a small printing press was already clacking, producing copies of the proposal for a formal vote. Weil hoped I Hmilra hadn't ordered the printing so fast that essential details would be left out and room for debate or even disobedience remain.

He had not. The ink was still wet on the paper, but everything was there. Seven thousand groundfighters north, to hold an enclave on the Bhir. A thousand with naval support to remain behind in the island off the coast of the Matriarchy, to observe and if necessary offer relief to the homeless and the hungry. The bulk of the Fleet to remain wherever it seemed most likely to forward its mission, the interests and neutrality of the Island Republic, and the revelation of plots against it by any and all persons of any or all lands.

Most of the Captains waited just long enough for the ink to dry a trifle more before signing. The junior captain collected the papers (with a wink to Weil as he passed by; he'd been the open supporter among the last four, no doubt because of the lively work it promised his hot-for-combat torpedo-carrier crews) and handed them to I Hmilra. He shuffled, counted, coughed, and rose.

"Nineteen to seven for Captain Weil's proposal. Do all consent to be recorded as having spoken?"

"Ayes" rose in order from around the table, some clearly reluctant, all audible.

"Then I declare this ordering of the Expeditionary Fleet to be lawful and binding. Let us commence the development of it."

"Development" meant filling in all the details, as Weil had expected. She had not expected, until she came back from the head to find everyone waiting for her, that she would now lead the discussion.

Law and custom both made sensible this Kertovan

eyes while she did this, and it was those eyes that gave her the lifesaving warning.

They widened suddenly, the mouth followed, in what should have been a scream but came out a gargle and a hiss, and Tuomitti heard over that pathetic sound stealthy footsteps behind and to her right. She half-vaulted, half-rolled over the wounded Farer and came up with her knife in hand.

"Owerigo!"

The single shrill tribal battle cry set off an eruption of sound. Someone shouted a curse, in Alobsi, Tuomitti thought, but in what seemed a Drylander voice. Someone else let out a wordless shriek and leaped forward with a spear held ready to thrust down into the fallen Farer. Tuomitti got inside the spearman's guard with her knife, sank it between his ribs, jerked it free, and thrust again to cut his throat almost to his spinal cord.

The night was heavy with blood-reek—then night faded before the light of hand flares, as the people in the trenches started igniting them. In the next moment a mortar coughed, and a more powerful bomb-flare burst high overhead. Then the crankgun in the bastion opened fire.

The bullet stream whipped just over Tuomitti's head, close enough to singe her fur. She wished she could make herself as thin as a sheet of paper—but then, she'd probably dissolve in the mud—

The crankgun chopped air again, and this time something more solid. A death-scream died away in a gurgle, somewhere beyond the edge of the light, a death-scream that could come from no Drylander. Tuomitti slid under the wounded Farer and began half-carrying, half-dragging him toward the left, out of the crankgun's line of fire.

That put her squarely in the path of a groundfighter squad lumbering out of the trenches, making more noise than mating dreezans and carrying their rifles so that if anyone tripped he was likely to shoot a comrade.

ing for their boats to come around to the gangway and return them to their ships.

In dress uniform she couldn't carry her binoculars, and they wouldn't have been much use anyway. The mortar flares were lighting up the ground battle quite nicely for the camp, but *Valor* lay too far out to let the unaided eye make out much by flarelight.

One or two Captains suggested that they form their launches into a patrol force, sweeping the anchorage for hostile boats. More prudent voices spoke in favor of not giving enemies easy prey and friends problems with identifying targets. Weil sweated in silence, knowing that *Lingvaas* was likely to be the first target for any such enemies, lying as she did close inshore, immobile, and crucial to the defense of the camp.

The firing died, followed by the flares, and Weil discovered that the whole battle hadn't lasted as much as a single beat. The mixture of relief and alertness kept her silent until the launch carried her back to *Lingvaas*—where the relief vanished the moment she mounted the gangway.

Crouched in the shadows of the railings and the fore and aft gangway were nearly a hundred of the Matriarchy's people, mostly women and children, and with a look that would have told Weil they were refugees even without that. Fortunately Second Captain Sharil Kund was on hand before she could ask rude questions of those without answers.

In spite of Weil's impatience, Kund began his story at the beginning and only came to the refugees near the end. The fight on shore had been too short for *Lingvaas* to take any action, but he'd called all hands to battle quarters. All guns were loaded and the searchlights were fully crewed but not turned on, and two more boilers were coming on line so that the ship was at half a beat for getting underway.

"I also had Mr. Borlund turn out the landing party and get up steam in the launch. When no call for assistance

make enemies, then exploit that mistake."

Weil would not normally have let such cynicism pass without comment, but she was too tired. All she said was, "We'll want a commander's conference in my quarters as soon as everybody's awake. Meanwhile, feed the refugees, don't let them wander around the ship, and wake me up if Mr. Borlund reports anything unusual aboard the ferry."

"Aye-aye, ma'am."

SUNBRIGHTEN WAS ONE OF THOSE SULLEN, COLORLESS affairs that frightened the Farers new to southern seas. Sky, sea, and land all seemed to flow into one another.

Even Ehoma Tuomitti might have found it hard to tell up from down without the help of the smoke columns to the north. The fires set in the night's fighting were mostly still burning, and every so often a new dark plume would scar the horizon.

At least there was no smoke from Rinbao, save the usual grayness of wood-fueled forges at work, and an occasional white puff as someone fired a signal gun or let loose at some phantom of their imagination. Dar stood pristine on its bluffs, although the river was still dotted with boats, carrying fugitives one way and soldiers the other. (Tuomitti had even heard tales of working parties on barges, laying a boom loaded with mines across the river to keep out *everybody's* Fleet.)

She wrinkled her nose as a puff of breeze surrounded her with the reek of bodies left unburied in the heat for the best part of a day. She'd thought the caked mud from last night made her the foulest-smelling thing around; now she knew better.

Arms went around her from behind, even as she heard the footsteps there.

"Greetings and good health, hero."

She turned and thrust the palms of both hands against Zhohorosh's ribs.

"How so?"

laughter at the same time. Zhohorosh might be no school-taught commander, but he had the wits not to pick more fights than he could handle.

He continued. "*Byubr*'s one of the stay-behinds, so. . . ." This had quite a list of consequences, including Zhohorosh's being chief over a new shore party to relieve all Farers whose ships were sailing north.

"We'll probably blow up the camp fortifications tonight and leave the mainland to the people with a taste for that sort of fighting," he concluded.

"Here I was hoping that my people would be on their way back to the ship, thanks to you."

"There'll be time," he said, grinning, then picking a clot of mud out of her crest. "After a bath, though."

She punched him in the ribs. "Don't worry about that, I'll just swim out to the ship."

From seaward a whistle sounded. She looked, and even without straining her eyes, she could see a string of flags soaring up to *Valor*'s masthead.

SOMEONE STINGY WITH EXPLOSIVES (BORLUND suspected I Hmilra) chose instead to strip the camp of everything movable, then burn everything burnable, with a few drums of stove oil to hasten the fire. The foul smoke drifted offshore in the breeze and reached *Lingvaas* even at her new anchorage, to trickle below.

Borlund was trying to finish a sponge bath between fits of coughing when Barbara Weil walked into the bath chamber wearing a robe and a bath bag slung over one shoulder.

"My bath drain's blocked," she said. "An artificer's trying to work it clear with a worm-pusher."

"What about steam or air?"

"The engineers don't trust some of the piping," Weil said. She unslung the bag, took off her robe, and hung them both on hooks.

She wore nothing under the robe, and the sight of her nude was hardly a novelty to Borlund. However, he did

drew apart, and Borlund was quite sure that it wasn't only his anatomy that showed signs of arousal or his breathing that was a little irregular.

"Actually, I wanted a bath and to talk to you about something else," Barbara said finally. She turned on the faucet and filled her own bucket, then tossed her sponge in the water. "I wanted to ask you to be *Lingvaas*'s shore-party commander."

"That's turning into my speciality, it seems."

"Do you have a problem with that?"

"Well, the younger Fleet commanders I listen to say it's not a common road to higher postings."

"They're assuming we'll run our Fleet the way they run theirs."

"What Fleet?" Borlund asked.

"Given time—" she began, then shrugged. "I suppose there are arguments on both sides. At least they're letting you listen, which can't be a bad sign."

She'd wetted her skin, which made it gleam subtly— and now desirably. She soaped herself, and as she did, she went on.

"The stay-behinds would have to garrison one island, preferably one with a high peak for an observation post. The assigned groundfighters would provide most of the garrison, although each ship would also be represented.

"The ships would also have to assign smaller parties, to embark in the shallow-draft vessels of the squadron— not just the torpedo-carriers; they burn too much coal and their engines are delicate—and patrol the rest of the archipelago."

"Looking for what?"

"Anything that might affect the Republic's safety or neutrality."

The whole Fleet of Kertova would be too small to make that thorough a search, Borlund pointed out, and Weil didn't contradict him. She did add that she'd picked him because he was experienced, popular, and unorthodox.

without running aground on the Matriarchy's brawls and intrigues.

If Alikili's last letter was true, he would receive some honor even if nothing came of completing the voyage to Eneh. He had no difficulty conjuring up words that he'd read a dozen times.

The ones who call themselves "the best sort" seldom call on me. But our servants and their servants are busy folk indeed, and much passes between them.

By what I am told, these people have more confidence in you than they would in most other Fleet Commanders. They believe you love action at sea so greatly that you will steer past anything which might draw you into shore fighting.

Of course, this overlooks the fact that we have no declared enemies in the south and none of them have any seapower worth the name. Also, that when the day comes for the Fleet to uphold the Republic against the Empire or the Saadians (whom these folk sometimes speak of in one breath), it will hardly do so by great battles on the open oceans.

However, folly in some has often left an opening for the wisdom of others. May it be so in these circumstances, is my most earnest wish, next to your swift, safe, and honorable return. . .

I Hmilra laughed too softly to be heard above the churning bow wave and the rumble of the engines. "The power behind the throne" was a name sometimes given in the chronicles to rulers' lovers. So far no one had been so minded to apply it to Alikili.

He would not be surprised if the day was not far off, however. Nor, in truth, could he deny that she had power—only that he had a throne, or that she was behind it.

interlude

THE BHIR DELTA, SECOND FULLRIPE:

Whips cracked, team drivers shouted, and every sort of hauling creature except slaves gave tongue in their own fashion. Ungreased wheels and overburdened metal and wood added their notes to the concert.

Given a choice, Jossu I Hmilra would rather have listened to the apprentice musicians of Fort Huomikki practicing. However, the choice was not his. The fort and all the rest of Saadi were half a midtide away.

Also, the din now assaulting his ears meant that the landing of the expeditionary force in the Bhir Delta territory was almost complete. Drawn by ten-pair teams, the heavy guns were going ashore. By tomorrow's sunbrighten most of them would be emplaced, in locations the gunners were keeping so secret that they did not even show on Jossu I Hmilra's maps.

When that was done, the Fleet would be free to deal with any Imperial efforts to cut it off from home, whether by intrigues in Rinbao-Dar or by open force. The groundfighters would be able to block any Imperial advance by land around the northern edge of the gulf, while extending a hand (actually, patrols) north up the Bhir to the southernmost outposts of the Regality of Eneh.

It all looked very fine on maps, but Jossu I Hmilra

lic's flag, or all the short tempers and long memories in Rinbao-Dar would again be inflamed.

The breeze shifted direction while the shore parties wrestled with barges. It had been blowing mostly from the land; now it blew along the foreshore, from the open water to the east. The water was as hot as the land, so the breeze was no cooler, but it now carried fewer ripe smells. Seven thousand groundfighters and a thousand hauling beasts had done their best to add to the rich odors of a tropical foreshore; I Hmilra drew in a deep breath from sheer relief.

"Permission to come on the bridge?" he heard from behind. Turning, he saw the bridge guard looking dubiously at Leader of Scouts Juinjijarsa, who was standing at the head of the port ladder.

"Be welcome, Scout," I Hmilra said.

"I am grateful," the commander said. She was about equally of Enehan, Rinbao-Daran, and tribal blood, and the mixture had given her longer legs than most folk. Indeed, at sunfade, from a distance, she might have almost been mistaken for a Drylander.

That mixed blood would have kept Juinjijarsa from even being considered a lawful resident of Rinbao-Dar, except that one of her grandmothers had been the First Matriarch. Fewer questions were asked about one of such blood; fewer still when she proved to have a natural genius for the demanding work of the mounted scouts.

She had volunteered to accompany the Fleet north, saying that her kin would rather have her aiding the northerners than be a standing target in the cities. That this was not the whole story, Jossu I Hmilra had known, when some twenty more Scouts ("kin-bound or oathsworn," she said) and their blooded ariyoms came north with her.

"Reporting that our mounts and gear are ashore, and asking permission to join the scouting line," Juinjijarsa

Matriarch-kin but could think of no words that would make that plain without usurping the authority of the groundfighters' Captains.

Juinjijarsa seemed content with the letter when she read it, however. She even repeated the oath of heart's blood before she climbed down the ladder to the launch ready to take her ashore. I Hmilra watched her go, then watched the last gun barge sliding off the beach. Meanwhile, a double hauling team and fifty groundfighters heaved on the ropes of the barge's load, a fifteen-line bomb-thrower, to get it across the sodden ground of the foreshore to where a steam tractor could take it in tow.

I Hmilra wondered. Could there be a way of building a steam tractor inside a boat's hull, with the wheels acting as paddles in the water? Such a machine could move from water to land without stopping, even if it might not be able to carry the heaviest loads.

And suppose one also built shallow-draft ships, with their engines in the rear and most of their hull one long hold? Perhaps even a hatch in the bow, or, better yet, doors, so that they could run up on sloping shores, open their bows, and let beasts and men, guns and tractors, run straight on to dry land?

Such a vessel might be too expensive to build strictly for war—but would it not have other uses? River ports were often shallow and ill-equipped. Also, those who wished to have rock-oil more widely available had been wrestling for ten Greats with the problem of keeping the flames of a boiler's firebox apart from the cargo of inflammable oil. Would not putting the engines aft serve the purpose?

I Hmilra could not leave *Valor*'s bridge at once, not while the unloading continued. By the time it was done, he had mentally registered a half-score new designs and devices, and made his kin so rich from these registrations that he could leave everything else he owned to Alikili without their uttering a word of protest!

some truth to the most common opinion: they could not worship the Lord of the Waves at all and worshipped the Lady of the Rocks under other names.

But not complete truth. She had heard Jossu talk in unguarded moments; she had even studied some of his confidential correspondence. Some Drylanders clearly worshipped the male principle, which they called Jeshu, Ullah, Bowda, or Lurd (which last might be a title rather than a name). Others worshipped a Lady Muri. Most did not worship at all, or at least pretended not to.

Why anyone should pretend to have no faith at all (as opposed to merely pretending one and believing another, as was sometimes necessary in the City-States) was a mystery Alikili could not solve. But then, no doubt the best minds of every folk who had met Drylanders these past fifty-odd Greats had struggled with that mystery with equally little success. She would not solve it in the short time before they reached the godhouse.

The godspeaker for the Lady was in good voice this morning. The godspeaker for the Lord barely had a voice; he croaked, wheezed, and coughed as if lung-rot would take him off in the next moment. Alikili hoped not, for the orphans' sake as well as his own. They lived cold and hard in the winter, and it was no secret that too many of them died young from wasting diseases.

The godspeaker coughed again.

"Bless most particularly those commonly in the care of your kinswoman, who are among us today. For they have stepped forth from the Rock to serve among those who ride the Wave. They do not ride your creation themselves, but honor them for all that they have done and bless them that they may do more."

Alikili did not dare twitch an eyebrow, let alone turn her head. But she felt glances boring into her like crank-gun rounds, and not only from the Women's Squadron. She suspected that if she had looked around her, she would have seen the same question on a score of faces.

Is someone at work, to allow the Women's Squadron

considerable land and financial interests in half a score
of different enterprises.

To complete confusion, Quiusa I Shtuur was as
proven fertile as a woman could be without actually
having borne a child. Her family had threatened to dis-
inherit her if she joined the Women's Squadron, but her
reply had routed them with enviable speed.

"If I have no inheritance from my blood-kin, then I
will have my inheritance from the honor of the Fleet in
which we serve," she had replied. That had given her a
case for serving that few dared dispute. As she had also
quickly won promotion to Farer First Class on sheer
ability, she now had more than a nimble tongue fighting for her.

I Shtuur looked no better than anyone else who had
been on duty since sunbrighten was a distant gray spot
on the horizon. She blinked as she held out a message
pouch to Alikili.

"Thank you, Farer I Shtuur."

"It is from your—from the I Hmilra estate. The duty
commander said that she would authorize emergency
leave if necessary."

That was hardly tactful, in hearing of the Squadron's
Captain herself, but it was not maliciously meant either.
I Shtuur had merely spent her whole life in circles
where no one dared take offense at anything said by
someone of her name. It was a miracle that she had
more wits and courtesy than the average.

"I agree," the Squadron Captain said. "If you care to
read it now, I can arrange for you to return with the driver, or even go directly to the station and find an earlier
train."

Alikili would rather have taken off her clothes than
read the letter with so many eyes on her, but the Captain's suggestion had the weight of an order. She
unsealed the pouch, opened the letter inside, and read.

Her face must have said what her lips held back. The

his weapons, a heavy bush knife with a saw-toothed edge, and an extra canteen.

He would gladly have carried little and worn nothing, like the mythical Father-god avatar Adam—or the first human, depending on if one followed the Rationalist or Observant orthodoxies. The Adinisis seemed to form a barrier to the slightest breeze, as well as a ripe collection of tropical stenches that the nonexistent breezes let accumulate over them like flies over a dunghill.

There were some of those, too, near the refugee camp whose care and maintenance had quickly become the largest single work for the observation force. A thousand groundfighters and the crews of *Lingvaas, Bybur*, nine torpedo-carriers, and several transports had been expected to be more than ample for the work to be done.

But the refugees who clambered aboard *Lingvaas* the night of the riots were only the vanguard of an endless (or at least not yet ended, even if diminishing) flow. Not all of them remained on the islands under Fleet care, of course. Some had money or were sent it by their kin in Rinbao-Dar to buy them safe passage until the Matriarchy was quiet again.

Even those needed at the very least food, water, and transportation to their destinations. One of the torpedo-carriers was serving practically full-time, running up and down the coast with refugees clinging to practically everything above-decks except the funnels and the torpedo warheads. Two other torpedo-carriers had escorted the light-transport *Juumsan* down the coast to the town of Dlee, on a voyage that began with five hundred and six refugees aboard and ended with five hundred and ten (one dead and buried at sea, five babies born).

This left a mere two thousand or so camped in improvised shelters (less improvised each day, thanks to both the Kertovans' efforts and those of the refugees), fearing or believing that they had no place to go. A few Kertovans and even some humans muttered that the refugees

contributing her quota of guards to both camp security and the distant patrol ever since the camp went up, but this was a different matter.

"I want to see how fast we can get thirty people ashore with a crankgun on wheels, supplies in pack saddles, and everything else for a serious fight," she said. "I want to see how many of those thirty know their arses from their elbows about groundfighter work, and make sure the ones who don't stay ashore.

"And I want to find out just exactly *what* our Kertovan friends may really be doing in the camp."

Borlund had nodded, there being nothing to say. He and Barbara still had few secrets from each other, as short-tempered as they had both grown. They both knew that more than a few troublemakers in the Matriarchy accused the Fleet of keeping the refugees in camp against their will, of using them for forced labor or worse, and of trying to make them serve Kertovan interests in the cities.

Borlund and Weil thought this was nonsense. But other humans, not just in the Study Group, might do so. Then all the suspicions of the motives of those humans who had accepted the Fleet's invitation to honorable service might erupt like a geyser, scalding the reputations of everyone serving aboard *Lingvaas* or training for Fleet service.

Losing so much to the gaping mouths and empty heads of Rinbao-Daran demagogues was unbearable.

So as the quick sunfade of southern lands swallowed the shore, Sean Borlund strode up the beach toward the road to the camp. It had begun as a forest trail, been widened to a path by trampling feet, and then widened and smoothed further into a proper road by work parties from both camp and Fleet. Ahead of him marched four Farers with their rifles held at the ready, as if they were moving in hostile territory. (Weil had picked those four herself; none were too quick to shoot but all could hit with the first round when they did.)

not wide enough for us to march abreast, more's the pity. And I command, if anybody needs to."

That shouldn't be necessary, as the patrol commander was always someone senior to both Borlund and Tuomitti. That seniority might even help twist an answer out of Tuomitti or Zhohorosh, about why *Byubr* and *Lingvaas* were carrying out the same training exercise on the same evening.

The single combined column had covered about two-thirds of the distance to the patrol line, with the lights of the camp's fires fading into the forest behind them, when Borlund heard a single flat crack from ahead. It was too loud to be a twig snapping, but didn't sound like a shot.

Had some of the camp children found another box of old fuses and decided to throw them into a campfire? That had already happened once, a few nights ago, although mercifully with no damage except to adults' nerves and children's bottoms.

The crack came again, loud enough to raise echoes. As the echoes died, Borlund heard a peculiar metallic *clang* that sounded like a spring-loaded metal door slamming.

That could hardly be a children's prank.

The next sound ended all doubt. It was an explosion—a shell burst, Borlund thought, maybe a dud but at least a six-liner.

No children, and nothing on the patrol line or even friendly. The nearest Kertovan artillery was on Outpost Flanker, four-liner pack guns. They'd hardly be firing into the patrol line.

Somewhere up ahead, those folk with evil intent and silent feet were coming.

human or Kilmoyan, but a helpless one was doomed and a dead one skeletal unless rescue came quickly.

The column had just started off again when two of the Scouts hurried back, carrying a wounded Kertovan groundfighter between them. A healing-trained Farer stepped forward from the *Byubr* party, although even dim lantern light showed too much bleeding for there to be much hope.

Tuomitti and Zhohorosh deployed the two parties so that they wouldn't be an irresistibly large and vulnerable target for whoever was slinging shells out of the darkness, or even for prowling snipers. Borlund interrogated the Scouts.

"We came up to where the telegraph line to the artillery crossed the trail," one said. "We saw a dead gunner lying on the ground. We started to spread out, but somebody shot Stark. Sniper, I think."

"Local weapon or—?" Borlund asked. This might be violating security, but rumors of Drylander snipers were all over the Fleet. Ignoring them was bad leadership and plain stupidity.

"Local," the other Scout—Klimova, from the name on her shirt—said. "It had that heavy black-powder boom to it. Big slug, though. Stark's head just came apart. Then somebody else started lobbing shells—too big for grenades—and one hit close enough for the fragments to hit Ruag. Pedersen and I were already on the ground, but Ruag was trying to spot the sniper."

Another distant *clank*, but this time a dull *thud* followed, along with cracking branches, instead of an explosion. Pedersen bit his lip and stared wildly about him, but said nothing. Klimova was clearly doing the better job of keeping her nerve. Borlund remembered that aboard *Lingvaas* she was an oiler who worked every day with hot, fast-moving machinery.

"Nice to know that they sometimes have duds, too," Borlund said, pitching his voice to be heard by everyone

he stepped off the trail after Klimova, Borlund's final thought was *If something that potent is that cheap, whoever has it is a serious menace. Whoever they are, and wherever they learned how to make them.*

THE WIRE-SPEAKER NOW DIRECTLY LINKED THE WAN'WA Crossing station and the I Hmilra estate. It had done so, in fact, since before the last snow melted. But along several passages through forest and along one stretch of road where no forest provided windbreaks, falling branches and snapping poles could break the wire as easily as a string asked to moor an armorclad.

So Alikili had no way of telling the house when she reached the station, near the end of sunfade. The first train she could have caught from Saadi was a local that actually arrived later than the next one, an express; she decided to wait for the express.

However, its railsteamer broke down halfway between Gaanaus and Wan'wa Crossing. Since the line was single-tracked, the fastest way out for the passengers was in carts hauled by steam tractors hastily gathered from the nearest builders' camps and road gangs. Alikili was glad she carried no baggage, but hoped that they would clear the line in time for what I Shtuur was sending after her to reach the house tonight.

Not all of it was material she cared to leave at the mercy of fate and strangers. Still less did she want it exposed to strange or hostile eyes as well, for a whole common.

Her uniform seemed to speed matters, and certainly helped one of the tractor drivers recognize her as Jossu I Hmilra's tuunda companion. Ignoring indignant protests, he allowed her to ride in the cab, but himself protested when she wanted to relieve the stoker—who seemed hardly more than a boy—at his work.

"A lady shouldn't have to do that work," he muttered.

It would have been quickest for Alikili to reply that she was no lady but a garcik, and if he doubted her word

wings of gray stoopers or the strength of the legendary giant Sovmraaki. He felt a grievance at this lack of accurate information.

He also felt sweat pouring off him, and half a dozen muscles strained or torn. Being not only the commander but one of the largest and strongest Drylanders in the party meant doing his share of the brute-force lifting and hauling or maybe a little more.

All the force of all the brutes in the party, however, managed to move the crankgun no more than three hundred paces before Borlund had to call for a halt. Along that trail of sweat and straining, they had made so much noise that he was sure only the continued mortar bursts had kept the enemy from marking every step of the crankgun's progress.

If an enemy attack did burst out of the forest now, he suspected that nothing would save *Lingvaas*'s landing party except the enemy's laughing themselves into a fit at the sight.

Borlund wasn't too short of breath to give a few orders, however. The Farers of both races weren't too weary (or perhaps were too afraid of the chiefs) to obey them. They heaved the crankgun around until it was aimed across the largest stretch of open ground in sight, perhaps two pistol shots wide and half that long. They loaded a drum of the thumb-sized brass-jacketed slugs, then locked the hammer back while they cranked one into the firing chamber.

After that, it would take only the flick of a thumb and a hand on the crank before the gun started spewing death. Of course, it would help if there was somebody to spew it *at*, and Borlund had begun to wonder if anyone would be willing to provide the legitimate target.

The mortar barrage seemed to have ceased. He heard the random round-popping of sniping and skirmishing, but hardly any explosions. Even those were the flatter, milder *craaak*! of hand grenades or homemade throwing-charges.

spawned worse than bandits, seeking more than money. Why shouldn't they take to the roads in search of prey?

Before Alikili could even finishing drawing her pistol, let alone aim it, the four riders were up with her. Without slowing, they trotted on past. She would have sworn that one of them was a woman, and that they had a fifth dreezan, a pack animal humped with a heavy load, clattering along behind them on a lead rein.

But she couldn't be sure of any of this, before the loudest thunderclap yet burst over the landscape. Then landscape, riders, and everything else more than ten paces away vanished.

It seemed like the Skyfall Rains had come again. Alikili abandoned compassion and thrust in her spurs. The dreezan quivered, took one step that an infant might have equaled, then halted again. It raised its head and began a plaintive grunt, instantly lost in more thunder.

Alikili did not try to outcurse the thunder. But in her mind she cursed the whole race of dreezans, the hire-stable owner's son and all his line to the last generation of the world, all powers commanding weather, and the whole household staff who couldn't find their hindparts without her drawing them a map!

After that, she felt sufficiently eased to dismount. She would lead the dreezan until the rain or at least the thunder ended and its nerve returned. The satisfaction of doing something lasted three or four breaths, until the water lying across the road spilled over the tops of her shoes, so that she squished as well as splashed at each step.

Sadly, she realized that she had exhausted her stock of curses.

WITH CLANGS AND CRASHES, THE CRACKLE OF SMALL branches breaking and the thud of something heavy bouncing off larger ones, the mortar's projectile plummeted down onto Borlund's party.

outpost off to the right, to watch the way they'd come, back toward the trail. The guards he'd posted on the trail had either fallen silently or met no enemy, but four Farers couldn't watch much besides the trail. More flank protection—even if in the end, Borlund suspected he would have more flanks to protect than Farers to protect them.

The messenger from the outposts volunteered to return, to warn them of the crankgun's shift of position. Borlund realized that the outposters needed to know this, but didn't want anyone wandering around alone. He asked the messenger to pick a companion and go quietly, then turned his attention to the mortar projectile.

It did look like a large tin can, the kind used aboard ship or in eating houses for cooking oil or vegetables. From one end sprouted a long metal rod, strengthened with three flanges set equally around it. At the end of the rod was a circular plate, lightened by several cut-out sections.

The thing did not look particularly strong, and from the fact that it had dug only a shallow hole in the ground it could not be very heavy, either. The can was probably light cast iron or, more probably, rust-barriered sheet steel, filled with explosives. Borlund had no idea where the fuse was, why it hadn't gone off, or what it would take to set it off now.

He very much wished that one of the *Lingvaas* landing party was a gunnery expert. Even a senior gunnery chief would know more than Borlund did about things that flew through the air and were expected to go *bang* when they landed.

Zhohorosh was the closest thing to a gunnery expert with Borlund's party. However, he was also the farthest leader from Borlund himself. Calling him back from the outposts now was hardly practical.

A hope and a necessity remained. The hope was that someone among the Drylanders had acquired contaminating knowledge of weaponry, and would be willing to

of friendly smokeless ones, once the sharper crack of a grenade, but no *clanks*, no crankguns, and no war cries. The screams of the wounded and dying, yes, but nothing to give away anybody's position or identity.

Borlund liked that even less than he liked the attack itself. That kind of discipline smelled of trained Imperial groundfighters or the best of the Rinbao-Darans. He hoped Zhohorosh could do as well with his outposters and confuse the enemy as badly.

Then one scream found an echo—several echoes. What seemed half a hundred throats were all tearing themselves to pieces with screams that might have been war cries or might have been the plaints of damned souls in Hell as Bridget described it. (Borlund was briefly glad that he did not have to believe in Hell, if it made people scream like that.)

The screaming went on, and now thudding feet and cracking branches swelled the din. Borlund drew a pistol and wished he had a rifle; the ranges would be short but the more accurate rifle would reduce the danger of hitting friends.

Then as if a theater curtain had risen, the far side of the clearing suddenly boiled over with hurrying, armed groundfighters. Half a dozen paces behind them, conspicuously taller than the rest, came an unmistakable human.

THE RAIN DID NOT BEAT ON ALIKILI'S SKULL HARD enough to stop her thoughts. She could spare a few, from the work of leading the dreezan "not into error and vice," as the Reverence gave it, and not herself stepping off the road into the ditch or even into the larger potholes on the road.

There was no law that said a woman could not be riding abroad tonight, with three companions and a packbeast. To say otherwise was to think like the hire-stable owner's son, which was hardly thinking at all.

instead of an impersonal force like the pull of the ground threatening your handhold on a cliff or fire and smoke ready to end your life with no more malice than they would show toward a mite.

Alikili promised thank-offerings to all concerned with giving her a modern cartridge pistol that could be trusted in wet weather. She rummaged in her cloak pocket, for the ten spare cartridges, which gave her a total of fifteen.

Then she crawled behind the dead dreezan, conscious that her back was still exposed as well as sodden. It still felt better to be crouching with a weapon in hand rather than lying wondering what hit her, and that her movement hadn't drawn a third shot was encouraging. Random shooting in this murk needed luck to do damage, and luck played no favorites.

Borlund managed about three steps before the enemy reinforced their attack. Crushed bushes crackled as nearly a hundred Kilmoyans shouldered their way forward, trampling fallen comrades as they came. Few of them wore any insignia, many of them wore hardly any clothing, and more than a few of them had no firearms at all, only spears or long two-handed swords. Most of them also had empty sacks slung over their shoulders.

Borlund recognized locally recruited tribal levies when he saw them. He knew that they might have been carried away by misplaced enthusiasm for battle, rushing forward against orders. He also knew that if their enthusiasm carried them to close quarters, those blades and spears could do appalling damage.

The crankgun roared.

Its crew had reached the same conclusion as Borlund, moments earlier. An entire drum of rounds staggered the enemy line, soldiers, militia, and levies alike dropping from crippling wounds or knocked off their feet. So many went down that the second drum found fewer targets.

The third drum spewed as a few hardy souls tried to arm and throw hand grenades. One grenade bounced off a tree, slicing the air and several living bodies with fragments. Three others fell back into the enemy ranks and exploded there, maiming more of the throwers' comrades than the throwers' enemies.

The combination of three drumloads from the crankgun and the self-inflicted grenade damage ruined enemy marksmanship. Even those who survived to use their rifles and pistols mostly had black-powder single-shot weapons. Quite a few bullets flew toward the defenders; few hit. Borlund had only moments to be aware that the enemy seemed to be able to miss even a target his size. Then suddenly the battle turned hand-to-hand, and Borlund was glad of his size. Previously, towering over the average Kilmoyan had made him self-conscious. Now it gave him a survival edge.

which the attack had come. "It looks like a Drylander matter."

"Another Drylander in Imperial colors?" was all Borlund could say.

It was hard to tell when a Kilmoyan's eyebrows were rising, particularly when they had as much facial hair as Zhohorosh. The watch chief still radiated surprise, and Borlund realized that he might have given away too much.

"Was there one up here?" Zhohorosh asked.

"Yes, and I think we killed him. Have a search made for the body, and when you find it, guard him."

The two chiefs saluted, and Borlund remembered just in time to respect the chain of command by repeating the orders to the human chiefs. Then he lurched to his feet.

"What is back in the trees, if it's not a Drylander, alive or dead?" he asked.

"Nothing I've ever seen," Zhohorosh said, "nor any of the groundfighters either. We think there was a second, but the people with it got clean away."

"A second what? Zhohorosh, are we talking about their portable mortar, or something else?"

"You can call it a mortar if you want," the chief said. "But it's like no mortar I've ever seen. It looks as if it tosses bombs with a spring."

"A *spring*," Borlund repeated, glad that this time surprise didn't turn him into a soprano. "I have to see this."

"Then follow me," Zhohorosh said.

ALIKILI WAS CERTAIN BY NOW THAT SHE HAD CROUCHED behind the dead dreezan through the whole night, and that sunbrighten must be close. She also suspected that the first storm had blown out, and that its third or fourth successor must be blowing now. Or had there been another Skyfall, which was the only thing that could have produced so long a storm . . ?

She shook her head, half expecting water to spurt

of age. She hoped that the enemies of the Republic would continue to find him impossible to kill, and that he would die in his own bed from the sheer weight of the Greats pressing him down into the Lord's realm—

The first shot aimed at her in some while made a *wheet* as it flashed overhead and a *chunk* as it tore into a tree. Then the sodden darkness ahead was darker still, with solid shapes. No, not solid, but wavering—which Alikili realized came from their moving fast.

She was ready to empty the pistol into them when she remembered Jossu's tales of disastrously mistaken identities. There had also been some training—one common of lectures, another common of exercises—in Watch duties. The Women's Squadron was not expected to see combat, but neither were they expected always to be able to call on male Farers to guard their quarters or their offices, and had not been issued pistols and quick-healing kits for their personal adornment.

Alikili tried to make herself invisible, inaudible, and invulnerable all at once, which would have let her rank with the great magic-workers of legend if she had succeeded. Before she could so much as draw breath to laugh at the conceit, the running figures stormed past, making as much noise as a galloping herd of unbroken dreezans.

Then lightning blazed, showing Alikili the receding backs of several hooded heads. Darkness returned quickly, and as her night vision did the same, the sky's thunder again crashed across the land.

Not sure if she was safe or if she could hope to *be* safe tonight, Alikili didn't move until she became aware of someone standing over her. Even then it was only to draw in a deeper breath, so her mind would be clear and her hand steady when she aimed her pistol at one who probably would shoot first and at this range could not miss—

"Greetings, Farer Alikili."

It was unmistakably a woman's voice. Alikili looked

to stand here arguing much longer. "If I have to walk the rest of the way home, I will. I will not trust myself to anyone who will not tell me what I need to know." She held up a hand. "And do not think to take me by force. That would prove you a poor friend to the Captain-Born."

"I was not thinking of any such gross stupidity. My oath to both Lady and Lord upon this," the woman said. "Are you fit to ride?"

"I think I have doubled my weight with mud and water, but if you have a stout dreezan—"

"We captured several."

"Good. Then mount me on one, and perhaps you can tell me what I need to know as we ride home."

SEAN BORLUND HAD BATHED, EATEN, AND CHANGED clothes since coming back aboard *Lingvaas*. He had not slept, and did not dare even rest his chin in his hands, for fear of dozing off.

He had to be awake and even coherent right to the end of the commanders' meeting. He didn't know if he had led the bloodiest ground action since the Drylanders came to the Island Republic. He hadn't even read all the public histories, and the secret ones might hold almost anything.

He definitely held the ground-combat record aboard *Lingvaas*, the first and so far only Drylander-crewed ship of the Fleet. This made him the center of attention for now, even if the future might reduce him to footnotes.

The bath had helped, although he still thought he smelled of the battlefield—leaf mold, human bodily wastes, gunpowder, and other undefined odors. So had the meal, although he hadn't been able to eat much. The queasy stomach he'd dreaded during the shooting came afterward.

He'd therefore been able to look everyone in the eye while giving his report. Sometimes he saw underneath the sweaty, weatherbeaten faces the ruin a bullet or

loss of surprise won't make much difference, in the next fight. And the actual crews may have been perfectly well trained, just not knowing where we were and trying to—what's the term—scout by shooting?"

Nobody was groundfighter enough to correct Borlund, but he detected some sideways glances. Knowing too much about war had been at least a social offense on Esperanza since before the first subassembly for *Ramparts* reached orbit. Maintaining that standard on Kilmoyn had been a rearguard action since within days of the landing. It was now about to become an exercise in complete futility—but some of those glances were from people too senior to Borlund for him to tell them that, to their faces, in public.

"That's a point," Kund said. "But even then, the Imperials seem to have had problems with discipline among their levies. What if they depend on the levies for ammunition bearers?"

"The levies could be replaced with militia or even Imperial regulars," Borlund said. "As you said, this was an outpost action. Perhaps the local Imperial commander didn't have the regulars to spare.

"Also, the levies did their duty until they ran into the crankgun. By then, they'd kept their oath to bring back their weapons bloodied or die trying?"

Kund's face hardened with frightening speed. "How did you learn that?"

From the faces around him, Borlund knew his stomach wasn't the only one twisting. He wished he could interpret those faces. Were the other commanders just surprised, or ready to take sides, and, if so, which?

It would not help if they wound up taking sides, even if some of them took Borlund's. Every commander aboard *Lingvaas* was here. Weil had made it clear that missing this meeting now or being indiscreet about it afterward would be a beaching offense.

"The people from *Byubr* had interrogated some of the

being extremely discreet, so that the Fleet does not suspect we are trying to hide anything from them."

That drew nods from all around the table. Borlund was relieved to see everyone apparently united against stupidity, even if they might not agree on what would be good sense.

"Yes?" Kund looked as if he would agree to dance on the table if it ended this embarrassing situation any faster.

"Help us in the matter of identifying the Imperial humans and their weapon," Weil said. "With your own resources, those of your friends, and those of anybody you report to. I will even let you use Fleet facilities for messages using—ah, private codes—if it will bring us more intelligence faster.

"As you yourself said, anytime the identity secret is in danger, we all have to bend the rules a trifle to defend it."

Borlund felt a perverse combination of a stomach twisting again at the thought of the investigation, and a head so light it threatened to float off his shoulders at being able to do serious work on tonight's mysteries. Possibly the identity secret wasn't directly in danger, but cooperation between Fleet and Drylander easily could be. Then the Fleet would have more reason than ever to be curious about matters they had let lie for two generations.

More reason—and more resources, if Jossu I Hmilra had anything to say about the priorities. Borlund hoped his face would not crack from the effort as he tried to smile.

"As the central exhibit in the investigation, I'd like to vote in favor of the bargain. The only thing I ask is to advise the investigators on how to question the *Byubr* Farers without giving up secrets. There's probably not much that Tuomitti and Zhohorosh don't know about Drylanders, and that's not counting anything their commanders or fellow chiefs might have learned."

attack the house or tried to carry them out and were defeated.

Or broke through Kekaspa's guard and took the house, Alikili reminded herself. She remained aware of that possibility, for all the other woman's reassurances that the house was hardly more than bait in a trap that could be expected to do all the necessary work.

She was not sure how strongly Kekaspa felt about having the household left ignorant, lest some of them talk where hostile ears could hear. Therefore, Alikili had resolved to tell her people as little as allowed them to remain safe—but to tell Kekaspa nothing at all about speaking to the people.

That would only ignite an argument. Such an argument would go nowhere and yield nothing—except perhaps a loosening of Kekaspa's authority over her companions. Alikili doubted that even the most remarkable of men could be wholly free of doubts about obeying even the most remarkable of women, particularly in Saadi.

When Kekaspa replied, it was in a somewhat remote voice.

"My mate is kin to a family that once gave Saadi five princes. He holds to the old notion that both sire and bearer must breed courage into the babes. So I tell him much about dangers but little about where they come from, and he thinks I am braver than I am.

"But at least the old tales seem to have it right. Our babe healed swiftly after his little swim, and thrives now in my sister's care. I know he misses me, and I hope he knows that I miss him, but where he is, it will be hard to make a hostage of him."

Alikili almost softened to the point of abandoning her resolve of silence. Moi Kekaspa might end leaving her mate and babe alone, if she did not know everything the house would have ready for its enemies.

"He also thinks it is better I serve where I do," Kekaspa added, with a twisted grin that bared excep-

Probably not now, he decided. The Kertovan knack for compact, high-powered steam engines had reduced the market for expanded uses of electric power. On the other hand, those handy little engines would make wonderful generators, particularly if they could be adjusted to burn "rock oil"—and the technical journals had mentioned that this was being worked on.

It shouldn't be long before electricity was in sufficiently widespread use for various "inventions" to be made without contaminating Kilmoyan culture—assuming, that is, that the stay-behinds had not sold themselves to the Empire (with or without the aid of the Confederation) and embarked on a systematic program of inventions. After two generations in exile, the ragged handful of stay-behinds must be ready to contaminate anything and everything, if it could give them leadership among the humans of Kilmoyn.

Unless their ancestors had stayed behind not out of a desire to play Gods from Space, but out of a genuine disagreement with some of the principles of the *Ramparts* group? That had not occurred so clearly to Borlund before.

The more he thought about it, the clearer the possibility became. Also the greater. If systematically lying to your hosts to protect them from your imagined power to harm them had begun to look like a cure worse than the disease to someone like Sean Borlund—who was definitely no scholar. . .

To puzzle that one out, Borlund decided he needed fresh air. He shaved quickly and went on deck.

It would have been an exaggeration to call the air "fresh," but an occasional puff of morning breeze blew away some of the sweat and stench. It also brought the smell of wood smoke from shore, where the watchfires were dying down and the cookfires were starting up.

They had the cooking for the refugees well organized by now, Borlund recalled. But sooner or later the area around the camp would be stripped of firewood. Then

ing your conversion in the streets where the Study Group can hear you?"

"A long time ago. Or it seems that way, at least. Besides, a lot has happened now that hadn't happened then."

A whistle blew off to greenward. Another torpedo-carrier steamed past, towing a smaller barge also piled high with logs.

"What are they doing?" Borlund asked.

"Getting out a boom across the mouth of the anchorage," Weil said. "We don't know what the Empire has on or around the island. But *Byubr* and *Lingvaas* are all the heavy guns we have now if the camp is attacked."

"Do we have enough chain to make something that will hold in a storm?" Borlund asked.

Weil nodded, acknowledging his prudence, then shrugged. "We only have to keep torpedo-carriers out of the anchorage for a few days," Weil said. "And the weather seldom gives worse than rain at this time of year. Once Jossu I Hmilra returns, we'll have plenty of searchlights and guns for a more active defense.

"But it wasn't big guns I was thinking about when I carried you off. It was the bomb-throwers. You mentioned that Chief Zhohorosh is a gunnery expert. Can you and he work together on the local investigation of what the—the Empire has come up with?"

Borlund thought that they ought to send one of *Lingvaas*'s gunners and said so. Weil shook her head.

"It's not expert knowledge we need to send, it's someone our friends trust."

"If I go with that label pinned to me, the Study Group people will be watching me every step of the way."

"Afraid of the Study Group suddenly? Sorry, that was not well said. But I have to meet with Captain Impanskaa of *Byubr* and Commander Shvotz of the ground-fighters this morning. I'd like to be able to report as much progress as possible."

chapter 22

EHOMA TUOMITTI USUALLY slept unclothed when she did not sleep alone or when it was almost too hot for a sane Farer to contemplate sleep. Tonight was the second sort of night.

She shared a cabin with three other watch chiefs, but two were women and Huusen the devoutly faithful sire of eight children. She did not fear temptation, only drowning in their own sweat.

The *Illik*-class vessels had never been designed for warm waters and hot winds, when there was a wind, which there usually was not (as tonight, for example). What could be done with clockwork-driven fans, windsails, and sleeping on deck had been done, but the first two were falling apart and the third was no longer safe. Since the Imperial attack, the only Farers allowed on deck were those clothed, armed, and on duty.

Tuomitti rolled over, with the care needed not to jostle the Engineer Chief in the bunk above. The woman was a light sleeper and ill-tempered when awakened.

Spending half the day in the boats and the other half with a work party in the chain locker had taken its toll. Tuomitti found herself yawning, then felt vision grow dim and muscles slacken. Then she was floating along on a current of luminous purple water that seemed to form a border between waking and sleeping.

She thought she saw her father floating not far from

swimmers were half-legend, half-rumor, but there'd
been suspicious incidents that could hardly be explained
otherwise.

They were one reason the Island Republic's ships did
not anchor too far up the Hask, even in City-State
waters. They were also one of several good reasons for
the three days of backbreaking labor to lay the boom
across the mouth of the anchorage.

Tuomitti slid out of her bunk, landing with her heel on
a rivet in the deck. Pain burned the oath out of her mouth;
she groped blindly and felt Huusen holding her up.

"Easy, there, girl," he said.

"Girl?" she snapped, then remembered that his eldest
daughter was only a few Greats younger than she.
Except for wanting to be part of this last great voyage
to Eneh, he would doubtless be home with them, and
their children.

She'd do her best, Lord and Lady helping, to see that
he went home afterward.

ALIKILI COULD NOT SLEEP AND WONDERED WHY.

It could not be that she was alone in the bed she had
so often shared with Jossu. She always slept poorly for
a few nights after he went to sea, but he had been in
southern waters much longer than that.

Nor was it injury or illness; she had not so much as a
dripping nose or earache from her battle on the storm-
swept road. Perhaps it was just that she had slept so long
the first night at home that now her body needed less
rest than usual.

Certainly she had little enough to do. Coming home,
she had found that the house was as ready for defense as
could be contrived, short of spikewire in the hedges or
crankguns on the roof.

Either Moi Kekaspa had been lying about keeping the
situation secret from the house, the house had drawn
their own conclusions and taken their own measures, or
Kekaspa's people in the house had talked freely whether

looked like one of the old Farers in the house, who spent more time laying fires and shifting crates and barrels than he did bringing refreshments to the lady. He was immaculately clean, though, and both his muscles and his garments bulged reassuringly.

"Aught else?" he asked, with a pronounced Saadian accent.

"Plenty of greenmist in the hoeg, say half," she added.

"You'll not sleep, after that," the man said.

Alikili grunted in frustration. She hadn't had this many nursemaids when she was a newborn babe!

"I should think there's enough to keep anyone awake," she replied.

"Mayhap," the Farer said. "But if they come, it won't be tonight. Quiet, clear, and those of us who need to be awake will stay that way."

Alikili muttered a Drilion oath that made the man's ears twitch. He would not meet her eye as he backed out, but his shoulders shook.

It was only after the door closed that Alikili discovered that the inkpot was dry. She lay back on the pillows, setting herself to compose the rest of the letter in her mind. When the hoeg came, it would be soon enough to ask for fresh ink.

UNDER OTHER CIRCUMSTANCES, SEAN BORLUND would have said that he was wandering. On a larger ship with a broader deck or even aboard *Lingvaas* on a night when he had fewer duties, he might actually have done so.

But tonight each change in the direction of his steps, from redside to green and back again, was deliberate. He wanted to keep an eye on the lookouts, who probably didn't need a commander or even a chief looking over their shoulder to make sure they were intently watching the sea. He also wanted to look out into the darkness himself, if only to reassure himself that noth-

the darkness, and then at the launch on the davits. The canvas cover was snugged down tight, to keep rain out.

Find out when the cover was last undone, to give the launch an airing. Tropical molds and fungi had a voracious appetite for damp, closed spaces, like the bilges of a launch too long sealed.

That kind of detail was really the chiefs' duty, but it never hurt for a commander to remind them that he knew about the details. Borlund thought he'd finally learned to walk the fine line between standing back so far the chiefs thought he was careless and standing so close that they thought he was doing their job for them out of mistrust.

At least Zhohorosh said so. Borlund sometimes wondered if Zhohorosh's praise of him these past few commons was sincere. The Kertovans certainly seemed to be engaged in the next thing to a conspiracy of tact, to assure the humans that finding Drylanders among Imperial troops didn't make them distrust the Farers of *Lingvaas*.

Borlund now walked aft, studying the lashings of the launch's cover. All snug, none showing any signs of being undone to let a pair (or more) of lovers crawl into the launch for a quick meeting.

Zhohorosh said that was a problem, in tropical waters after a midtide or so. "Something in the air," was how he'd put it.

Human sexual codes should make that less of a problem aboard *Lingvaas*—but "should" was as important a word here as "less." Borlund had noticed a few exchanges of the same kind of looks he exchanged with Barbara Weil, when they were absolutely sure nobody could see them.

For a few commons he had found himself aroused at the thought of what might happen if nobody could see him and the Captain for a really long time—even half a watch. But that was letting himself grow frustrated over the absence of a miracle—he found himself using that

lic's ships visible from several-score casts farther than they would have been otherwise. Only slowing still further could douse the seaglow now, and some of the ships could not maintain steerageway at any lower speed. The half-empty coal-carriers and at least two of the transports were among these.

Then it seemed for a moment that the sea off the redside bow caught fire. Seven parallel lines of green fire seared across the dark water, as if a seven-fingered hand had clawed at the sea. I Hmilra gripped the railing so tightly that his knuckles ached by the time the first of the Seakin blew.

Seakin. *Not* Imperial torpedoes or some mystery out of Farer legend. I Hmilra knew quick relief, unclamped his hands—then heard the other six Seakin blow also at precise intervals. Too precise, to have any meaning except one.

This was a message party.

"Send for the Speaker to Seakin," I Hmilra said.

The watch commander saluted with great discipline and grinned with equal triumph. "Already done, Lord. Do you want her up here or down on the bow?"

"Down on the bow, with relay talkers to a Farer on the whistle."

"That could warn the Imperials as well as tell the rest of the clan."

"Not being able to warn the rest of the Seakin risks offending every last one of them in the Gulf, at least," I Hmilra said.

"At least?" the commander asked, plainly controlling irritation at being ignorant in front of both seniors and juniors.

"The message we received before the Fleet sailed south was said to be from the entire race of Seakin. *If* they communicate that well, and if the Speakers know their—"

"I assure you that the Seakin do communicate that well," came a level voice apparently from around I

jerked the whistle cord again. Anything the commander might have been about to say was lost in a triple blast. The Seakin replied, each with a single blowing, and sounded.

"As I was saying, Captain Over Captains," the Speaker resumed, "they did come to warn us. They said that those not Landkin—I do not like that translation, but—"

"Does that poor word affect the truth of what they told you?" I Hmilra said. "I too delight in a fine choice of words, but not when time presses, as you seem to be saying it does."

The Speaker looked annoyed. I Hmilra swore to himself that if she was angry enough to sulk until he had counted to ten, she would never sail with the Fleet again. (The Speakers had a powerful guild, so that was the most he could do; throwing her overboard would be only briefly satisfying and doubtless end his career nearly as quickly hers.)

At the count of seven, the Speaker was continuing.

"Those who are not Landkin have come against the rest of our tribe in—it translates as the south. Not Luokka, the people off Rinbao-Dar, on that island I never could remember and the Seakin have no name for—"

"Puyasa," the watch commander put in,

"Thank you," the Speaker said, more graciously than before. "On Puyasa there is—or will be, I can't be sure—fighting. The unfriends have come by sea but will fight both on land and on the sea. The water is too shallow for the Seakin to help, if their—we call it *law* but it's really not translatable—"

This time I Hmilra held his tongue as the Speaker went off into a long display of her erudition. She might be telling him nothing that he needed to listen to, but she was giving him time to organize his thoughts.

"I thank you," I Hmilra said at last. "Signalers!"

The Speaker understood the dismissal and looked as

chapter 23

EVERYONE ON *BYUBR*'s deck was still on duty. Not all were clothed, because they had scrambled on deck hastily. Nor were all armed, because not all had duties that allowed them to carry personal weapons.

Ehoma Tuomitti wore enough for street decency and more than enough for battle modesty; she also carried her pistol. It was on her belt now because she needed both hands free to signal or push her anchor section into position.

Whistles, shouts, anything that made noise—Captain Impanskaa had forbidden them. His plain intent was to have *Byubr* fully alert and ready to open fire without giving any sign of this to the enemy.

If there was an enemy.

On the prow, forward of the capstan and just above the tarnished scrollwork on the stem, Tuomitti had as good a view as anyone on the main deck and better than most. For all she could see, the Imperial combat swimmers might have vanished back into legend or at least into the dark sea.

They might also have left gifts behind them—water-proof explosive charges tied to the boom, or mines set adrift in the anchorage. Or they might even now be swimming for shore, to slit the throats of sentries at the refugee camp, or for *Byubr*, to board and grapple, shielding themselves among Farers too afraid of hurting

On *Byubr*'s decks, discipline strained but did not part
its moorings. The one anchor Farer who raised her voice
above a whisper stared briefly down the muzzle of
Tuomitti's pistol, then nodded and turned back to her
work. Around the main gun, the crankguns, the searchlights, everyone gripped ammunition, tools, or handles,
posed with them for a moment like a troupe of hill
dancers, then eased their stances.

They had just done this when a second explosion
sprayed water and flame across the beach in front of the
camp. The roar echoed around the anchorage, joined by
screams from the camp.

From pain or fear? Tuomitti wondered.

Byubr's seaward searchlight snapped on. From
beyond the boom, the spitting yellow flame of a crankgun replied—or, rather, from beyond where the boom
had been. Searchlight and gunflash together showed a
gap wide enough to pass three ships the size of *Byubr*
steaming abreast.

Fire sparked in the darkness of the forest-covered
point to the north of the anchorage. An enemy landing
party trying to clear the way for their comrades, or Kertovans moved so secretly that *Byubr* hadn't been told,
trying to defend the anchorage?

No bullets touched *Byubr* or her Farers from land or
sea. That left Tuomitti and everyone else still ignorant
of who was shooting at whom, but usefully informed
the crankgun crews that they did not have an identified
target. The four crankguns with clear bearings remained
silent.

The searchlight's beam lifted now, briefly gilding the
funnels of two unmistakable Imperial torpedo-carriers,
both of them now using their crankguns. Tuomitti
shouted to her people to be ready to lie down. The
enemy could find the range at any moment, and sweeping an enemy's decks with crankgun fire was listed in
most books on tactics as a preparation for boarding.

If the crankguns lacked range or targets, the same

This time Tuomitti heard the *wheett* of bullets passing, and the *spanngg* of them hitting metal close by. She
did not hear any cries of wounded Farers, because
Byubr's crankguns opened fire, now sure of their range.
Their bang and clatter made a din fit to kill the living as
readily as to wake the dead, and drove silence back to
the same remote corner of the world as darkness.

Tuomitti had to ask the messenger tugging at her arm
to repeat himself three times before she understood that
Byubr was going to weigh anchor and get underway.
The main gun fired a third time as the anchor section
took their posts, knocking them down again without the
shell's hitting anything. The fourth shot drowned out the
clanking of the capstan, and this time a Farer went down
so that he would have been caught in or maybe under
the chain if two others hadn't snatched him clear—

Tuomitti saw a fifth shot going into the main gun, and
this time remembered to open her mouth as well as clap
her hands over her ears. Without the orders she'd forgotten to give, two of her section pried the hatch off the
chain-locker and scrambled down, to be sure that the
chain was coming in properly.

Then the main gun fired its fifth round.

BY THE TIME ALIKILI FINISHED COMPOSING THE LET-
ter, she hoped the hoeg was scalding hot and loaded
with greenmist. Otherwise she might not be awake long
enough for the servant to bring the fresh ink, let alone
finish the letter.

She also wanted to be particularly delicate in her
choice of words. Jossu would not object to her new
sense of duty to the Women's Squadron, unless he
thought that meant diminished regard for him. He con-
cealed his pride under the Captain-Born's customary
armor, but it was there and capable of being wounded.
Nor could he wholly ignore the gap of so many Greats
in their ages, not when he was alone with his conscience.

She could be sure of one thing. Jossu I Hmilra would

She ducked and shot, so that the lantern missed her and she missed the new attacker. Then the lantern crashed to the floor, shattering as it did, spewing flames and the stench of rock oil.

Alikili felt the scorching at her back as well as the stench pricking at her nostrils. If she stood to escape the flames, she would be silhouetted against them. If she crawled around the end of the bed, she would be a slow-moving target. If she crawled under the bed, she would die a coward.

So she slipped the pistol down the front of her nightrobe, then lay flat, feigning being stunned or frightened into helplessness, watching with half an eye as the second attacker stood by the bed.

Would he draw another knife, use his comrade's, or risk the noise of a pistol? Three shots must have waked the whole house by now, and every loyal soul in it must be rallying. He was big, though. If it came to a grapple, Alikili doubted she had much chance. Pistols evened that kind of odds, but only if you could hit with them—

The man climbed onto the bed and stood, looking down at Alikili. Rage at muddy boots ruining her bedding nearly drove her prematurely into action. But she waited, until he flexed at the knees, ready to jump down and subject her "corpse" to a close examination.

In the moment that he was off-balance, she rolled over, drew her pistol, and fired at the largest target, the man's belly. The heavy bullet knocked him back and down into a sitting position, which for a moment was all that told Alikili she might have hit him.

Then the man started screaming.

In a part of her mind, Alikili both marveled and stared in horror at her own self-command, rising to examine the knifeman and find him dead, then realizing that if she wanted a live prisoner the second attacker had to be kept alive.

But not screaming like that. Not anywhere under the rule of Lord and Lady, screaming like that.

But there was no time for the bath, if she was besieged in her own home. As for the hoeg, she took one look at the Farer who'd been bringing it, face-down in a puddle that mixed his blood with the spilled hoeg. She would have heaved again if her stomach hadn't been too dry and empty.

It would be whole Greats before she could order hoeg again.

IT TOOK LONG ENOUGH FOR EVERYONE ABOARD *LINGVAAS* to become thoroughly uneasy, before they learned the strength of the attack from the sea.

Lingvaas's Farers would have been worse than uneasy if they hadn't been busy preparing their ship for action. At least that occupied their hands; but to Sean Borlund they seemed so well trained that they could run out and load the guns, stock the dressing stations with bandages and splints from the sick quarters, and so on, without thinking.

Borlund was able to keep both hands and mind busy. Battle Stations was an all-hands job; good commanders were expected to work up a sweat if necessary. With his size and strength, Borlund was able to find it "necessary" quite a few times.

At last the ship was ready for action, and his good luck did not desert him even then. Signals swarmed in from the scouting line. Some were broken, some fragmentary, and many hard to tell from the gunflashes.

Barbara Weil had a notebook full of signals within a few beats, and summarized them for every commander within hearing.

"Eight-plus large merchant vessels, one with heavy guns on deck. Several torpedo-carriers and unidentified light vessels, some towing barges. Looks like a major reinforcement for the island, obviously."

"What kind of troops?" Borlund asked. "Imperial Regulars or more tribal—"

He wanted to say "scrapings," but that would dishonor

"If they scatter, that will delay them. Delay them, and our groundfighters can post sentries on every beach with access to a trail. The Imperials will have to fight their way off the beaches.

"I'll wager half of them will still be on the beaches when *Valor* and the rest of the Fleet come back. Then we won't have anything more to worry about."

Borlund was inclined to agree, if only because *Lingvaas* might not be afloat or her Farers alive by then. But they had a fighting chance, against even a heavily armed vessel with no more armor than they had and almost certainly inferior gunnery.

That was not underestimating the enemy. That was a realistic assessment of risks, unless the Empire had bought not only ships but entire crews of trained gunners from the Confederation. Borlund decided to keep *that* possibility to himself.

Weil had finished while Borlund was assessing risks. He had decided that he was dismissed along with the rest—*Lingvaas* was already heading out to sea—when Captain Weil signaled with one hand.

In the shadow of one corner of the bridge, she gripped his hands and looked down at his feet. "I hope this comes off. I hope the Kertovans will stop worrying about Drylanders not making good Farers. And I hope we come through it, so we can keep our promises."

She did not kiss him, because a messenger scrambled up the ladder just as she swayed forward to do so. The messenger was Roald Chaykin-Schmidt, with a look on his face that said he had heard everything and was disappointed not to see more. Borlund's glare sobered him quickly.

The boy was hardworking and a promising Farer, but his "uncle" was still Directorate Security.

IT NOT ONLY SEEMED ONLY A BEAT OR TWO SINCE JOSSU I Hmilra had lain down on his bunk to try sleeping. It actually had been.

chapter 24

E HOMA TUOMITTI HAD too much else to do to follow the path of the fifth round. As the gun blazed, the anchor started moving, the vibrations in the deck told her that the propeller was turning, and every drum, trumpet, and whistle aboard *Byubr* signaled "Getting underway."

Being half-blinded by the muzzle flash and more than half-deafened by the discharge didn't help either.

She crouched by the capstan, closer than she would have allowed most Farers, alternately watching the chain come in and shouting reports on the ship's position to the Farers below. Two more of the section wielded a hose hooked to the foredeck pump, washing the mud and filth of the bottom off the chain as it came in. *Byubr* generated enough reeks and smells of her own without help from the southern seas.

The last of the section was mounting guard but had no other work until after the seventh round. By then *Byubr* was backing down slowly, and the anchor chain was so taut that Tuomitti heard the winch groaning and squealing under the strain. She supposed that the Captain knew what he was doing; backing down would put the ship in water too shallow for torpedo attacks and open arcs of training for more crankguns and searchlights.

She still fought the urge to order the Farers in the chain locker back on deck. If the chain snapped under

A large insect would have been sighted trying to board now.

Then *Byubr*'s engines shifted from slow back to slow ahead, and from that swiftly to one-third, two-thirds, and at last full speed. The main gun fired three more times before Tuomitti saw a decent bow wave, but after that the stokers must have shoveled like fire-sprites. *Byubr* was throwing spray higher than her anchor when she passed through the gap in the boom.

Tuomitti stared around her, wishing that some of the spray would splash high enough to wash her face. She felt ready to shave her hide bare, if nothing else would get it clean.

Crankguns raved again, from out to sea, from the north point, from *Byubr*, and from alongside. Tuomitti watched spray rise from the shallows, sand and gravel from the beach. Running figures also rose from the shallows and ran toward the camp. But groundfighter rifles on land and crankguns aboard *Byubr* and a Kertovan torpedo-carrier chopped them down like mad cane cutters.

It was not a good night for the war swimmers.

The main gun ceased firing, and a stretcher party came forward to pick up the gut-slit Farer. She was mercifully senseless now, from the blood lost before one of her comrades packed the wound with an emergency dressing. Tuomitti hoped the woman would never awaken—then started and nearly slipped in the pooled blood.

The beach on the north point now swarmed with dark figures running with as little apparent purpose as fingernippers in a panic. Fires in the trees and flares overhead showed up the runners as Imperials. The Kertovan defenders seemed to have fallen back on the camp, with only a few fire-sparks in the trees to show where the rearguard stood.

The river-steamer lay broadside to the beach, hard aground. Bodies littered her decks, blood streaked her

She walked aft, past the main gun with its bent stanchions, scorched paint, and gunners black as if they'd been rolling in the coal bunkers. She waved; they'd done well enough that she could forgive them the ringing in her ears and the bruises where they'd knocked her down.

In fact, she'd have been almost content, if Zhohorosh had been aboard to share the coming sea fight.

WITH HER BACK SAFE FOR THE MOMENT, ALIKILI TURNED to the work of keeping the bedchamber from going up in flames. Fortunately the lantern's rock oil had not fallen on anything that would burn like dry tinder such as the bed hangings.

In the bath, Alikili soaked a blanket until it was dripping, then flung it over the heart of the fire. A servant with an equally sodden pillow attacked the rest. Then more of the household appeared, sooty and grimy, holding mostly empty buckets, which they promptly ran to fill.

They were even sootier and grimier by the time the fire was at last out, as well as coughing from the smoke. Alikili thought of opening a window, then realized that with the room lit from within, this would tell anyone lurking outside exactly where to strike, with gun or bomb.

She would have given much to be able to chop a hole in the floor. The firefighting water lay toe-deep even where the rug had soaked up some.

More water that hadn't drenched the floor had ended in Alikli's wardrobe chests. She had a long search for clothes that would preserve decency, keep her warm, allow her to move quickly, and not make her as plain a target as if she wore a Lady's headdress set with candles!

By the time Alikili was dressed, so many people had come into the bedchamber that Kekaspa had to chase some of them out again. Leaving too much of the house unguarded or gathering too many people into a single unmissable target seemed less than wise, although Alik-

"Let me get a heavier pair of boots."

Aliliki was sitting on the ruined bed, pulling the boots on, when Kekaspa knelt beside her and handed her a slim envelope.

"Guard this carefully. It's what I had time to write down about tonight's enemies that is not in the files that Jossu knows."

"If you fall, I will be the next place they think to look for it." Alikili realized that might sound like fear, so shrugged. "So let's agree to live out the night."

"And many nights beyond this one," the other woman said. "Oh, and you almost forget these." The bag she handed Alikili *clinked* faintly, and Alikili realized that it was all the spare cartridges from her nightstand drawer, for the pistol that she had only begun to reload when everyone suddenly claimed her attention!

SEAN BORLUND COULD NOT CONSOLE HIMSELF THAT HE was not a commander, as *Lingvaas* headed seaward. But at least he was fifth (or was it sixth?) in the line of command. *Lingvaas* was likely to be sinking or sunk before he had to take command of her survivors.

Not to mention that at his battle station amidships he was standing on one of the most likely targets. Some of his seniors were far more likely than he to survive tonight if it came to heavy action.

Borlund knew that it would, unless by sheer ill-luck they could not *find* the enemy. Then solemn curses on Drylanders in the name of the Lord and Lady and more ancient powers would be the most charitable response from the Kertovans. To say nothing of the kin of the Rinbao-Dar refugees, or the refugees' own spirits.

Spirits. Something he was not supposed to believe in. But on this night, on these waters, he found it easier than ever to wonder if those who spoke of gods, spirits, and other supernatural entities might not have grasped another part of the same truth that the Rationalists thought they knew entirely.

couldn't ask the Kertovans to abandon the refugees, even if they were helping them for the wrong reasons."

Another new believer in the complexity of the Universe—or at least of Kilmoyn, Borlund decided. Saying that out loud would sound condescending, so he smiled and nodded.

To seaward, complete darkness had now returned, along with silence. Double and even triple lookouts kept every wave and patch of sky watched every moment, and listened for any sound lounder than fissioning jellyfloats.

Borlund turned Barbara Weil's decision to go for the armed transport over and over in his mind, as if it were a problem set in a tactics class. Except that he had much less than half a watch before the answer had to be in, and every prospect that a wrong one could kill a great many Farers.

No, not quite. *The Captain* faced those limits. Fortunately, so did the Captains on the other side, and it could be they who came up with the wrong answers.

Barbara Weil was making sense, Borlund decided. Without their escort, the other troop-carriers might not be able to fight off *Lingvaas* or *Byubr*. They would probably be unable to bombard the camp or Kertovan groundfighter defenses. They would be more vulnerable to torpedo attack, even if *Lingvaas* herself did not survive the battle.

Borlund wondered how many others aboard realized that Weil's plan called for treating *Lingvaas* and every Farer aboard her as expendable. That kind of thinking was clearly labeled "militaristic" everywhere Borlund had seen it—at least in Drylander writings.

But if the plan brought a victory, the Kertovans would raise strenuous objections to punishing anyone for winning it in the wrong way. If the plan failed, there would be very few from *Lingvaas* left for the Directorate to punish.

The Study Group would hardly follow dead Farers

Borlund tried not to stare wildly around him, searching for what made this engine-wracking command wise or at least safe. Quickly, he saw and understood.

Dead ahead, a high-sided dark shape was sliding past, a silver curl of water at her bow. Almost as dead astern, a column of smaller shapes slid past on the same inshore course. Borlund thought he saw something even smaller, about the size of a torpedo-carrier, trailing the column.

Lingvaas was exactly between the two columns of the—

The enemy?

The passing ships were no hallucinations, but their shapes were too vague to identify. Had I Hmilra sent transports on ahead, while he turned toward the Imperial shore of the Gulf to patrol against seaborne intruders?

All Borlund's sweat was suddenly as cold as the ice water only dreamed of for much too long.

Then a reminder came that the enemy always has the same problems you do. A searchlight blazed from the column astern. Its beam painted a glowing line across the sea all the way to the other ship, then began groping about, seeking what some lookout must have vaguely glimpsed.

Before the beam touched *Lingvaas*'s mast, it had settled the question of the strangers' identity. In the yellow glow, the brown and red sword-and-sceptre flag of the Empire showed up plainly, at bow, stern, and after-masthead.

Before the beam swept lower on *Lingvaas*, Borlund heard three separate voices shout a single order.

"Commence firing, all guns bearing!"

A MESSENGER BROUGHT JOSSU I HMILRA WORD FROM the lookout, that gun*flashes* as well as gun*fire* could now be made out. Definitely to the southward, on about the bearing of Puyasa. No Seakin in sight.

I Hmilra swore to promote the lookout. No Seakin

expect the Empire to show itself so arrogant on the high seas either."

"This is hardly beyond coastal waters yet, Captain. As for arrogance, I think our Fleet has a few proven cures for that."

the equipment of her repair party with uncommon care. From time to time she also walked forward to see how they were coming along with swabbing the blood from the deck by the capstan.

Each time she walked forward or aft, she passed the main gun. The gunners were now hard at work oiling and greasing the breech mechanism, training gear, and hoists, adjusting the sights (with judicious taps of a small hammer), and making sure that the ready ammunition locker was watertight, flash-tight, and full.

Then it was always back to her repair party and its supplies. She could count woven-fiber mats, compressed-fiber and wooden plugs, patches, props, and shoring for weakened bulkheads and pierced plates (in all, enough wood to build a small house), entire baskets of hammers, saws, axes, and smaller tools, and a metal can of fastenings varied enough to make the landbound builder claw her hair. Not to mention two hoses, six buckets, a breathing helmet for entering flood or smoke-filled compartments, and a hand-cranked air pump to make sure the helmet lived up to its name and the wearer lived to breathe the Lord's and Lady's air again.

She could also count eight seasoned Farers, two from the anchor section and six others whose battle station was repair from beginning to end. The pile of repair stores was in good hands able to put it to proper use, save it from fire or flooding, at the last resort throw the lumber and fiber overboard to help swimmers keep afloat, and at no time to steal so much of it that she or the repair chiefs would have to notice what was missing.

Tuomitti wished she could be sure that this lull in the battle meant the situation was also in good hands. It wasn't out of doubting her Captain that she doubted this. It was also not as consoling as it had been, that the enemy was probably as confused from stumbling ashore as the island's defenders were from being attacked. Ashore the enemy had the edge in numbers; afloat the odds were still anybody's guess.

verability, and draught. They were also intended to keep torpedo explosions a safe distance from her vitals. Now they proved they would do the same for shells.

The enemy shell burst against the redside bulge well aft of Tuomitti's position. Fragments of shell and hull plating whistled in all directions, including harmlessly upward and outboard, as well as less harmlessly inboard. Tuomitti heard screams from Farers as if they had their mouths against her ear.

She heard more distant screams from the enemy. Looking through a new gap in the railing, she saw the Imperial gunboat slewing bow-first toward *Byubr*. She was either out of control or trying to ram, with steam pouring from her deckhouse and driving overboard Farers who had survived the shell's explosions and the spraying with crankguns.

The enemy's main gun—ten lines at least, Tuomitti thought—was still crewed, though. It fired again, before *Byubr*'s second shot. The aim was high, but the shell punched a hole in *Byubr*'s deckhouse and passed almost all the way through before exploding. Most of the blast and fragments wrecked empty cabins or flew out to sea.

Some of both flailed the crew of *Byubr*'s main gun from greenward. Tuomitti heard more screams, also the sound of a butcher's cutter as one fragment bounced three times and ended in the skull of a repair Farer.

Then *Byubr*'s main gun fired again.

Shot or shell, it was impossible to tell which. It struck the gunboat's main weapon squarely on the muzzle. One or two explosions—again, no way of telling—flung bodies and fragments masthead-high but also poured out smoke that hid the worst of the shambles.

Flame spewed from the heart of the smoke cloud. This time the whole gun rose higher than the gunboat's bridge, hung in the air long enough for Tuomitti to see the peeled-back muzzle, then plunged into the water. Smoke hid the whole enemy vessel for a moment, but

But until tonight the pistol had been mostly a mark of rank. Now she had killed with it. Shouldn't this make a difference?

Apparently not. She wondered if this was good or bad. Turning into a warrior was a fate to which she was now resigned. But there were good warriors and bad warriors—most especially, warriors who could tell friend from foe and those who could not.

Jossu had made this entirely clear. What he had left darker than the hall before her was how to tell the two kinds apart. He had not even hinted at how to keep from becoming the bad kind oneself. Alikili felt a moment's grievance against Jossu, even as she felt it knowing that it was unjust. He had not anticipated the fighting coming this close to her. Neither had she. The fault, if any, was shared.

Also, Moi Kekaspa might be able to give a better answer. She must have made her first kill many Greats more recently than Jossu. And she was jouti, walking out alone into a land from which her kind was usually supposed to be barred.

They were a good deal closer to the entrance hall when a muffled shot sounded from somewhere above. A second followed quickly. Then a scream and five lighter shots replied from outside.

Everyone stopped. Most stared at Kekaspa. Some looked as if they would have liked to flatten themselves into the carpet, like roofworms. Some of those staring seemed to want Kekaspa to turn into a magical war engine out of the old tales that came from before Skyfall.

Alikili tried not to stare but would have rejoiced at seeing the woman so transformed. She wondered idly if the Drylanders had such tales. She had never learned enough of their history to know how much of it they lost at the time of Skyfall.

Jossu was more likely to know that than to know how she could train herself as a warrior. She hoped his

sources, even among men and women. Also, she would *not* sound like a woman ready to throw a jealous fit.

If anything could ensure her being sent out into the darkness, denied the right to defend her home, it would be making Kekaspa worry about her back as she crept up on the sniper!

"ALL GUNS BEARING" INCLUDED ALL THREE HEAVY guns, forward and aft, and the crankguns bearing forward. The midships five-liners and Borlund's crankguns couldn't bear on any target within range.

The din was still ear-battering. Borlund hoped all the noise led to some results. Forward, he was pretty sure it would. The big armed transport was within rifle shot, let alone heavy-gun range.

The transports aft were a different matter. They were a third of a league off at least. Borlund only hoped the guns there would hit something even if it wasn't what they were aiming at.

Gunners, Zhohorosh had once said, came in three kinds. One could hit only with modern sights and calculation arcs, one could hit only by Farer's eye, and one couldn't hit anything at all.

It would appeal to Zhohorosh if *Lingvaas*'s gunners could hit the old-fashioned way; he was of that school himself. But with the latest sights on all of her guns, if her gunners couldn't use them, *Lingvaas* faced the unappealing prospect of hitting nothing and probably being sunk in the next few beats.

The opening salvo destroyed what was left of Borlund's night vision and left a whine in his ears. He could still see the torpedo-carrier close alongside, and someone leaning from the wing of *Lingvaas*'s bridge and shouting to it. As his hearing returned, he recognized Barbara Weil's voice but not her words.

She was shouting in pure Saadian, and as the next salvo drowned out her words he understood why. There were almost certainly Kertovan speakers aboard the

She was coming down fast, to ram *Lingvaas* and put this pesky opponent forever on the bottom of the Bishak Gulf, or at least out of the fight.

The lookouts and steerers aboard *Lingvaas* were working together too well for that. The two ships passed broadside to broadside, with *Lingvaas* able to hurl everything that two heavy guns, two light, and four crankguns could produce into the transport. In the lulls Borlund heard riflemen shooting in both directions; if he'd been nearer the railing he could have probably hit the transport with his pistol.

If *Lingvaas* had carried torpedoes, they could not have missed. They also might not have had time to arm themselves.

The transport's crew was still working their guns, but *Lingvaas* was so close alongside that everything was flying even higher overhead than before. It was a long burst from a crankgun, more easily depressed to reach a low-flying close target, that first drew blood from *Lingvaas*.

A series of sharp explosions tore at Borlund's ears. Screams followed. So did the *whup* and *wheet* of more flying fragments passing him on all sides, and not passing some of the people around him. More screams shrilled, practically in his ears; he saw Farers reeling, bleeding, falling.

He also saw a gaping hole in the transport's redside quarter, with torn and split plates all around it and steam trickling out. He didn't know if he had a voice or anyone around still had ears to hear him, so he waved as well as shouted.

Both of the midships guns still had crews; they did not fire together, but both shells tore into the transport close to the torpedo hole. The steam turned from a trickle to a cloud. The transport began to lose way, as the crankguns that would bear raised their muzzles and sprayed the transport's decks.

Then the two ships had passed each other, *Lingvaas's* after guns both had a target, and they let go together. It

He no longer wore much of a shirt, but he stripped off the powder-blackened rags that were left and twisted them as a tourniquet around the bloody stump. Then he unpacked his own dressing and started tying it over the wound.

An explosion that came from no gun rolled across the water. Borlund looked up from his healer's effort to see the enemy transport brightly lit by several fires, most on deck but one gushing flames from ports below and aft. She was also nearly dead in the water and noticeably down by the stern.

It would take longer than a night for the transport to become a fighting ship again. If sunbrighten found her afloat at all, it would be good work from her crew. The thought of how many Farers and groundfighters might be struggling amid the bits of wreckage made his stomach twitch for the first time since the battle opened.

He calmed it, rather to his own surprise, by calling for a muster of his own division. Yoshino and some others answered from the deck, and some did not answer at all. Borlund could put not only a name but a history and a personality to all the still, blank-eyed faces. When he knew all the names, he felt a little better about the coming fate of the Imperials aboard the transport.

He even felt a trifle better about his own people, once he started preparing a list of the dead and wounded. The doctor would need it, and so would Captain Weil—or her successor (a thought which nearly destroyed the barely regained calm).

Then he heard Weil's voice from near the ruins of the bridge, calling to the torpedo-carrier.

"Fine shooting. We're going after the other transports. Can you keep up?"

"We need a couple of fresh stokers. Two of ours are down and the survivors of *Number 67* aren't fit yet."

"I'll call for volunteers."

What she should have said was, "I'll keep you from being swamped by volunteers." There was no time for

thinner," she said with a forced smile. "Two fingers less of me astern, and nothing would have happened. Now I can't even say I have an honorable scar. Or at least one that I can show."

"Those of us who were here tonight won't insist on proof, and it's nobody else's business."

"Thanks, Sean."

Weil laid one hand against his cheek briefly, and he felt the sweat on it mingling with hers. He also felt the tautness in her muscles, and remembered that buttock wounds were more than embarassing. There was a lot of flesh and nerves down there, the pain would be serious and long, and meanwhile *Lingvaas* would have a Captain who could lie down or stand up but not sit!

"Now, let's see about getting a repair party on the bow gun," Weil said. "A captain shot in the stern is one thing. A stern chase with no bow gun is another."

"Aye-aye, ma'am," Borlund said. He turned another impulse to kiss Weil into a regulation salute, then headed back toward his post.

IT DID NOT TAKE JOSSU I HMILRA LONG TO MAKE A SUM of the lookouts' reports, from *Valor*'s tops, both cruisers, and the torpedo-carriers on either flank.

Somebody was in action to both the southeast and the southwest, off Puyasa and also well out to sea.

Further calculations suggested that the fighting out to sea was not the rest of the Fleet encountering an enemy. It seemed to be closer than the westward squadron could have been, unless they had sighted an enemy invisible from *Valor*, closed, and engaged.

If so, no harm done. The westward squadron had less than half the torpedo-carriers but considerably more than half the armorclads and heavy guns. Nothing that the Empire and the Confederation put together could send into these seas would stand against them.

I Hmilra leaned back in his chair on the wing of *Valor*'s bridge (time to get behind armor in the stifling-

chapter 26

EHOMA TUOMITTI WAS too busy with her repair work on the bulge to pay much attention to her ship's maneuvers. But she had the vague notion that *Byubr* was wandering up the North Channel toward the open sea. She was certain that the main gun was firing toward the island every dozen beats or so.

She hoped they were not going to waste too much ammunition on what could be hardly more than a gesture as far as she could see. The shore was a mass of trees with not even a patch of glow-moss showing, let alone fires or anything that might have been a battle.

That dense a forest would soak up the fragments of a shell before they'd gone twenty paces. A solid shot would do nothing except to the tree it hit, and if the tree was big enough, not much even to that.

Keeping up the hearts of the groundfighter ashore was hardly worth even a single round for which they would surely find better targets soon enough. Unless the groundfighters had been driven back out of the forest to open ground, where weight of numbers and tribal fierceness might count?

Tuomitti jerked her mind away from that thought and swung her sledge with extra force as if to crush it thoroughly. That kind of a retreat almost certainly meant Zhohorosh's death. Otherwise he would have stood behind the cowards with pistol or even sword, threaten-

Tuomitti reminded herself that the night could bring far worse than Zhohorosh's death.

The torpedo came out of the darkness with only a single wordless cry that held both fear and warning. Any further cries were lost in the explosion of the torpedo against the greenside bulge.

No glare dazzled Tuomitti's eyes this time, but a waterfall poured down all over *Byubr*'s decks. The shock of the explosion made even her fat hull flex and twist, and Tuomitti went sprawling.

The explosion faded into echoes rumbling back and forth between the two shores. Tuomitti gripped a stanchion, slashed her palm on a jagged end where it had spilt, then lurched to her feet.

Beside her one of the repair party lay moaning, one foot at an implausible angle to his leg. Explosion shocks could sprain or even snap ankles. Tuomitti was relieved to discover that both of hers could support her weight. They ached, and those weren't the only aches, but apart from her hand she was fit.

One-handed, she fumbled a dressing out of its wrapper. By the time she'd done that the Farer with the broken ankle had recovered enough to help her dress the wounded hand. By the time they were done, Tuomitti could see that *Byubr* was still lower in the water, and listing to greenside.

Steam roared up from the funnel, as the engine room vented a boiler. That meant likely enough a cracked boiler shell or a cracked steam line. Tuomitti hoped that they could keep enough boilers on line to steam *Byubr* into water shallow enough to beach her.

The Captain's voice cut across the roar of steam. "Main gun, stand ready. Do not fire without my orders. Repair parties, lay below to the greenside boiler room."

Tuomitti winced. Even one-handed, she could still climb down the ladders if her Farers needed her, which they probably would. Nobody enjoyed being in the engine spaces of a torpedoed ship, with steam already

either side, against the walls. That seemed a compro-
mise that everyone could live with, except the snipers—
and their opinions didn't matter.

Another *skritch* of plaster, and the muffled sounds of
shots from outside. Alikili could now tell that that the
outside now had rifles, pistols, and shotguns in actions.
To her, that suggested friends—the game guards would
certainly have turned out with their game pieces.

Kekaspa had been lying with her head to one side, listening as intently as a healer to a sick child's breathing.
Then she turned and gave Alikili the signal.

First finger curled into the base of the thumb—enemy.

The next moment, Kekaspa leaped up and plunged
forward. Alikili felt herself lifted as if by invisible
wires, and jerked forward in the other woman's wake.

She did not know or care who followed her. She
slapped her free hand down on the wardrobe chest laid
across the doorway and vaulted into the room a breath
after Kekaspa. Bullets raved through the air toward her,
then gouged dust and splinters from the walls and kept
on going.

Something seared across the back of Alikili's left leg.
She rolled, coming up with the pistol aimed at a shape
half-hidden in the faded and ragged curtains over the
window. The half she saw let her recognize an enemy,
and gave her a target.

She'd fired three times before the enemy started to
fall out of the curtains. Then screams and curses jerked
her around, to see Kekaspa grappling with two opponents. One of them was holding his rifle by the barrel,
to swing it and smash Kekaspa's skull with the butt.

Instead, Kekaspa wrestled her pistol free and shot the
rifleman at such close range that Alikili saw the bullet
rip out of his back. The other man now broke away and
fired his pistol into Kekaspa's back.

He had time for only two shots before Alikili shot him
through the head. She would have tried for the larger
target of his body if Kekaspa hadn't still been too close.

A farmyard din of voices ended with a sharp, wordless command.

Then:

"Stand in the window, Alikili."

Before anyone could protest, she obeyed, throwing back the curtains and holding up the lantern to light her face.

No bullets tore into her. Instead, she heard, even with battle-stunned ears, sighs of relief. Then someone cheered, and a second, a third. In another moment everyone seemed to be cheering.

Alikili stood motionless, glad that everyone was too far off in the night to see the tears trickling down her cheeks. All she could think of was that this cheering wasted time that might bring healing to Moi Kekaspa. But her voice had left her.

It was finally one of the household who stepped forward, broke through and beat down the cheering with Farer's oaths, and brought a healer forward to the main door.

LINGVAAS WOULD NOT HAVE HAD MUCH OF AN EDGE IN speed over the transports unless she had been able to hit one or two of them. With them undamaged and her own engineers treating her engines delicately, she closed so slowly that it was hard to see that she was closing at all.

Furthermore, she was chasing at all in order to keep the transports nervous and try overtaking them when they slowed for the mouth of the North Channel. With no bow gun, she could not even chance an occasional harassing shot without yawing to open an arc for one of the undamaged after-guns. That would cost too much distance, and also turn her broadside to an enemy not so nervous they couldn't strike back.

One of the transports at least had a long-range light gun, probably one of the river-fortress antiboat guns on a shipboard carriage. The shot it fired left a hole hardly

be getting dragged into the pages of the history books, feet first and protesting. It would also be his duty, which somewhat reconciled him to having another complicated situation to untangle.

Weil looked over the side to where the torpedo-carrier was keeping station with no apparent effort. Her crankgun was crewed, and rifle-armed Farers perched on the empty torpedo-launchers.

"They picked up a prisoner from one of the transports up ahead," Weil said. "He confirmed what we suspected—a landing to take the Puyasa and kill the refugees, or use them as hostages. Either way, the Empire would have the high hand in Rinbao-Dar, which would cut us off from Eneh."

"The Directorate might not like that highly intimate pronoun 'us,' " Borlund said.

"Oh, flush the bilges with the Directorate," Weil said, in a voice that shook with pain and fatigue. "The secret of our stay-behinds helping the Empire will be all over the Republic by the time we drop anchor back in Saadi. The only way we can keep it from blowing us up too is to make sure everyone knows we're too valuable to be destroyed or exiled."

"Tonight's battle won't hurt."

"No, and neither has everything you've done before you joined *Lingvaas*. The Directorate may never admit it, but you've done more good work for them than you could have in ten years on that damned rock."

Weil shifted a foot and winced. Then she started. Borlund did not, because his ears hadn't quite recovered from standing so close to the guns.

But he did see the flashes. He combined memory with a look at the compass and realized that one set of flashes was off the mouth of the channel. Another was well to the north. Neither seemed to be the enemy transports, unless they'd altered course or increased speed—which was perfectly possible, of course.

Planning for the enemy's capabilities instead of esti-

career have survived being relieved of command, which I Hmilra was prepared to do.

Again, lookouts aloft aboard both *Valor* and *Relentless* saw the gunfire before the torpedo-carriers did, and the torpedo-carriers both ahead and astern saw it before I Hmilra did. He ordered no course changes, because the squadron was already headed where it had to go and in formation to fight in any direction from which an enemy might appear.

It was only when the trailing torpedo-carrier and *Shuumiba* both reported transports overtaking from astern that I Hmilra ordered the helm put over.

Valor heeled as she turned hard to greenward, *Relentless* following in her wake, torpedo-carriers maneuvering to cover both the seaward flank of the heavy ships and the mouth of the channel.

"What about the command tower . . ?" The Captain sounded as if he was embarrassed to remind I Hmilra that there was such a place.

"Wait until we know who they are," I Hmilra said. He moved to the wing of the bridge and braced himself so that he could use both hands on his binoculars. He willed the darkness to lift as he peered into it, even for the moment that would let him tell friend from enemy.

Then a searchlight thrust out from *Relentless*. It lit up a high, rusty gray hull hung with netting and topped with boats swung out ready for lowering. A gilded broadwing topped a straight bow, and the railings were crowded with brown-capped figures.

Imperials.

I Hmilra thought it, the Captain and others shouted it, and those with hands on lanyards or cranks acted without thinking or speaking. Suddenly the searchlight was only one light among many, and not even the brightest one.

then only another one to nod (she refused to salute such
a painful order) and say:

"Aye-aye."

ALIKILI BROUGHT ALL THE RESCUERS INTO THE HOUSE,
in her mind performing rites of aversion that there
should be no more traitors or enemies among the new
arrivals. However, they could do harm as easily outside
as inside, and any stray gun-toters or knife-wielders
from the first attack could strike much more easily if she
kept everyone milling about outside. There were too
many stone walls and bushes in the garden that would
allow slipping up to shooting or even stabbing range.

This did not make her think the house's stone walls a
solution to all her problems. She posted armed sentries
on stairs and in halls to block any attack from the rear.
She posted the two best rifle shots on the roof, and had
torches set out on the lawn to reveal anyone trying to
attack from the front. She used her own and the household's knowledge of the ground to take several other
precautions that she hoped she would remember well
enough to describe in detail to Jossu.

By the time she was done, the only ways to attack
would be light artillery, or else a bomb in the rear of the
house powerful enough to knock the front down as well
or set everything on fire. If the enemy commanded such
weapons, then Lord and Lady had forsaken her and her
people. She would just have to make the best fight she
could when she had lost even much hope of its becoming a tale told to those in Greats to come.

When she had done all this, and thought she could
command her voice, she went to see Moi Kekaspa.

They had laid the wounded and the dead in two of the
guest bedchambers. The master chamber was unfit for
anything except laying out the enemy's dead. Two heal-
ers attended the wounded, and a gardener and a cook's
helper who had learned some quick-healing helped them.

came from no strains, and discovered that his left hip and calf were peppered with tiny fragments and splinters. Some hadn't even penetrated clothing, let alone skin. Others had gone in far enough that he could anticipate a little while in sick berth with his trousers down and the attendants yanking at him with tweezers and smearing him with salve.

Meanwhile, he hadn't lost a dangerous amount of blood and he wasn't going to before the next round of shooting began. He intended for the bow gun to be pulling its weight by then, even if he had to lift its entire five tons himself.

By the time the gun was back in action, he felt as if he had very nearly done so. He was stripped to the waist to keep from ruining his uniform even more thoroughly than it was already, and the clothes he still had on were clinging with sweat. He kept his boots on, however; they helped support a half-sprained ankle and keep loose bits of metal and wood out of his feet. The deck crew had swept down fore and aft, but working in darkness they couldn't possibly have found everything.

He put his hat back on so that he could salute properly when he reported to Captain Weil that the bow gun was ready for action.

"Well done," she said. "Somebody's engaging the transports already, in case you hadn't noticed. It's time for us to join the party.

"Gunnery Chief Gann is back on duty—it was just a scalp cut. Let him take over the bow gun, and you get back to your own battery. Don't worry, I plan to take us in to biscuit-tossing range. Those crankguns will have all the targets they can use."

"Aye-aye."

Borlund had barely pulled on his shirt when the bow gun fired. The blast snatched his coat out of his hand and set it whirling overboard, and made the ladder he was climbing sway like a mast in the wind. He could hold onto something like that now with one hand,

shouted, to the three crewed midships guns and the three working crankguns:

"Open fire as your guns bear!"

IF THE ENEMY HAD AN ARMORCLAD OR EVEN ANY HEAVY guns among the transports, Jossu I Hmilra hadn't seen it. He feared, however, that *Valor* had done herself as much damage as a serious opponent might have done.

The steam line to the training engine for the after turret had carried away on the third broadside. No enemy metal had come within a cable of it; the concussion of Valor's own guns had done the work. Fortunately the loading gear was hydraulic and pressure in it kept up by a second engine, so the turret could still fire, but it could not turn to follow a target, and the transports seemed to be scattering like a flock of sea fliers.

"Signal to *Relentless*," I Hmilra shouted. He was shouting as a matter of course now, because even when the guns weren't firing everybody on the bridge was half-deaf. Being inside the command tower might have shielded ears, but it would also have blinded eyes. When the enemy had nothing that could hit *Valor* at this range I Hmilra preferred a good view.

"Signal to *Relentless*?" someone asked. Without looking to see who had replied, I Hmilra ordered the cruiser to steam out to sea, steering a course to pass to greenward of the transports and hitting them at close range as she did.

That would reduce the transports' chances if they turned and fled back the way they had come. Meanwhile, *Valor* could maneuver off the mouth of the channel if the enemy tried to press on through. With her five-gun broadside reduced to three, it made more sense for the enemy to come to her than for her to chase them.

Besides, any more high-speed steaming and she might cripple more than a training engine.

The signal lamp flashed. I Hmilra hoped it could be

could see the splashes in the water. The enemy wasn't returning fire either. All hands seemed to be amidships, around the torpedo launchers. Tuomitti hoped that meant they had a faulty torpedo or launcher, preferably both.

Then it seemed as if the door opened in her face, flinging her outward against the railing. The gouged and nicked railing gave under the impact and she felt herself in midair. She had time to thank the Lord that the bulge was now nearly submerged and she would not break too many bones by falling on it. Then she plunged into the water.

When she broke the surface, she saw what had hit her. Firing abeam, with its muzzle thirty paces from her, the main gun had hit the torpedo-carrier squarely amidships. It was a solid shot, two Farers' weight of chilled steel, aimed high.

Not too high to do its job, though. It had cleaned one torpedo launcher off the carrier's deck like a knife trimming the stem of a squan-fruit. Air blast and fragments had swept the crew off the decks. More fragments had certainly pierced the funnel, possibly riddled the bridge, and perhaps even reached the engine room.

Certainly the torpedo-carrier was steering like the last and drunkest Farer back from leave as she vanished into the darkness.

Tuomitti swam only a few strokes before her left hand struck something solid. The pain sharpened her senses; she realized she had swum onto *Byubr*'s bulge. She used her right hand and both legs to push herself onto the rounded iron, scraping one knee on a rivet.

Then she stood up—and as she did, she saw a silhouette hard to mistake, well out to sea but lit clearly by her own gunflashes—and then suddenly, by two searchlights as well.

Valor was out there, in among the transports.

Crankguns snarled, aimed to redward. The main gun fired again. The next sound to pummel Tuomitti's ears was an explosion from well clear of *Byubr*. She tried to

as inevitable, like the rise and fall of the tides," the commander said.

He turned away and shouted some orders whose words Alikili understood but not the sense.

"We have the other half of the company coming up on a sunbrighten train," he said, answering her look. "A messenger is returning to the station to tell the guards we left there that we have matters here in hand—"

"That you *found* matters here in hand," Alikili said. Had her voice been steel, the commander would have been clutching a bleeding throat.

"That we found them in hand at the house, and are now scouting the country for any fugitives or folk too stupid to know defeat?"

Alikili could not help smiling. "I can accept that. But do not pull ruffs in every village and farmstead within a day's march. Jossu enjoys peace with his neighbors."

"We will let him enjoy it when they are at peace with him," the other said. "When they are not—both of you are too precious to the Republic to put foolishly in danger."

Alikili had no reply to those words, and after a moment decided that this was no great loss.

SEAN BORLUND HAD ONLY TWO MIDSHIPS GUNS LEFT now; one had a round go off from the heat in the open breach. Only one Farer was surely dead, but some of those sprawled dark shapes below looked as if they would be a long time moving.

However, healer-attendants were working on them. That was oddly encouraging; it meant that everyone below was either dead or at least fit to be left alone briefly.

The greenside gun was ready to fire again when Borlund recognized something in its target.

"Hold your fire! That's *Shuumiba*!"

Somebody sounded ready to argue, but the redside gun also had a target and let fly, drowning out the

might take longer, and probably had to be fought with just as much determination.

Otherwise the Directorate's opponents of humans going to war and the Republic's opponents of Drylanders going to sea would have time to form an obscene alliance to deny *Lingvaas*'s Farers any reward for what they had done this past Great *or* tonight.

EHOMA TUOMITTI DISCOVERED THAT SHE HAD NO LIVE company in the water. But the top half of a body floated close enough for her to recognize the Imperial cut of the ruff and the tattoos above either ear where the scalp had been shaved bare.

It was supposed to honor dead foes, to think about those who would mourn them as your kin would mourn you. It was pleasing to the Lord, and those who obeyed the Lady more than most Farers thought it was nearly a duty.

But Tuomitti decided that such thoughts now would more likely addle her wits. Tonight had been the longest fight of her life, and the bloodiest. She tried to climb back aboard *Byubr*.

Unfortunately, one hand wasn't quite enough for climbing. The roar of the guns out to sea kept everyone's eyes turned that way and deafened everyone's ears to her croaking calls.

So she squatted on the bulge and looked at the body, and decided that she might as well honor him as not. She might be keeping company with him for much of the night.

Be well, Farer who fought us. Be well, you whose kin will mourn. Be well, kin who mourn.

Those ritual words were over too quickly. Tuomitti thought of questions she would have liked to ask the living Farer, if they had met at some drinkshop.

I never served aboard a torpedo-carrier. Ours have a reputation for cramped quarters. But yours was bigger

tower—where you could not see well enough for the fine maneuvering ramming needed!

"Everyone off the bridge, except the lookouts. Command tower party, to your stations. Maneuver on my orders!"

For a moment he thought the battle roar had cost them their wits as well as their hearing. For another moment, he feared, if not mutiny, at least rude remarks.

Discipline held, though. They went in silence.

Now, if my voice and the speaking tubes hold so that I don't have to ask for messengers. . .

Valor heeled in another sharp turn, letting the after-turret fire—encouragingly, with both guns. I Hmilra gripped the railing, wished that it was possible to keep one's night vision in a night action, and started picking his first ramming target.

SHUUMBIA'S SEARCHLIGHT PICKED OUT A BATTERED transport nearly dead ahead. The enemy was brightly lit, by three fires and a searchlight of her own.

Her decks were also crowded with brown-uniformed Imperial groundfighters, and her railings seemed pierced for too many guns. Crankguns or light artillery at most, but solid splashes to either side of *Lingvaas* said that the artillery at least had the range.

The cruiser was turning now, hard to greenward, to pass the transport astern and rake her deck. The signal winking to *Lingvaas* told her to pass ahead of the enemy, meanwhile engaging her on the broadside.

Once more Borlund would have given ten Greats of life to have torpedoes aboard *Lingvaas*. That wasn't the only discontent, either. He heard muttering from below.

"Hope they don't rake when we're in the line of fire."

"Awful careful about us not hitting friends. Maybe they'll take their own advice."

Something about Captain Fobeen that would, not too many Greats ago in Kertovan history, have demanded a blood-duel.

scream. But he didn't hear the sounds of wholesale slaughter, as if *Lingvaas*'s decks were being scoured clean of live Farers by the debris from the explosion.

He gripped what was left of the railing and pulled himself to his feet. The transport was still afloat, but with her bow half blown away and fires burning all over the rest of her. Astern, *Shuumiba* was vanishing, beyond the transport was another Imperial ship, even bigger, and something loomed even farther away, with a mast like a warship's.

"Cease-fire, all midships guns!" Borlund yelled. "All" was only one, for now, but that was too many to have firing into a tangle of ships that certainly weren't all enemy.

VALOR WENT ON WREAKING DESTRUCTION WITH HER reduced battery even as she maneuvered to ram. Her gyrations kept opening the arcs of fire for the immobilized after turret. It kept firing. I Hmilra even authorized them to use shells if they ran out of solid shot. He dreaded the Imperial casualty list after too much of that, but they weren't surrendering and his ship was now in crankgun range.

Fortunately both sides had crankguns. What bothered I Hmilra was the times when he was within rifle range of troop-crowded decks. It was just as well that there were only three people exposed on the bridge at any moment, although the lookouts had been changed twice. He knew that he'd felt bullets clip his clothing, and he knew he'd gone far beyond what Alikili would allow to pass without a few sharp words. As for what his tailor would say—

Well, the little dear will have her profit either way. Either a complete outfit of new uniforms for further service, or a chance to create a masterwork for my burial.

The searchlights were dying on both sides now. Shattered by crankgun rounds or shell fragments? Abandoned by crews too weakened to crank them? Without

It was still a near thing, as *Valor* careened across *Lingvaas*'s bow at pistol-shot range. But Weil had lost none of her shiphandling skill. *Lingvaas* was turning hard away from the collision point. It would have been a glancing blow at best, although not well done, in the moment of victory, with damaged ships far from a friendly dockyard.

We have to do something about that, if we are going to keep the sea route to Eneh open year-round, I Hmilra decided.

The bridge suddenly seemed to grow people. He decided that he could forgive their coming out with no orders. Victory ought to be celebrated in the open air.

Not fresh. Death-stink all around, every kind of smoke. Lord of the Waves, forgive what we've done to your air.

The last intact signal lamp was flashing, and *Shuumiba*'s reply came back quickly.

BYUBR GROUNDED TO PREVENT SINKING. SERIOUS DAMAGE AND CASUALTIES. THREE TORPEDO-CARRIERS MISSING. ONE ENEMY TRANSPORT KNOWN SUNK, ONE ASTERN DEAD IN WATER, NOT SURRENDERED.

I Hmilra replied:

REQUEST TRANSPORT ASTERN TO SURRENDER IMMEDIATELY ON PAIN OF BEING SUNK. IF OBLIGED TO SINK, PREPARE TO CARRY OUT RESCUE OPERATIONS. GOOD SHOOTING ON OUR FRIEND WITH THE MAGAZINE EXPLOSION.

It seemed a long time before the cruiser replied:

TRANSPORT ASTERN HAS SURRENDERED. MOST LIKELY CAUSE OF MAGAZINE EXPLOSION GOOD SHOOTING BY *LINGVAAS*. WILL CLAIM ASSIST, HOWEVER.

I Hmilra stared from *Shuumiba* to *Lingvaas*, and then to the transport they'd been arguing about, which looked as if she would need a rescue operation before long. Her ruined bow was already nearly level with the water.

So Captain Fobeen had enough honor to overcome his dislike of Drylanders and praise them for what they

epilogue

PUYASA'S ANCHORAGE WAS no longer as crowded as it had been a half-midtide ago when several hundred refugees were returning to Rinbao-Dar every common. A single paddle-wheel-steamer lay off the beach, with a steam launch towing a barge carrying more lumber than people heading toward it.

Few signs of the battle remained. The hulk of the river-steamer lay rusting where she had grounded that night. A gallant effort, Jossu I Hmilra realized, but without a victory at sea a futile one.

The groundfighters had been too scattered in landing to attack the camp before the Kertovan defenders rallied. Their thin line held until sunbrighten, when word came (or was sent) of the disaster at sea.

Even then, a few Imperial commanders whose heads held so much honor there was no room for brains wanted to continue the fight. Most of these fools had their wish of death before surrender, even if some of them died at the hands of their own fighters.

The rest of the battle marks were trees shortened or trimmed by shells or burned by the fires of unnatural lightning. The refugee camp was not being abandoned; the Kertovan garrison on Puyasa would use it. But the quick-growing vegetation of this warm land was already blending its outline into the landscape.

The next set of answers to the querulous wire-posts

squall. Nonetheless, the future holds you—and so may I, before much longer.

Not being a poet, I cannot find words to say how much I have missed that. Nor can I say how frightened I was at the thought of losing you, without seeming more of a coward than I wish to sound even to you.

All blessings to you, and my hopes that *Valor* will outspeed this letter homeward.

I Hmilra read over the letter, realized that the weight of what he could say on paper had made him sound awkward, and blotted the letter nonetheless. Alikili could read well enough what he did not say, even though she might feel like boxing his ears for not having said it.

A whistle blew, to seaward—one I Hmilra did not recognize. He peered out the port.

The high red hull and the green banner floating from the third of the four stubby masts were unmistakable. The new Enehan ship (in fact, the only seagoing steamship under the Enehan flag) had arrived.

Even though this was not her first visit to Puyasa, her coming called for I Hmilra's presence aboard her sometime before sunfade. He called for his steward and pulled the water jug toward him.

ABOARD *BYUBR*, EHOMA TUOMITTI, ZHOHOROSH, AND twenty other chiefs and senior Farers stood at attention, while a trumpeter and a drummer rendered honors to the Enehan ship.

They remained that way until Tuomitti was certain that her good eye was going to melt and her saluting hand become as weak as the wounded left one. They remained that way, for what she knew was half a common longer.

Then at last the Enehan ship blew her whistle five

"We bought Puyasa to have an offshore base on the way to Eneh. It needs a station ship. Either we bring one all the way down from the north, or we use one that's already here.

"*Byubr*'s here, and she's not going to fight again. Not without a pot of gold sent on repairs. So the pot of gold is going to the cities, to pay the 'maintenance fees' for keeping her afloat."

"Another bribe," Tuomitti said. "Has Fleet worked out a bribe for us, to make us stay?"

"The tales run that everyone aboard has their choice of taking their pension and staying, or going home to a post of their choice." he hesitated. "I will go where you go, my friend. Or stay where you stay."

She looked at him. He shrugged again. "I am too old to put love into stronger words. My heart might not stand it. You might even tell me to go. That one eye sees pretty clearly."

She tucked his arm through hers. "I see a good man. That isn't the most common sight. Maybe I can do something with him."

"I won't fight it if you try."

LINGVAAS STEAMED IN THE REAR OF THE FIRST CONVOY bound north from Puyasa to Eneh. The convoy carried a good part of what would be needed to build the fort, repair the canals and railroads, and establish permanent harbor facilities on the north shore of the Bishak Gulf.

Or at least as permanent as the Empire allowed. The Aloboliri still had more than enough groundfighters that they could in a purely military sense write off their losses in the Battle of Puyasa. Their pride might make scrap of purely military calculations.

Hence the convoy, with *Relentless*, four gunboats towing torpedo-carriers, and *Lingvaas*, for ten merchant vessels, two of them smaller than *Lingvaas*. Provincial viceroys could be replaced with remarkable speed when the Empire's ministers wished it, and a purely land route

"What didn't you tell him?" Having helped compose the report, Borlund wondered that there was anything she'd left out. Certainly it couldn't be enough to save her from the Directorate, if they caught her outside Fleet jurisdiction for long enough.

"Remember why *Lingvaas* can't become an independent Drylander community, even if the Fleet asked us?"

"No headroom," Borlund said. Service aboard any ship designed for Kilmoyans was a sore point with him. (Also, quite often, sore head from bumping or sore neck from ducking.)

"The real reason."

"Too small a genetic base."

"Exactly. Now, I've probably seen more secret material than you have. But even what I've seen doesn't give the stay-behinds more than two hundred people. That's sixty years ago, so all but the handful of children will be going or gone. Two-thirds of them were men."

Borlund needed only a moment's mental arithmetic. "A small population. Village-sized, if that. Much more inbred than we are, no matter how hard they try. Getting more so with each generation, too."

"Precisely. So small that even if each one was an Einstein or a Feisal, they'll know that time is running out for them.

"They've never had numbers on their side. Now they don't have time. They may be desperate. What happens if desperate stay-behinds find an Imperial ally smarter than those Emperor's bad bargains we just fought?"

Borlund decided not to suggest making a free gift of this knowledge to Jossu I Hmilra. It might not be knowledge, anyway—just a guess, not even a probability.

He liked it no better for that.

"Speaking of gene pools," Weil said, "ah—how to put this? I'm old-fashioned in some ways. I want your bearer-partners' permission to—court you."

"Court" was a ludicrously delicate way of describing what Barbara Weil wanted to do with him and he with

had taken her child. Good people all of them, and not ones Alikili would have cared to have as enemies.

The grass was too sodden for the ritual prostration. Instead she knelt, head bowed but eyes raised so that her spirit touched both the memorial here and the earth fifty leagues away that actually held the woman's body.

"Shimosh Kekaspa shall be raised by his kin, on both sides. This is right and proper, for they know the ways of Saadi and I do not.

"Yet I swear this, by all who listen, who uphold oaths and punish oathbreakers.

"What the child may need to become all that he may wish to be, and his kin cannot give, I promise to give it."

That was the easy part. Now came the part that had cost her sleep, although she knew that the oath would not be complete without it.

"If Jossu I Hmilra, by word or deed, does what might cause me to break this oath, then I will consider his oaths to me and mine to him likewise broken. This too I swear by all who listen and who uphold oaths or punish oathbreakers."

She rose, and felt the wind on her face. She also felt a wind blowing inside her, from nowhere to nowhere, a wind that seemed to chill and warm her at the same time.

For a moment she felt as if she held within herself a space as vast as all the seas of Kilmoyn.

CITY-STATES
Loose federation of petty states between the mouth of the Hask and the border of the Empire.

CLEARSKY
The sunniest and warmest season in Kertova; roughly equivalent to summer.

COMMON (TIDE)
Day; 28.62 hours.

CONFEDERATION OF DHANDARA
Dominant political unit on the eastern continent of northern Kilmoyn; a militaristic oligarchy more friendly to the Empire of Alobolir than to the Island Republic.

DAUGHTER OF THE ROCK
Sworn servant of the Lady of the Rock; allowed to preside over Reverences in her honor.

DILGAO
Quasi-bovine southern draft animal; enormous strength when fed a high-sugar diet.

DISSTUL OIL
Inflammable extract of the sap of a Luokkan tree.

DREEZAN
Most common riding and draft animal; resembles a long-legged rhinoceros, about 1.8 meters at the shoulder.

DRILION
Minority in Saadi; descended from an extinct City-State and consider themselves oppressed by Saadians.

DRYLANDER
Common name for humans, based on their cover story

FLOWER FOWL
A Luokkan bird known for its spectacular plumage and evil-smelling droppings.

FUGITIVE *OR* STAY-BEHIND
Negative human term for those who did not sail to Kertova. Also called "tribalists."

FULLDARK
True night.

GAISOL
Synthetic fireproofing compound; one of the first products of the rock-oil industry.

GARCIK
Obscene term for a sterile female; implies that her sterility was the result of vice or neglecting her health.

GHATYS
Luokkan pirate knife with a heavy curved blade and a single razor-sharp cutting edge.

GIGNEL
Edible root, usually served either pickled or baked into a pie.

GREAT (TIDE)
Year; the Kilmoyan year is 355 Standard days.

GUIT
The Saadian male nature spirit.

GRAVELTOES
Rude but not quite obscene term for one who does not go to sea.

HOST
Army or other large aggregation of groundfighters.

JOUTI
Kertovan term for a fertile female.

KANIK
Kertovan obscenity; implies incest.

KERTOVA
Republic ("the Island Republic") occupying most of the islands between the Imperial Coast and the Greater Sea. The principal seafaring power on Kilmoyn.

KILMOYN
Best possible transliteration of the Kertovan name for their homeworld.

KRIMO
A common seaweed with a mild nicotine content; harvested with the help of Seakin and cured for smoking in pipes.

LINE
Kertovan unit of measurement for the bore of a gun; roughly two centimeters.

LORD OF THE WAVES *AND* LADY OF THE ROCKS
The principal Kertovan deities, also known as the Gray Lord and the Green Lady.

LADYSOUL
For the Kertovan believers in reincarnation, a honorific term for someone whose soul has been in existence since the original creation of the world by the Lord and Lady. Usually applied to a female.

RAMPARTS
Starship whose drive failure marooned the Esperanzan colonists on Kilmoyn; in a cometary orbit around Kilmoyn's primary.

RATIONALIST
One who rejects any of the traditional human religions.

RECUIN OIL
An edible nut oil.

RIISVAL TEST
The basic Kertovan test of female fertility.

RINBAO-DAR
A pair of cities on the Bishak Gulf loosely controlling territory north to the border of Eneh. Also see "Matriarchy."

SAADI
Formerly a theocracy opposite the mouth of the Hask, constantly at war with the City-States. Now a protectorate of Kertova. The name can refer to either the city or the whole territory.

SEAKIN
Omnivorous mammalian pelagic species resembling small orcas; highly social and recognized as sapient by the Kertovans.

SHTRUG
Epithet; feeble-minded.

SKYFALL
An asteroid strike on Kilmoyn c. 1000 years before the opening of *Eneh*; massively destructive to civilization and life in general.

TUUNDA
Kertovan term for a sterile female (non-perjorative).

UKKIO
Kertovan demigod; the discoverer of navigation.

WATCH
Kertovan unit of time; approximately 4.77 hours.

WIRE-POST/WIRE-SPEAKER
Telegraph/telephone.

WATCH CHIEF
Petty officer.

WATCH COMMANDER
Junior officer (equivalent to lieutenant).

YERIS
Domestic animal resembling a small, long-legged pig.

YPROGA
Island holding principal human settlement in Kertova.